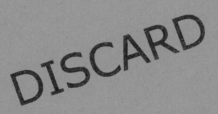

ASK ME

ASK ME

Kimberly Pauley

Published in the United States by Soho Teen
an imprint of
Soho Press, Inc.
853 Broadway
New York, NY 10003

Library of Congress Cataloging-in-Publication Data

Pauley, Kimberly.
Ask me / Kimberly Pauley.
pages cm
ISBN 978-1-61695-383-6
eISBN 978-1-61695-384-3
[1. Oracles—Fiction. 2. Missing children—Fiction. 3. Murder—Fiction.
4.Grandparents—Fiction. 5. Florida—Fiction. 6. Mystery and detective
stories.] I. Title.
PZ7.P278385 Ask 2014
[Fic]—dc23   2013038340

Interior design by Janine Agro, Soho Press, Inc.

Printed in the United States of America

10 9 8 7 6 5 4 3 2 1

To the Music and the Musicians who make it

ASK ME

SUNDAY

Let's be honest. I hit him on purpose. I was driving and half-listening to her once again yammering on and on and on about how I should apply myself more in school and how I should try harder with my dad and how—I don't know—I hadn't mentioned how cute her new skirt was or some stupid shit like that. And there he was, some old Cuban guy, walking along the edge of the road in the middle of the night. Eight ball, corner pocket. I found myself wondering if that would shut her up. Spur of the moment, but that's how some of my best decisions have always been made. I barely had to swerve to hit him.

One satisfying thump, a squishy bump as the back tire went over him, and that was it. I kept driving, but she didn't shut up at all. Instead she started screaming. He hadn't even screamed, and he was the one who'd been hit.

"Oh my God, oh my God! You just hit that guy! You have to stop! Turn around! Oh my God! Do you think he's okay?"

I slowed down and looked in the rearview mirror. It was dark, *but the moon was out. He wasn't even twitching. "Pretty sure he's dead," I said and stepped on the gas again. "No reason to stop."*

That actually shut her up. For about a minute. "We can't just leave him there. We have to tell someone. We should call the police."

"Why?" I asked. "They can't do anything for him." I was regretting it now. Not the hitting him part; that had actually been the biggest rush I'd had in ages. I could still feel the adrenaline running through my body. I felt more alive than I had in months. I shouldn't have done it with her in the car, though. Now she was never going to shut up.

She was quiet for a few peaceful moments, huddled over against the passenger's side door. Staring at me.

"You hit him on purpose, didn't you?"

WHO CARES WHAT THE QUESTION IS?

The problem with prophecy is that someone has to actually ask the right question at the right time for me to produce the answer to it. Otherwise, I'm as adrift in the world as anyone else. Maybe more. The day that changed my life and the lives of everyone around me started the same as any other day, though technically things had been set in motion the night before. I just didn't know it then.

It was a typical morning with Granddad Porter reading the paper or, more likely, studying the dog pages for the track. I sat down at the old wooden table in our tiny dining room and poured myself a glass of juice from the carafe. I took a sip and grimaced. Granddad gave me a knowing grin and tapped the side of his coffee mug, even though he knew I couldn't stand coffee. I might need to develop a liking for it, though, if I had any hope of keeping my taste buds. Grandma Ellie's juice concoction was far too heavy on the grapefruit that morning. She always said it was good to start the day with something sour, so everything else would seem sweet after. But truth be told, I think her taste buds gave up in disgust years ago.

"I'm thinking I might try getting the Powerball numbers out of you again," Granddad said. I rolled my eyes. He'd been working on that ever since I'd moved in with them when I was thirteen, but my prophetic "gift" apparently didn't want us to be independently wealthy. It didn't seem to matter how he asked, the answer always came out as a cryptic riddle he could never figure out until after the numbers were picked. It wasn't my fault, though. I'd tell him the numbers if I could. He knew I had no control over my answers. I think he enjoyed the challenge. It was like a running family joke between us.

"You leave the girl alone, Porter, you hear me?" Gran called from the kitchen. "She doesn't need any of your foolishness before school." She poked her head in the doorway and waved a wooden spoon threateningly in his direction. "Pancakes and sausage in three minutes, Aria. Don't fill yourself up on juice." She disappeared back into the kitchen.

Granddad leaned forward and whispered to me, glancing at the kitchen as he did. There was little enough privacy in our house, but after the door between the kitchen and dining room had rotted off its hinges a few months ago, it was even worse. I could see the swish of Gran's skirt as she whisked back and forth between the stove and the counter. "So, Aria . . . we could use a spot of help this month, even if it isn't the lotto. Don't want to worry Ellie about it." He gave another furtive look toward the kitchen. What that really meant was that he was going to ask me for something that she wouldn't want to participate in. She didn't believe in divination for personal gain, even when we were flat broke. Gran had lost her ability to prophesize years ago when she turned seventeen. She still cast the stones, but the only answers you could find that way were far more general than specific. Not the kind of help Granddad was looking for.

I nodded, and he scooted his chair a little closer to the table.

"So, could you tell me who's going to win the third race?" He leaned over to put the tip sheet in front of me. I waved it away. It wasn't necessary.

I let myself go loose so I wouldn't interfere with the answer. Usually I'm trying to hold it back, and it felt strange and freeing to let it all go. "Your gambling away may bring loss easily. Question it," I said, then paused to gather myself. "Sorry, Granddad. I guess that won't help much."

I sighed. It was times like these I wished I had *any* amount of control over what came out of my mouth. Gran may not approve, but giving tips to Granddad was the only way I had found to contribute. Money had been tight since I had moved in, and it wasn't like Mom or Dad ever sent any funds our way to help out with things. It had been months since I'd heard anything from either one of them and that had only been a birthday card signed by Janice, Dad's second wife. He hadn't even bothered to scribble his own name on it. No money in it either, just a generic card with a teddy bear on the front. Apparently, they still thought I was seven instead of seventeen.

"No, no, I think that might do it," said Granddad, chewing on his stub of a pencil. "The long odds are on a dog called Y Gamble? Clever. The odds-on favorite is Bonnie Ballyhoo, but I think I'll put my money on the other fellow." He grinned and winked as he leaned back in his chair. "Just don't tell Ellie."

"Don't tell Ellie what, you old dog?" Gran came in with a platter full of pancakes and sausage.

"Nothing!" said Granddad loudly. I mumbled something under my breath about fools and money that probably neither one of them would have wanted to hear. That was a trick I used all the time. People were always asking questions, and the only way I could leave the house and go out in public without attracting too much attention was to go ahead and answer as quietly as I could. One of the names the kids at school called me was The Mumbler. It was one of the nicer ones.

Not answering a question I overheard wasn't possible. The longest I'd ever made it without answering had been ten minutes, and that had been on a small, inconsequential question. Those minutes had been the most uncomfortable moments of my life. Well, most physically painful, anyway. If we wanted to talk emotional pain, I had lots of stories to tell, stretching back years, back to when I'd first been cursed with the "gift" of prophecy at age twelve.

"Hmmmphf," said Gran. She set down the plate and picked up the paper, pretending not to notice as the dog pages fell out onto the table. Granddad swept them onto the floor and kicked them under the table where chances were he'd forget them.

I took two pancakes and poured some honey over them, grateful Gran hadn't tried to pass off one of her homemade orange marmalades on us this morning. She never used enough sugar. The fact that the few tourists who came through Lake Mariah bought them never failed to amaze me. I supposed "quaint" counted for something. Either that or they were charity purchases. Probably the latter. It was pretty obvious to anyone that came by our roadside stand that we were terminally broke.

"Oh," said Gran. She put the paper down on the table.

"What?" I asked. There was something about the way she'd said it that made me think of how she sounded when she talked about my mom, her absentee daughter.

"A hit-and-run." She slid the newspaper even farther away on the table, like she could push death away. "One of those farmworkers of Dale Walker's. Happened near Laurel Creek last night . . ."

"An illegal, I bet," said Granddad. He wasn't a big fan of Dale's or his business practices. He had a reputation for being cheap and cruel to his workers, at least according to Granddad. We heard about it a lot at the breakfast table. Living in a small town meant everything was everyone's business. Besides, Granddad had worked on a farm when he was young, and he still complained about the blisters. I think it morally offended him that Dale never actually broke a sweat himself. Slave labor, he called it.

"There's nothing here that says he was," Gran said, waving at the paper.

"What was his name?" Granddad replied.

"Armando Huerta," said Gran and I at the same time.

"But I don't see how that matters anyway," continued Gran sharply. "Same result. A man is dead, and he's left behind his wife, Gabriella, along with three young kids. It's a shame, is what it is." Gran bent her grey head down to say a quick prayer. I ducked mine as well, though I really didn't have anything to say.

"Yeah." Granddad was quiet a moment, though he didn't bow his head down like Gran. "Still, I'd bet good money it's Dale's fault somehow. Probably had the poor guy out working late or something. Wouldn't be surprised if he ran him over himself."

Gran raised her head. "Drop it, Porter," she said sternly. "You're like a dog with a bone."

"I'm just saying," continued Granddad, worrying his pancake into shreds. "You think Dale even noticed the guy didn't show up for work today?"

"No," I answered unwillingly. "Not until the police showed up." Gran threw Granddad a menacing look, but he was on a roll and didn't even notice he'd asked a question.

"You see," he said, waving his fork in the air, stabbing at nothing to make his point. "Who do you think even found the poor guy? Not Dale, I'd bet you that."

Everyday kind of questions didn't really have much effect on me, other than causing me to spew out some kind of answer. They were nuisances, like mosquitoes buzzing around my head, and were gone as soon as I spoke my answer. But big questions, life-or-death kind of questions or questions deeply felt, those had a way of hitting me directly in the middle. This one sailed right through me, leaving a dull burning sensation in my stomach. "Guts and blood—red is everywhere." I spit out. "Love lost. Anger fills her." I felt my face flush and then grow pale. "*Useless* . . . except rage takes away . . ." A small moan escaped my lips. Oh, God, the pain. For a moment I felt like the wife, staring down at her husband in a puddle of blood on a dirty road.

I fumbled for my glass and took a big sip, trying to ignore the way my hand shook until I dropped it, my pancakes cushioning the blow and saving the glass. Juice spread across the table in a sickly orange film. Gran jumped up to grab a towel from the kitchen.

"Sorry about that," said Granddad, dropping his fork into the sticky mess as he grabbed his own napkin to staunch the flow. "Always forgetting and running my fool mouth, aren't I?"

"Yes. It's okay," I said, breathing through my mouth, knowing that I wouldn't be able to drink juice again for a while, not that it would be a big loss. A metallic taste filled my mouth, like blood. "I need to get to school anyway. Sorry about the mess, Gran."

"No worries," she said, hurrying in with the towel. "You go on. Take another pancake with you. You need to eat, especially after that. Get something in your stomach." She whacked Granddad in the back of the head, and he nodded meekly.

I took a fresh pancake from the platter, knowing I would throw it away as soon as I was far enough down the road that they couldn't see me.

THIS IS THE TIDE

I rolled down the windows in my ancient Dodge Colt as I drove, trying to ignore the way my stomach was still twitching. Even this early in the morning, the heat in the car sucked at me, and I let myself sink into it like it was a blanket. The air-conditioning in the Colt had breathed out its last long before I took possession of it, and only three of the four cylinders actually worked. But it ran. Besides, even with no air and the slow pace, it was better than the hour-long bus ride to Lake Mariah High School filled with kids and their questions. I had been saving up for a car since my freshman year, though I still wouldn't have been able to afford one if Granddad hadn't traded our lawn mower and some tools with one of Dale's workers.

It was worth it. Every bus ride had been a small trip through hell. Whatever it was that made me answerable to everyone didn't care whether a query was actually directed at me, only that I could hear it. Answers burned inside me, even for rhetorical questions. Watching quiz shows on TV gave me a headache for days, and it had nothing to do with the annoying hosts. Grandpa joked that I'd clean up if I went on a show, but I knew there was no way I could survive it.

I tossed the pancake out the window when I reached the main county road, and my tires hit pavement. I watched in my rearview mirror as it sailed out into a copse filled with oaks and pines, dripping with Spanish moss. The pancake would likely be gone in an hour or two, devoured by any number of creatures. Florida may be full of retirees and tourists, but in the center of the state, the wilderness still ruled. Once you came in from the beaches and the sherbet-colored coastal towns, you were in old Florida. It had teeth.

I was born in Michigan, in the cold and the snow, but four years here had made me a child of the heat. I did not miss the cold or the brittle stares of the girls who had once been my friends, before my gift had turned them against me. Who wants a friend who only speaks the truth?

We lived a good half-hour from town in our little shanty shack, which suited me fine, even with the long ride into school every day. The only time I felt at peace was out in the forests and wetlands. There the only sounds you could hear were the endless chants of the cicadas and the low buzzing whine of mosquitoes. They, at least, were honest bloodsuckers. They never questioned me.

Too soon, I pulled into the school parking lot. I parked in the no-man's-land by the mosquito-filled drainage ditch, grabbed my drab, army green backpack, and put my headphones in. I just had a cheap, store-brand MP3 player, but it was the one thing that got me through the day still sane. I turned it on and cranked it up before I headed into the main building. Even with it on, I kept my eyes down and headed straight to my locker. You never knew when someone might shout out a question—"Hey, how was your weekend!"—loud enough to break through the music. Mumbling answers mostly worked, but it definitely wasn't foolproof and if I was sufficiently surprised, my answer always seemed to come out too loud. If I could get away with listening to my MP3 player in class, my life would be a lot easier.

Someone bumped their shoulder into me, dislodging my backpack and one of my earphones. I looked up into the sneering face of a boy. Hank? No, Tank. A nickname, I assumed. Surely his parents would never have guessed that he'd turn into such a hulking specimen when he was first born.

"Freak," he said and slammed his shoulder into me one more time for good measure, knocking my backpack the rest of the way off of my arm and onto the floor.

I stumbled, catching myself on a girl's arm to keep from falling, making her spill the contraband soda she was carrying. It splashed all over the front of my skirt, missing her entirely. She threw me off with a look of absolute revulsion, making me wish I actually did have the plague or leprosy so I could pass it on to her.

"What's your problem?" she said. "Get off me."

"I can only live the future, not see it," I said.

Probably a deeper answer than what she was looking for,

but she walked on without waiting for a response, anyway. I put my stray earphone back in and flicked the volume louder. Then I went after my backpack, which had been kicked farther down the hall by some of Tank's friends. I snagged a shoulder strap before anyone else could kick it again and turned against the crowd to go to the bathroom to see what I could do about my soaked skirt. I was sure jokes about me having peed myself were swirling around me, but all I could hear now was The Dandy Warhols. I let my hair fall around my face as I nodded my head in time to the music, my eyes downcast and half closed.

I pushed the door to the bathroom open. There were two girls standing in front of the one mirror that hadn't been completely defaced by Sharpies. The blonde one was leaning over the sink, shoulders shaking. The brown-haired one turned her head as I came in, a pained look on her pretty face. Delilah Jenkins, which meant that the other girl had to be Jade Price. Delilah never went any-where without Jade. Or, rather, Jade never went anywhere without Delilah following along behind. Delilah said some-thing to me, gesturing wildly at the same time. Against my better judgment, I stopped and pulled an earphone out.

She pursed her lips and blew out a stream of air, exasper-ated with me already. "Get out," she snapped. "Can't you see we're busy?" She glared at me as I stood half in, half out of the doorway. A mother hen protecting her chick.

"I only see pain and tragedy," I said softly, but appar-ently loudly enough that Jade heard.

Jade lifted her head to look at me, her blue-green eyes red-rimmed. She looked strange and wild with her hair hanging lank around her face. I was used to seeing her smiling and perfect, always in control.

She hiccupped once and put a hand on Delilah's arm. "It's only Aria," she said, her voice raw. She'd been crying for a while. "Leave her alone, Delilah." Gracious even in her sorrow, she waved a welcoming hand at me. "Don't mind me, I'm just—" she hiccupped again "—having a crisis." She managed a watery smile.

Even though she was popular—maybe even the most popular girl in school—Jade had always been, if not exactly my friend, at least kind to me. On a few occasions, my defender. I wasn't the only one. She had risen to her adored status within the school not by climbing over the backs of others, but on the strength of her personality and her kindheartedness. Of course, it also helped that she possessed that brittle kind of beauty that made you want to protect her even as she protected you: those wide-set eyes set within a delicate, heart-shaped face, all framed by wispy pale blonde hair.

"Sorry," I muttered. I went to a sink. Delilah sniffed but ignored my presence and went back to rubbing circles on Jade's back.

The front of my skirt was soaked. I grabbed a handful of thin brown paper towels from the dispenser and dabbed at my leg. Luckily it was early enough in the day that there were actually still towels to be had. By the end of the day you were lucky to get toilet paper.

Being here with Jade reminded me of the first time she had saved me. As a freshman, before I had discovered that music would allow me to roam the halls relatively unscathed, I had spent a good deal of time in bathroom stalls, cursing Gran for not letting me be homeschooled any longer. She said that someone who had barely finished high school herself had no business teaching "higher subjects." But really she wanted to force me into dealing with people. She said I couldn't hide at home forever. Instead, I wound up hiding in the john.

Then one day, snotty Shelley Roman asked me what my problem was. I stood wedged in the corner by the trash can, pretending to look at nothing. She had been watching me in the mirror as she put on mascara, her mouth half-open in a perfect moue. Bad timing for that particular question: my period had arrived early and with vengeance that morning. My answer said as much. Jade had been there, too. Instead of cackling with embarrassment and delight like Shelley and her crew, she'd kicked them out, given me some pads and ibuprofen, and stood guard at the bathroom door so I could have privacy until I was done. She ran off before I could even thank her. I wondered if she even remembered.

"Just tell me what happened," Delilah said, bringing me back to the present. I got the feeling from her wheedling tone that it was the same thing she had been demanding of Jade before I arrived. "It can't be *that* bad. Why won't you tell me?"

My memories had gotten the better of me. I should have put my earphones back in, especially in such a small space. I whispered, "Some things can only be confided to the earth."

Delilah had chosen to fall silent at exactly the wrong

moment. "Are you eavesdropping?" Her voice dripped disbelief.

"Yes," I said, wanting to say no. I didn't look up from brushing at my skirt, though the cheap paper towels had actually made the mess worse rather than better. They had disintegrated into shreds of muddy brown and were now plastered to the rough cotton of my skirt.

"What did you say, Aria?" asked Jade, her tone more curious than confrontational. Gentle, even. It occurred to me that perhaps she had been kind all these years because she, too, thought I was touched in the head.

I gave up and dropped my skirt, looked directly at her, and repeated: "Some things can only be confided to the earth." Not that I had a choice.

I shrugged, a slight apology for intruding where I wasn't wanted. I had nothing to add, no explanations. I didn't know what it meant. Who talks to dirt?

They both looked at me, Delilah slightly bug-eyed and Jade with her eyes swimming behind more tears.

"Yes," Jade finally said, nodding slowly. "Some things are better left unsaid, aren't they?"

"The damage has already been done," I responded. "What you choose now only determines the extent." My voice rumbled and caught, my throat burning. I didn't know what her secret crisis was, but it had to be a big one. I swallowed to alleviate the sudden dryness in my mouth. Jade was staring intently at me, like she could find an answer in my ravings. I threw the remains of the paper towels in the garbage. "I'm sorry," I said again, eyes down. "I should go. I hope your crisis works out. Sorry." I grabbed my book bag and hurried out the door, just catching Delilah's "What the hell was *that?*"

I squashed my lips together, but the word "truth" leaked out all the same. The swish of the door closing covered it up. I ran on to class, the hallways almost empty, my footsteps echoing and my skirt plastered wetly to my leg like a shroud.

FALSE ALARM

I didn't think any more about Jade until the next day. Delilah grabbed my arm outside of my fifth-period biology class while I was fumbling with my earphones. Tank had elbowed me in the back as he shoved past me through the door. Perhaps I should paint a target there to make it easier for him and his friends. Twenty-five points for a dead-center hit. Ten for a shoulder. Fifteen if they catch a rib and make me wince.

"Have you seen Jade?" Delilah asked me, her bright red fingernails cutting into my elbow.

"Not me, no, not I. Not today, not today, she's gone away." I bit my tongue, hoping there were no more verses. I hated the singsong answers most of all.

Delilah dropped my arm. "God, I don't know why I asked you anyway." She backed away from me, like my weirdness might rub off on her. But I could see worry in her eyes.

Before I could reconsider, I touched her shoulder as she turned away. "Is something wrong with Jade?" It was dangerous, inviting conversation. On the other hand, Delilah was taking a social risk seeking me out.

"I don't know," she said, eyes darting up and down the hallway, searching. "She's not here today, and I haven't been able to get her on her cell since she left school yesterday. I thought you might know something after that thing in the bathroom, whatever that was." She paused in her hunt to look at me, but I shook my head and she returned to scanning the halls. "If you see her, please tell her to text or call, okay? I'm worried. She was really freaked out, and she wouldn't tell me anything. I'm sure it's *his* fault." She glared down the hall and then stomped away in the other direction, ending our brief moment.

I followed her glare, but I wasn't sure which "he" she meant. Alex Walker was hunched into his locker, trying to shove an over-full gym bag inside, and Will Raffles was strolling toward me down the center of the hallway.

I understood, though.

Alex was only a junior like me, but the word in the halls was that Jade was doing more than tutoring him in statistics. (He was also Dale Walker's nephew, the same Dale Walker Granddad loathed and wouldn't put past a hit-and-run.) Everyone had been buzzing about Alex and Jade, because Jade had been going out with Will off and on since freshman year. If the rumors were true and she and Will were over, as a senior, she had crossed an invisible class line.

The two boys were alike and unlike at the same time. It

was easy to see why Jade could be interested in both. Will had perfect sandy blond hair; Alex's curly hair was dark brown and unruly. But each had a physical presence about them that few other boys in school approached. Where Will's manifested in a casual swagger, Alex was a big guy and comfortable with it: imposing and physically *there.* You felt that presence when either entered a room. Kings among men. Men among boys.

As I watched, Alex managed to shove the bag into his locker and slam the door shut.

He straightened and glanced up and down the hallway once as if he, too, was looking for someone. Maybe Jade? His eyebrows were drawn down and his lips pressed together in a thin line. It was hard to tell what he was feeling. For all I knew, he was constipated. He glanced in Will's direction and straightened his back, pushing his muscular chest out at the same time, but the display was for nothing. Will didn't even spare him a look.

I had never really spoken directly to either of them. Still, I knew things about them that other girls would love to know. Random answers to overheard questions. Like how Will often slept in the nude and Alex's favorite poem was *The Love Song of J. Alfred Prufrock.* Or how the smell of mint made Will inexplicably happy or how Alex felt deeply guilty for that time he'd played mailbox baseball with some other guys from the team. In the end, though, these snippets were just jagged pieces of a meaningless puzzle. I couldn't put them together into a bigger picture any more than I could for the other kids who roamed these halls, Jade included.

ALEX WAS IN MY final period art class. He always seemed out of place there; his big hands delicately grasping paintbrushes when they were genetically predisposed to handling a ball of some kind. He wasn't as beefy as Tank, but he was well over six feet tall and solid, like a tree trunk. He dwarfed poor Kirby Williams, who sat next to him, one of those funny vagaries of alphabetic seating. Kirby weighed less than I did. Not that Alex ever did anything intimidating, and he never seemed to notice Kirby's discomfort.

The two of us were alike in one respect; neither of us talked to anyone else in class if we could help it. I knew why I didn't, and I could guess why Alex chose silence, too. He was well-liked enough for his athletic prowess. You could tell the changing of seasons by the changing of his uniforms. Then his link with Jade had pushed him even higher. But he had a big reason to hide. It was no secret that his father, Frank—Dale's older brother—was an alcoholic. But it wasn't something you mentioned in Lake Mariah. Not given the circumstances. After a weeklong drinking binge a couple of years back, a fire burned down the Walker house, killed Alex's younger brother, and drove their mother away. No charges were ever pressed—it turned out to be faulty wiring, nothing to do with Frank's drunkenness—but everyone in town still knew, and everyone in town blamed Frank for how the family fell apart.

MRS. ROGERS, THE ART teacher, actually allowed me to use my MP3 player during class so long as she wasn't giving a lecture. Today I left it off to save my batteries. Lucy Monroe sometimes sat with me at our table in the back, but she was absent today and I didn't really need it. Not that she talked to me anyway. She was a friend of Shelley's. Besides, everyone was working on the mixed media self-portrait project Mrs. Rogers had assigned us last week. The quiet in the room was broken only by the scratching of pen and pencil and paintbrush.

I had gotten nowhere with mine. My canvas was blank save for the background. I had spent two days so far covering the white with alternating layers of grey and green. It was a dismal mess with no form. Mrs. Rogers was always telling us art had to come from inside us, and as long as I was doing *something*, she would let me be. Apparently there was nothing inside me that wanted to come out that wasn't a blobby muddle of bleakness.

I went to the "salvage" cupboard and was debating a spool of flaxen thread almost the color of my hair when someone reached over my shoulder to pick up a handful of white feathers. I dropped the thread, and it rolled under the cupboard. I dove for it and managed to catch an end, but the spool kept rolling, the thread unwinding. I lay down on the floor and stretched my arm out, but I couldn't quite reach it. Pulling on the thread made it unravel more.

"Sorry. I didn't mean to scare you."

It was Alex.

"You didn't scare me," I said, looking up. From my

vantage on the floor he looked impossibly tall. "You just . . . startled me."

"Here," he said. "Let me." He pushed against the side of the heavy cabinet, lifting it up at an angle. I grabbed the spool and retreated, putting the bins between us. He set the cabinet back down, letting out a big breath as he did. I began the task of winding up the thread.

"Thanks," I offered.

Alex dug into a box and came up with a handful of feathers. It looked like he was holding the remains of a plucked chicken in his big hands, the way the feathers poked out between his fingers. He paused for a moment. I prayed he would walk away and leave me be, but then he asked, "What are you going to do with the thread?"

"Weave a web, a tangled curtain, end to end, with no beginning. Knotted and twisted, snarled and straight, tying me, binding me, binding us all."

I didn't even try to explain. What was the use? There was a moment of silence as he watched me winding the thread. I thought about dropping it back in the bin and walking away, but I could actually picture in my mind what my words were saying. Maybe I had found inspiration for my portrait after all.

"What a tangled web we weave," he finally said, hesitantly.

"When first we practice to deceive?" I finished the line. I looked up at him. Was he calling me a liar? Freak I was used to. A liar was the one thing I definitely wasn't.

"Sorry," he said again, this time with a small private smile. "It was the only vaguely poetic thing I could think of that kind of went with what you said. Was that from something?"

"Sir Walter Scott," I said, though he was probably asking me about what I'd said and not the famous quote.

"Yeah, I know," Alex said. He shot me a quick glance. "We studied him in English."

"Right," I said. A silence started to build up around us. Should I keep talking? "Um . . . I like Edgar Allan Poe's stuff better." We'd studied him recently. His poem, "Alone," had really struck a chord with me. It felt like my life.

Alex nodded. I stared down at the thread. Any minute now the "freak" would be coming out. I should have stopped talking and let him walk away.

"Yeah. He's cool. I like how he did those things with those letter poems, you know?"

"Acrostics," I blurted.

"Right. Hiding the truth in plain sight." He dug through a bin and pulled out another feather. "Anyway, I think I see where you're going with your portrait."

I couldn't help but ask. I wasn't entirely sure myself. The image in my mind was too new and fluid. "You do?"

"Yeah. Well, it's a self-portrait, right?"

"A window into the soul," I responded. At least Mrs. Rogers had said something similar, so I didn't sound like I was completely coming out of left field.

"Right. And you're always kind of hiding behind your hair. That whole tangled curtain thing."

I looked down, and some of my hair fell forward over my face. I reached up to put it behind my ear, even though the movement felt unnatural. Maybe he was right, but still. I had my reasons.

"Not that your hair is tangled. I mean, it's not, like, ratty or anything. I mean . . ." he cleared his throat. "Sorry, I should just shut up."

I couldn't help it. I smiled. Usually I was the one babbling. Maybe it was this side of him, not the sporty jock that everyone could see, that had drawn Jade to him. I wondered what other hidden sides he had. Would it hurt to know more? "What are you going to do with the feathers?"

He grinned back. "I'm not sure yet. Maybe nothing. I had an idea, but it seems kind of stupid now." He dropped the feathers, and they floated down and spread out to land in a ring everywhere but in the bin. He laughed a little at himself as he crouched down to pick them up.

"What was your idea?" I felt so brave, asking questions. But it wasn't like he had to answer me.

He kept his eyes down as he picked up the feathers. "I was thinking something about an eagle. Or a phoenix, maybe. Sounds pretty stupid, doesn't it?"

"No," I answered. "You will rise from the ashes of your father's shame and be reborn stronger than he, and be your own man soaring free." A warmth started in my belly and spread through me.

His hand clenched into a fist, snapping the shafts of a few of the feathers, while the rest floated down unharmed to land on top of the pile of junk in the bin. I reached out my hand to pick one up and then drew it back at the look on Alex's face. I had given him a bitter pill.

"Sorry," I said. "I didn't—" I didn't what? I didn't know what I was saying? I didn't mean to insult his family? I didn't mean to open my mouth and insert my foot yet again? This was exactly why I didn't talk to people.

"I didn't expect that from you, of all people," he said. The open look on his face had disappeared. The door had closed. "I'll see you later, Aria."

I hadn't even known that he knew my name, but I doubted if he'd be using it again anytime soon.

OVER MY HEAD

As I was leaving art class, I saw Delilah standing with a police officer and a worn-out looking blonde woman. They were going through Jade's locker. I walked closer, my embarrassment over what I had said to Alex forgotten.

The woman had Jade's eyes and nose, though a narrower, more pinched version in both cases. "Thank you again for calling, Delilah," she said. "I thought Jade was at your house last night, so I didn't worry when I didn't see her at breakfast this morning."

The policeman paused in his search, a copy of *Othello* in one hand. "Is it normal for your daughter to be out all night on a school night?"

"When the mood takes her or the boy calls," I whispered to myself, my chin tucked into my body. They didn't hear me, but I backed up a few steps anyway and stepped into something solid. Alex. He steadied my shoulders, but he wasn't even looking at me. He was staring at the three of them in front of Jade's locker.

Jade's mother bristled. "No, Officer, it isn't. But she told me she was going to Delilah's to work on a project that was due, and I trust my daughter."

"I'm not insinuating anything, Mrs. Price," he said patiently. "We have to ask every question in missing person cases. I hope you understand."

Alex's fingers clenched, and he released my shoulders. I stepped away, unsure what I should do. He didn't seem to even know I was there. *Questions*, the officer had said. I was curious but not that foolhardy. I put my earphones in and lost myself in The Fray. I hurried off to my car, leaving Alex standing and watching. Other students were beginning to congregate as well, circling like vultures.

I ARRIVED AT HOME that afternoon right after Granddad.

"Woo-hoo!" he sang out from the front porch when he saw me. I couldn't help but laugh as he kicked his skinny legs up and clicked his heels together like a grizzled but spritely leprechaun. He grabbed me around the waist as soon as I got out of my car and spun me around until we were both dizzy. "You did it, Aria! Our dog came in first. We won a thousand dollars!"

That was something to celebrate. We hadn't had that much extra cash in a long time. Gran and Granddad both got social security, but most of it went to regular bills and various medications. Granddad had a heart condition, though he ignored it (and his doctor's advice) most of the time. A scare a few months ago had hospitalized him for two days and cleaned out our cash reserves. I had even been thinking about writing Mom or Dad for money, but I hadn't been able to stoop that low.

Gran came out of the front door, wiping her hands on a dish towel. She must have heard him through the kitchen window. "Porter!" she barked at him. "You know how I feel about gambling! Aria should be using her gift for better things than that!" Her voice was tough, but I could see a slight smile working its way out. It was always the same. She'd give him a sound scolding and then put the money to good use. She was far more practical than puritanical, no matter what she said.

Granddad smiled, ran up the steps to grab her, and danced her around the porch. I hung back as they dipped and bobbed. Cutting the rug, that's what they called it. They had met years and years ago on a dance floor while Granddad was on leave. I never saw them happier than when they were dancing together.

"We are going out to celebrate this weekend," said Granddad firmly as they wound down. "No arguing either, Ellie. We haven't had a good night out in ages."

Gran opened her mouth to argue anyway, but Granddad swooped in to give her a kiss. They both wound up laughing and had to hold on to each other to keep from falling over. I slipped into the house to give them some privacy. I loved seeing them that way, but it made me jealous at the same time.

"IS SOMETHING BOTHERING YOU, Aria?" asked Gran that night at dinner. By the look on her face I knew she had asked it as a question on purpose, rather than rephrasing it as a statement. She was tricky that way. It was a good thing I had never tried to sneak around behind her back since I'd never get away with it. All you had to do was ask me what was going on, and I had to tell. A teen's worst nightmare and a parent's dream—or so you'd think. She'd been there once herself.

"Regret," I said, "that I did not do enough, that I did not do what I could, that I did not do anything but leave when I could have stayed." I groaned. If only I were a normal teenager. I could have just said "no" and been done with it. I wasn't even sure if I meant when I had seen Jade in the bathroom or when I had run into Delilah, Jade's mom, and the policeman after school. I may have answers, but I still didn't know what my subconscious meant. But the regret was there. I could feel it.

Gran leaned forward, waiting for me to explain. Granddad leaned back, staying out of it.

"A girl at school is missing," I finally said. "A policeman was going through her locker today." I poked at the stringy pot roast. Why Gran made winter food in the heat of almost-summer in Florida was a mystery to me. Maybe that's all that was weighing on me after all. It's not like I could have done anything in either situation. It wasn't my fault Jade was missing.

"Ah," said Gran. "And you feel guilty that you didn't try to help."

"No," I said, my own words this time. "I mean, not exactly."

"Well, maybe you should."

"Don't push, Ellie," said Granddad. "She'll do things in her own time, you know."

I shoved my plate away. The meat and potatoes sat heavy in my stomach. "I don't want to talk to the police," I said.

"Don't," said Gran. "Talk to me." She reached out a hand and curled her papery fingers around mine. "Did the girl run away?"

"Running from, running to . . . it's all the same." I pulled my hand away.

Gran leaned forward even more. "Where is the girl, Aria?"

"Nowhere," I said. I shook my head. This was useless. Why did she insist on doing this?

"Is she hurt?"

"Not now." We were playing at questions. "Gran, this is stupid."

"Aria, don't you think you'll feel better if you know?"

"Yes and no," I said. Well, that was clear as mud.

"Ellie," said Granddad. "That's enough. Let her be."

"Porter," retorted Gran, "she won't learn to control her gift if she never uses it."

"Control it?" I stared at Gran, my turn to lean forward. What was she talking about?

"Yes, control it. Aria, you're always trying to hide or bury it. You need to open up to it instead. Learn to channel it so that the answers don't surprise you or . . ."

"Or what?"

"Overpower you."

"Is that even possible?" Every time I had ever tried to control an answer it had always managed to come out anyway.

Gran seemed to know what I was thinking. "Controlling it isn't about repressing it, Aria. It's about letting it go and guiding it. I can show you how, if you'll let me. I still remember."

I shook my head. Letting it go was the last thing I wanted. It already controlled my life enough as it was.

Gran sighed. "You'll get it someday. I know you will. Why don't I get out the—"

"No." I stood up before Gran could finish her question. "I've got homework." Gran's eyes were disappointed, but she nodded as I left the room. Granddad gave me a pat on the back as I went by him. Sometimes, even though Gran was the one who'd shared this curse of a "gift," I felt like Granddad understood how I felt about it better.

MAD WORLD

I could tell at breakfast that Gran was dying to continue her line of questioning. Every time she picked up her fork or took a sip of that morning's horrible juice concoction (I'd only had to smell it to know I definitely didn't want any), she gave me a meaningful look. I silently chewed my grits, even though I knew they'd be a brick in my stomach by second period.

Turns out I was deeply regretting the grits by the time I pulled into the school parking lot. What I saw there didn't help. Someone—probably the cheerleaders—had made a huge banner: JADE, PLEASE COME HOME. They'd hung it across the chain-link fence. People had already stuck flower arrangements and white wooden crosses in the links, like they did when people died in traffic accidents.

I put in my earphones and cranked the volume up as loud as it would go. Students were gathered together in hushed clumps. For once, I could actually walk down the hallway without someone trying to put an elbow through my back. I passed by Tank and resisted the urge to accidentally knock into him.

My biology teacher didn't even notice that I left my earphones in, the steady drumbeat of Fall Out Boy providing the backbeat as I observed everyone in panic mode or pretending to be. Not that I was surprised, but it turned out our school didn't respond well to a crisis. I didn't stop the music for my next two classes either, but Ms. Samson was showing a movie, and algebra II had a substitute who obviously didn't give a damn that some girl he'd never met had disappeared, so he spent the entire class reading the paper.

I was starting to think I might be able to get away without a single question all day until my luck ran out in home economics.

Mrs. Pratt noticed the earphones as soon as I walked in the door. She smiled her I-don't-want-to-but-I-have-to smile and made pulling motions at her ears. I yanked on the cord and tugged both sides out at once, then went to a seat in the very back of the classroom. Home ec had a mix of every grade of student, all girls. I wasn't domestically inclined, but the school counselor, assuming I didn't aspire to any kind of real job, had put me in it. Delilah and Shelley were both in it, too, presumably for the easy A. Quite a few seniors were in the class for that reason. That, and Mrs. Pratt liked to concentrate on baking and everyone preferred her cupcakes to anything the cafeteria put out.

"We're making brownies today," she announced cheerfully.

"Those are Jade's favorite," said Delilah in a pitiful little voice. There was a moment of silence in the class as Mrs. Pratt looked a bit nonplussed. She was a relentlessly positive woman.

"Well," she finally said, "we'll be sure to save a plate for her for when she comes back."

"*If* she comes back," said Shelley. She looked smug, like she somehow imagined the world to be a better place now that Jade was missing. For her, perhaps it was. She seemed to delight in making other people miserable, and Jade had ruined that for her more than once. She certainly liked to make *me* miserable and had never let me forget the incident in the bathroom my freshman year. She called me Tammy Tampon whenever she saw me, and Jade wasn't around. Thank God it had never caught on with anyone else. I had enough nicknames as it was.

"*When* she comes back," said Delilah. I held no particular love or hate for her, but I had to admit that she looked lost without Jade and it had only been a day. Her normally perfectly straightened brown hair had been allowed to frizz, and there were dark circles under her eyes. She was probably going to look like an absolute wreck tomorrow if Jade hadn't reappeared by then.

"Why did she run away anyway?" asked Shelley, challenging Delilah directly. A few other girls in class nodded as if they couldn't imagine any reasonable answer to that question either. Other than the personal crisis Jade had been suffering under on Monday morning, I couldn't see why either.

"We all run from what chases us," I answered softly

and only to myself. Everyone else had gathered close to the front, especially after Mrs. Pratt had said the word brownies.

"I don't know," said Delilah defensively. "But—"

"Welllllll," said Mrs. Pratt again, drawing it out this time in an annoying little trill, "we'll be sure to ask her all about it over a plate of yummy brownies when she gets back. Now let's get cooking!" She picked up a wooden spoon and twirled it in the air like a wand, as if she could magic away any bad feelings or nasty tempers. She'd been stuck teaching home ec for so long she'd forgotten what the real world was like.

For some reason, Delilah turned around and looked right at me. I ducked my head, pretending to look for a pen, like we ever took notes in home ec anyway. I felt oddly naked without my earphones in.

Mrs. Pratt wrote out the ingredients on the board and began her spiel about the wonders of chocolate, like any of us needed convincing of that. I started pulling ingredients out of the cupboard while everyone else sampled from the block of chocolate Mrs. Pratt had on the front counter. There was an odd number of people in the class, which meant that I normally got to work by myself or team up with Mrs. Pratt for those things that actually required two people for something other than social interaction.

I was cracking eggs into my bowl when Delilah walked over to me.

"Can I work with you today?" she asked.

"Today is no more special than any other day," I said,

"and work is work, but this is hardly working, I'd say." Stupid, stupid rhyming.

She gave me a look but took my nonsensical reply as a yes. What was she up to? I passed her the bowl to stir. Mrs. Pratt raised an eyebrow then smiled, showing all her teeth. She evidently thought we were bonding over brownies. I didn't know what we were doing, but I was pretty sure nothing good would come of it, except maybe some decent baked goods for once. Delilah was a better baker than I was. I'd inherited my cooking skills from Granddad.

She stirred a few times and then passed the bowl back. "Why do you always say stuff like that?"

"Because I have to." I stirred furiously, not looking at her. "I'm not making fun of you or anything," I added quietly. Maybe I owed her that.

"Okay," she said. I was grateful she didn't roll her eyes. She started grating the chocolate, spreading out some parchment paper across the counter first. "Look, do you know anything about where Jade is or not?"

"No," I said. I thought that was it, but then more words came tumbling out of me, like an afterthought. "But try asking me again."

I felt a flicker of some strange joy. That had never happened before. Why would I ask someone to question me further? It had to be good, right? I fished a bit of eggshell out of the batter with a fingernail and licked the batter from my finger.

She was quiet for a moment. "So, do you know where she is or not?"

"No, I do not. Try again."

She blew out her breath and closed her eyes. I was amazed at her persistence. "Are you playing games with me or what?"

"Or what." My inner oracle was apparently feeling playful today. "No games," I added. "I'm sorry." I wouldn't have been surprised at all if she had walked away, but she kept on grating, the pile of chocolate growing ever taller.

"Are you going to tell me where she is?"

"Yes," I said, surprising us both. She stopped grating, and I stopped stirring.

"Where is she?"

"South of Laurel Creek. North of the oldest oak. East of no man's road. West of the wind."

"Laurel Creek . . . so she's not far." Delilah looked relieved but bewildered. "What's she doing out there?"

"Nothing." I was as confused as Delilah. I walked the woods all the time, and that was near the lake, though I didn't know exactly what I'd meant by no man's road. Was she hanging out at the swimming area? Hiding out at the bluff? Did her dad have a hunting cabin out there? A lot of local families did. It was best to wear bright orange when walking around during hunting season.

"How do you even know she's there?"

"I don't," I said.

Delilah shook her head, obviously annoyed. Chocolate curls scattered across the counter as the grater went across the top of the pile. "Okay, seriously, what the hell?"

"Hell is in the details," I whispered, stepping back. I couldn't really blame her, but I didn't know what else to say. There were no explanations I could offer that wouldn't damn me. Gran was always telling me to keep the truth of my gift to myself. I could hear her oft-repeated warning in my head. *Be careful, Aria. People will want to use you.*

"Girls!" Mrs. Pratt cried. "What a *scrumptious* mess!" Did she not know how annoying that shrill warble was? "Here are some paper towels for you!"

She held the towels out to Delilah, who just looked at me. I put my spoon down and took the roll. I pulled off a few towels and wiped ineffectually at the counter, managing to smear the chocolate rather than clean it up.

"Try some water, dear," said Mrs. Pratt, not budging.

Delilah glowered at her.

"Now, then, it looks like it is time to incorporate the chocolate." Mrs. Pratt smiled at Delilah, who grimaced but picked up the parchment and unceremoniously dumped everything into the bowl.

I sighed and picked up the spoon and started stirring again. Actually, I was a little glad Mrs. Pratt hovered over us with no intention of leaving. I had no idea what I was going to say to Delilah that would fix or explain what I had already said. Yet another example of why I could never talk to people.

UNHINGED

Delilah was leaning against my car when I got to the parking lot after school. I walked as slowly as I could across the steaming asphalt, hoping she was only taking a breather from the heat, but she didn't move as I approached. I stopped a few feet away.

"Were you lying to me earlier?" she asked, getting straight to the point.

"No," I said.

"So do you or don't you know anything about where Jade is?"

"Yes," I said, though that wasn't much of an answer. I held up my hand before she could ask another question or slap me. I knew it was one or the other. I had to think of something to say, something plausible. "I overheard her talking on her phone," I said.

Delilah opened her mouth, and I rushed my next sentence without really thinking it out.

"She said something about going out in the woods by the creek, that's all. I don't know who with. I don't know why. That's it."

I stepped forward and pulled on my door handle. It was open; the locks were broken and the Colt wasn't worth stealing anyway.

"That's all I know," I said. "Really. Okay?"

I forced myself to look in her eyes. *Don't ask, don't ask, don't ask,* I kept repeating in my head, even though I didn't have any hope it would work. It never had before.

She backed off and nodded.

I sighed and climbed in my car, slamming the door. The heat wrapped around me, and I drew in a deep breath, then wished I hadn't. My lungs burned with the stored heat. I turned the key and pulled out, watching as Delilah receded in the rearview mirror like an accusation.

GRAN SEEMED TO KNOW something was going on as soon as I walked in the door. Had she been casting the stones on me? She stood at the threshold of the kitchen silently watching as I dropped my book bag on the floor by the couch. Then she held out her arms, and I walked into them.

"So," she said, leaving it at that.

"Let's see if we can find out where Jade ran off to," I whispered. "Somewhere in the woods, that's all I know, really, so far."

"Okay," said Gran. She took me by the hand and led me to the dining room table. Granddad was there reading the paper. He folded it and put it down when we entered and regarded us both silently. I sat down.

Gran jumped right in, no preamble, no preparation. "Where is Jade?" she asked me.

"South of Laurel Creek. North of the oldest oak. East of no man's road. West of the wind." I shook my head. "That's the same thing I answered earlier. It doesn't say much, just that she didn't go far."

"Hm," said Granddad. I wanted to hug him; he didn't question a single thing. He simply got up and pulled a map out of the hutch. He unfolded it and spread it out on the table. It was tattered and ripped in a few places, but it was a pretty decent map of this part of Florida. I recognized it from when he took me out fishing.

"Good idea, dear," said Gran.

"I have one every now and then," he said.

I offered him a small smile and leaned over the table to look at the map. I pointed to Laurel Creek. It was actually the name of a whole section of land, which included swamps and scrubs and everything in between, and ran into a larger wildlife protection area. The creek itself ran around the eastern edge of the park far enough north to run into another larger river. There were a number of unmarked roads and trails running through it and tons of oak trees. Jade could be anywhere, though it would stand to reason she'd be somewhere with shelter. Maybe by Three Oaks? That was near the swimming area and one of the boat ramps.

"Well," said Gran, considering the map, "if you're talking about being south of the actual Laurel Creek, it would place her somewhere around here." She circled an area with her finger and then looked at me. "Is she here?"

"She's nowhere," I answered.

Gran considered for a minute and went in a different direction entirely. She reached out and took my hand. "Is she . . . alive?"

"Her spirit has flown," I said. "She's gone, gone, gone."

The words caught in my throat, burning and raw like I had swallowed acid. My vision darkened for a moment, Gran's concerned face receding and then looming large. I swayed and blinked, pulling back, Gran's fingers loosening. I fell off my chair and landed hard. I sat dazed for a moment and then let myself sink back onto the wood floor.

"ARIA! ARIA!"

I blinked groggily. What was Granddad yelling about? What time was it? It couldn't be morning yet. I opened my eyes to see both of my grandparents looking down at me. Behind their heads I could see a spider spinning a web in the corner of the ceiling, circling around and around. What was I doing on the floor? I sat up.

"You are okay now," Gran said awkwardly. No questions in it.

"Yes—" I stopped as I remembered why I was down there. Jade wasn't missing. She hadn't run off to the woods. She wasn't hiding out in an old hunting cabin or swimming in the lake. Jade was gone.

Granddad pulled me to my feet and helped me back onto my chair. The map had been pulled askew by my fall and suffered another rip, right across Laurel Creek, tearing it in two. I couldn't even look at it.

"She's dead," I said. Gran nodded, looking at me warily like I might pass out again. It had only ever happened a few times before. Only with the big questions. Like whether or not there was a God. Why we were here. Unknowable things. Or things I didn't really want to know.

"If you think you can do it, I need to ask you one more question," said Gran.

"About Jade?"

"Yes. To help the police . . . find her body."

I swallowed and nodded. Granddad put his hands on my shoulders, presumably to help keep me on my chair, just in case.

"Where is Jade's body located?"

"South of Laurel Creek. North of the oldest oak. East of no man's road. West of the wind." I closed my eyes to combat my nausea. Same nonsense as before. I stood up, surprising Granddad. "I need to lie down," I said.

He let me go. I stumbled to my room and sank down on my bed, then pulled my MP3 player out of my book bag and plugged myself in to K.T. Tunstall's honey tones.

Four songs later, Granddad came in and sat on the corner of my bed. I hadn't expected him. It was usually Gran that would come to me with her advice. Her plotting. I thumbed off the music and sat up.

"Aria," he said, "Ellie thinks we need to go to the police with this information."

I looked at him, not saying anything.

"Ellie thinks we should just waltz into the station and let you say your piece." I heard Gran snort from the living room, but she stayed where she was. "*I* think we should stay out of it. There'll be an investigation. Probably the state police. Who knows what. We don't need to be involved in that, not right now. Too many questions."

I couldn't agree more.

"But we are talking about someone's daughter here."

His rheumy eyes locked on my own. I sat up, scrunching myself against the wall and drawing my legs up under me. I pictured Jade's mom and how lost she had looked, staring into Jade's locker. Like she was looking through a window into a stranger's room.

"But we don't really know where she is," I said, trying to keep the whine out of my voice.

"True," he said.

"We could try again," called Gran from the other room, "with different questions."

With his back safely to the door, Granddad gave a barely perceptible shake of his head. I didn't like the idea either. I felt like I was insubstantial enough as it was. More questions were the last thing I wanted.

"I already told Delilah, Jade's friend, that I overheard Jade saying she was going into the woods near the creek. She's already talked to the police once. Maybe she'll tell them."

Granddad reached out to take my hand. I hadn't realized I was squeezing my pillow. He pulled me into a hug, and for a minute I closed my eyes against his shirt, breathing in the soothing scent of his Old Spice cologne. "Let's leave it at that for now and see what happens," he said loudly for Gran's benefit. Gran snorted from the other room again, and Granddad spoke more quietly this time, for my ears only. "There's no need to invite trouble we don't need."

Gran didn't like hiding or sneaking around, but I agreed with Granddad. There was no harm in letting things take their natural course. It's not like I could do anything for Jade now anyway. My shoulders shook as a sob escaped. Granddad patted my back, murmuring comforting words that did nothing to make me feel any better.

ON THE OUTSIDE

The next morning came too soon. I pulled into the school parking lot to find teachers directing students to go directly to the gymnasium rather than to class. The sign pleading for Jade to "come home soon" had been partially ripped down, like someone had been stopped in the middle of the removal or had thought better of it. Even more flowers were piled around it, along with teddy bears. The police must have discovered Jade's body. Of course the news had spread across town like wildfire. I wondered if Delilah had told them what I'd said or if they had figured it out on their own.

Gran had very obviously wanted to ask me more questions about Jade's death this morning, but I had refused. I still felt a strangeness about myself from the day before, like I wasn't quite all there. *What's done is done.* Jade was gone, and that was it. There was nothing I could have done then, and nothing I could do now.

Girls were crying, mascara tracks marking faces every direction I looked, even those who'd been eaten up with jealousy when Jade was alive. I drove around them, parked, and followed the line of students snaking into the gym.

It was the first time I had been in there outside of gym class for a long time. Needless to say, I avoided pep rallies and basketball games. The place always smelled of mildew, sweat, and defeat. Today it was buzzing with whispers and muffled sobs as the students quietly took their seats. I climbed to the top of the visitors' side and sat back against the cool, concrete-block wall painted with a giant constipated-looking Florida panther: our school mascot.

Lake Mariah High School had almost seven hundred students from around the entire county, but the gym seemed at least half empty with everyone clustered together on the lower bleachers. Jade's closest friends were huddled in a weeping mass toward the center of the home side. Delilah was the most vocal, practically wailing. There were no mascara tracks on her pale and shiny face. It was probably the first time she had set foot outside of her home without any makeup since the seventh grade. Usually I was the only girl in school without any war paint. I almost felt sorry for her, as if she were stripped bare and I was seeing her core, the lost girl on the inside.

Even Shelley was putting on a show nearby. Considering what I knew about her and how she had really felt about Jade—an all-consuming jealousy darkly tinged with hate—her misery was obviously a show put on for the rest of the world. I doubted if anyone was buying her performance. She dripped venom, and most people had been stung by it at one time or another. But Shelley wasn't the only one around with wicked secrets. The town was full of them. All places were. I'd learned that lesson before I'd moved here.

Principal James entered the gym and walked to the center of the court. He cleared his throat and tapped the microphone, sending a small boom echoing off the walls. "Good morning, students," he said and then stopped. He wiped at his forehead with the back of his hand. "As you all have heard by now, we've had some tragic news. Before anything else, why don't we have a moment of silence for our fellow student, Jade Price." He bowed his head, and the gym quieted until all you could hear were Delilah's shaking sobs.

I don't pray, but I closed my eyes for a minute. I tried to picture Jade as I was used to seeing her, laughing and smiling.

Principal James cleared his throat again and explained, with a lot of pauses and forehead wiping, that we were all welcome to attend free counseling sessions. In fact, he encouraged us to do so. There would also be a funeral service for Jade in a few days. She was to be buried in the local Lake Mariah cemetery, and everyone was invited to pay his or her respects. There would be classes the rest of the week, but attendance would not be taken, given the circumstances. (It was already Thursday, anyway.) His shoulders sagged. By the end of his speech, he looked wrung out and half the size he'd seemed when he walked into the gym.

"Please don't worry if you see some police around as

they investigate," he concluded. "I trust that you will all be cooperative."

That caught my attention. What if Delilah had told the police what I'd told her? Would they want to question me? The chances of that going well were slim. It would likely be a total disaster. I needed to find out from Delilah what, if anything, she had told them.

Mrs. Elmore, the senior English teacher, came out and took the microphone from him.

"Everyone, go on to class. Sign-up sheets for counseling will be on the wall by the cafeteria." She put an arm around Principal James's shoulders and pulled him away. He was obviously crying. That was when I remembered: he was related to Jade somehow. An uncle twice removed maybe? In a town as small as ours, there was a good chance you were related to someone else, except to me. Gran and Granddad had moved here when I came to live with them during middle school, after Mom said I couldn't stay with her and Dad had chosen his new wife over me. My grandparents had come to Florida to retire in Tarpon Springs, but when it became obvious having less people around would be far easier on me, we had moved here to the middle of nowhere.

I waited until the gym was almost empty before getting up. My dress caught on the corner of the last bleacher seat and yanked me back. I heard the thin cotton rip, and I swore under my breath at it. Hopefully it was mendable. If money was tight enough for Granddad to risk Gran's wrath over gambling, I didn't want to have to ask her to go out shopping, even if most of the dresses she bought me were from Goodwill. I didn't want them to use our wind-fall for something as mundane as clothing.

I unhooked myself from the bench and turned this way and that trying to figure out where the tear was. As I looked back over my shoulder, I caught a glimpse of Will Raffles standing in the open door of the gym.

For a moment, I thought he was staring at me and I felt the heat rise in my cheeks, but it seemed more like he was looking off into space, lost in his own world. I watched as some of the last stragglers walked toward his exit. They stopped when they saw him, ducked their heads, and turned to go out another door instead. He didn't seem to notice.

It was odd. Will had always been the golden boy. He hadn't needed Jade to boost his popularity, like Alex. He moved through the school like a panther or like a lion in the middle of his pride. He was universally admired without exception: the boys wanting to be him, the girls wanting to be with him. Even the teachers extolled his virtues in both public and private. Ms. Timmons, the American history teacher, had a very unhealthy crush on him. Someone had teasingly asked her whom she liked. Not that she would ever admit it out loud. She was as prim and proper as they came, at least on the outside.

I would have expected the group of girls to comfort him in his loss instead of avoiding him, but maybe they didn't want to intrude. As far as I knew, he and Jade had still been going out, Alex notwithstanding.

Then his jaw clenched. His steel grey eyes found mine for only a second, but it felt like much longer. I couldn't move. He turned and shoved through the door, slamming it behind him with a loud clank. My blush rose again in full bloom.

I stood there, willing my heartbeat to slow. What was I, some kind of silly girl unable to control herself in the presence of loss? I was no stranger to it, after all. I let out a bark of a laugh and went back to my dress, finding the rip along the waistband. Luckily it was a small one and definitely fixable once I got home. I shifted my backpack to cover the hole and left the gym through the same door Will had. Less than half a minute had passed, but he was long gone.

HERO / HEROINE

I got a closet filled up to the brim
With the ghosts of my past and their skeletons
"Hero / Heroine" by Boys Like Girls

I figured out why the girls had avoided Will as soon as I got to home ec. No one was making even the pretense of settling down, and Mrs. Pratt was fiddling with ingredients like nothing unusual was going on. It was her normal denial of anything unhappy, though it was hard to see how she could ignore the fact that Jade was, in fact, dead. Everyone was gathered around Delilah. As I squeezed past them to get to a seat in the back, she slammed a book on a table with theatrical flair.

Her tears were gone now, and only anger was left. "I'm telling you, there's no way this was an accident! She told me something happened last weekend, but she wouldn't tell me what. It had to be *him.* I know he's involved somehow."

"Yeah, sure," said Shelley. "*Him.* I heard she went out with Alex *and* Will last weekend." The way she said it made it clear what she thought of any girl who would go on dates with two boys in one weekend, though I was sure she would do the same, given the opportunity. "So, why are you pointing a finger at Alex? It could have been Will."

"Jealousy," I whispered under my breath. Delilah's jealousy of Jade? Or Alex? Or, more likely, of Jade dating Alex? I wondered if I should put my earphones back in before someone else asked a question. I held them in my hand, out and ready. I could barely make out the jingle jangly sound of Boys Like Girls. Mrs. Pratt wasn't paying much attention. I could probably get away with keeping my ears open a little longer.

"I just *know*," said Delilah. "Alex lives right near the lake, out that way. It was *him*. I know it."

"Shhhhh!" said Catherine Stevens. She was one of those girls who always strives to be part of the popular crowd but never quite makes it all the way in. "You don't know that for sure. Jade wasn't even found all that close to the lake. She was found south of the creek."

That checked out with what I'd told Delilah. I scrunched down in my seat in case she turned to look at me, but she was on a roll.

"I watch *CSI*," said Delilah. "He could have moved the body."

I could see some of the other girls nodding, like what Delilah had said was sage and true. But why *would* Alex have killed Jade? Who said anyone had? Maybe she'd had an accident.

"Okay. But there was that hit-and-run, too. I think there's a serial killer out there! Any of us could be next!" Catherine put a hand to her throat, like one was after her neck right now. Everyone ignored her.

"It wasn't Alex *or* Will," said Shelley, stepping closer to Delilah's desk. "She probably just went out in the woods and did something stupid. It happens. Stop being all dramatic and trying to pin it on one of her boyfriends." She stressed the plurality of the boyfriends again, in case anyone had missed it before.

Delilah threw a vicious look at her and stood up to poke a finger at Shelley's chest. "You're only saying that because you want to do Will."

I quickly hid a grin behind my hand. Delilah was right. On the other hand, half the student body wanted to sleep with Will, including one of the football players . . . including Delilah herself, for that matter.

"Girls!" said Mrs. Pratt finally. She shouldered her way into the center of the crowd. "That's enough of that. This is no way to act, especially today. Let's get to our seats. Maybe some cookies are what we need." She made shooing motions.

Shelley's face was purplish-red. I wasn't sure if it was in anger or embarrassment or both. She pointed a finger at Delilah but then backed away to sit down in a seat across the room.

"Mrs. Pratt, I need to be excused," said Delilah. She left the room without waiting for permission.

Mrs. Pratt just kept on waving students to their seats and told us to take out our measuring cups. She wasn't paying any attention to me at all. I took a deep breath and snuck out the door after Delilah.

I HAD A MOMENT of déjà vu as I followed her into the same bathroom I'd found her with Jade. She was staring at herself in one of the broken mirrors, her face fragmented into pieces, the cracks lacing her image like a spiderweb.

"What do you want, Aria?" she asked, not turning around.

"Peace," I answered. I cleared my throat and rushed on to my question before she could say anything else. "I wanted to know if you told the police what I told you."

"Yeah," she said, sounding drained. "Yesterday afternoon." She turned around and leaned back against the sink.

I slumped against the wall. That probably meant I was next for questioning. In that case, I was doomed. The police wouldn't make the weird teenage girl spouting random bits of poetry and nonsense answers into an honorary detective. They would lock me away in a loony bin.

"I didn't tell them who told me," she continued. "I just told them I'd heard she might have gone out into the woods over that direction. She went running with Alex out there sometimes anyway, and I told them that, too." She turned around and looked at me. "Why?"

"I'm scared," I said. True enough, though I hadn't really wanted to share that. I cleared my throat again. "I don't really want to talk to the police. If you could—" I looked down at the floor and then forced myself to look her in the eye again—"I'd really appreciate it if you didn't tell them it was me that told you. I just . . . I don't want to be involved." My eyes slipped back down to the dirty, beige tile floor.

"Okay," she said after a moment's silence. "But if you do know something else, tell me." She stepped towards me, her strappy sandals looking unaccountably cheerful and out of place. I involuntarily took a step back.

"I don't," I said. "That was it. I promise." I made myself look up again and resisted the urge to let my hair fall forward over my face. I had to look like I was telling the truth. Inside, I cringed at the partial lie, but I really didn't know anything more than I had told her. And I didn't want to know anything about it at all.

"Thank you," I said, meaning it. I reached behind my back to open the door. "See you in class." I turned and left, walking quickly and stuffing my earphones in my ears in case she called a question after me.

TRUTH

The day crept by. Even with my headphones on and the sound turned up loud, questions were flying in the hallways so fast and so often that I found myself muttering constantly, during every break between songs or lulls in the music. It was a mixture of nonsense and gruesome details. Whatever subconscious part of me provided the answers was apparently faster than my conscious brain. I couldn't keep track of which answer went to which question, and it all became a meaningless stream of noise passing through me like a river. The only concrete answer I could hold on to was when I stopped to catch my breath before lunch, letting the other students move on without me.

I had reached the end of my playlist and hadn't yet started the next one when a couple passed by me. "Do you think it hurt a lot when she died?" asked the girl, hanging on her boyfriend's arm as they trailed the crowd into the cafeteria. I didn't hear his answer, but I felt mine as it gushed out of me.

"Blood," I mumbled, "and pain. White-hot as the knife leaves the body. Again and again and again." A stabbing ache settled in my gut so suddenly I ran for a nearby water fountain and retched into it. For a moment, all I could think was how glad I was I hadn't eaten much breakfast. One of my earphones came out as I pulled my hair back so it wouldn't get wet. Jade's death wasn't an accident. It had been a murder, and a painfully bloody one at that, unless she had somehow managed to stab herself with a knife. Repeatedly.

I let my long hair fall forward again to cover me from any curious eyes, then I put my errant earphone back in with shaking fingers, using the back of my free hand to wipe at my mouth. I took a drink of the lukewarm water. I hit play. The long whistling introduction to a quirky, melancholy tune by Alexander began playing. The truth, indeed. My stomach clenched and gurgled, almost in time with the music.

I debated whether or not I should take advantage of the lack of roll call to skip out on school but decided I might as well stay since I had made it through half the day already. I also wasn't sure I could drive. My legs felt rubbery, like they might give out at any minute.

I went into the cafeteria and grabbed some crackers from the salad bar. Ms. Mabel, stationed at the register, looked at them and hitched her head to the right when I tried to pay. "No charge, sweetie," she said, her chocolate eyes kind. "You look a little pale. Were you a good friend of that girl?"

"No," I choked out. "I knew her not at all."

I took the plate of crackers with both hands, leaving behind the tray and Mabel's questioning look, and went outside. She was generally a good person, though I had learned to avoid the chili on Thursdays when she made it. She wasn't above using expired meat.

It was sweltering now, and all of the other students were inside in the air-conditioning. The heat didn't bother me. I was used to it since neither my car nor our house had air-conditioning. Granddad had salvaged an old window unit for the living room, but it wheezed out more noise than air. I welcomed the warmth, actually. It kept everyone else away. I walked slowly and carefully over to the one scraggly oak tree on the school's small inner courtyard. It was a deformed specimen covered in scars where kids had carved their initials and undying proclamations of love. All the lower branches had been broken off under the weight of backpacks, and the upper branches left didn't provide much shade. But it was the only option, other than a group of scrub palms, so I sat down at the base and leaned back against the scratchy bark.

I crossed my legs under my dress and put the plate on my lap. The crackers were going down okay, but that might have been because there were no questions to answer out here in the Florida sun. I had questions of my own now. Who had killed Jade? And why? But even if I asked them, I wouldn't get an answer. I was only a conduit for other people's desires.

"Can I join you?"

I dropped my saltine, and it broke into pieces on the

plate as my reply came, "You will." I hastily added, "If you want," to cover up the awkwardness of the answer. I looked up as someone came around from behind the tree, momentarily blocking the sun. A halo of light around blond hair blinded me for a moment, resolving in Will's face, looking down at me.

"Thanks," he said with a wry grin. "No one seems to want my company today."

He slumped down with his back against the tree, too. Our shoulders touched. I could only see his face if I turned my head so I settled for staring at him out of the corner of my eye instead. I had never been this close to him before. It was seldom I was this close to anyone, other than Gran and Granddad or Tank's elbow. Why was he here, sitting next to me?

He didn't say anything for a few minutes. I studied his profile as I picked up a sliver of broken cracker and continued nibbling. His eyelashes were long and darker than his hair. He had a strong chin and smooth cheeks with no trace of stubble. I was used to seeing him smiling, but today, not surprisingly, he wore a frown. He picked up a twig and drew a lazy spiral in the sand.

"I guess you're not a big eater," he said finally.

I looked down at my plate of crackers. "Not today," I said. "You either, I guess." He didn't have a plate with him at all.

"No, not today."

I itched to ask him what he was doing out here with me. To ask him about Jade. Instead, I picked up a new cracker and considered it for a moment before taking a bite. He leaned forward, his shoulder rubbing heat against mine as he did, and craned his neck so he could see my face.

"Ariel, isn't it?"

"Aria," I said. "A melody sung solo." I gave silent thanks that the answer hadn't come out any stranger than that.

"Oh," he said. "Sorry. I must have heard it wrong."

"That's okay. Everyone does that." I should have stopped after the first sentence. Now I sounded like I was asking for sympathy. "I mean it's a strange name. Not very common."

"Pretty," he said, still staring at me. "I like it."

I dropped my head forward so my hair formed a curtain between us. He wasn't having any of that. He reached out and tucked it behind my ear. I tried not to flinch, as if boys touched me in such a personal way all the time. I swallowed and resisted the sudden urge to lick my dry lips. Only girls in movies did that.

"I guess we've never really met before. My name is—"

"William Raffles," I said. Did he really think anyone in this school didn't know his name?

"You sound like my mom. Just call me Will unless you want me to think I'm in trouble." He laughed. "Or William Thomas Raffles if I've *really* done it."

"Will," I said, trying it out. It felt strange on my tongue.

"So," he said, and he leaned even closer, his grey eyes on mine, "do you think I did it, too?"

"*No*," I breathed, surprised at the rush of relief that swamped me as my answer registered.

"Good." He leaned back against the tree again. Our shoulders didn't meet this time.

We sat in silence, my crackers forgotten until the bell

rang. Will stood up and brushed himself off, then put out his hand to help me up. I took it, and he hauled me to my feet like I weighed nothing, even though I was nearly as tall as he was.

"I'll see you around," he said and walked off. Then he turned and gave me that same wry smile he'd had before he sat down. "Aria of the beautiful but lonely melody."

SOLITUDE

I spent sixth period gym on the bleachers watching the other girls jump hurdles. It hadn't taken much to convince Coach Townsend that I wasn't fit for physical activity. Someone had asked another question about Jade's death as I got to the locker room, and I had just made it to the toilet in time to lose the crackers I'd had for lunch. Coach Townsend had wanted me to see the school nurse, but I convinced her I would be fine if I could sit quietly for a while. She hadn't even made me change out of my dress, which might have been a tactical error on my part. Shorts and a T-shirt would have been better in the midday heat.

I snuck my earphones out of my backpack, hiding the cord in my hair. I flicked forward until Evanescence came up, and I turned the sound up until the plaintive voice of Amy Lee filled me from the inside out. The hurdlers shimmered in the heat, their flailing elbows and white gym

T-shirts making them look like ungainly egrets wanting to take flight.

Across the field, a group of boys were running sprints. Alex was among them but not. He was waiting his turn like everyone else, but there was a distance between him and the other boys. No one was talking to him or looking at him. He stood ramrod straight and still, except for his right hand, which flexed and unflexed in a fist. He was so big, taller and obviously stronger than nearly everyone else, much more like a man than a boy. A man apart.

Tank and one other boy broke from the loose line and went over to stand in front of Alex. I had no idea what they were saying, but it was clear that Alex didn't appreciate it. He shook his head, a frown on his face. Tank moved closer, his height a match for Alex's. He outweighed Alex by a good bit as well, but in such close proximity, he didn't compare well. Tank seemed like a pig fattened for slaughter while Alex was like a racehorse, muscles taut and ready.

After a few more heated words, Tank pushed Alex with both hands, making him stumble back a step. Alex pushed back, and Tank fell into the other boy, knocking him over. I leaned forward, not sure what to do, looking to see if any of the coaches had noticed yet. There was shouting now, but through my headphones I couldn't catch any words, just anger. I lost sight of Alex for a minute as Tank and the other boys surrounded him.

I stood up, then sat back down. What could I do? What should I do? Coach Clark—the baseball coach and Coach Townsend's male counterpart—had finally noticed and had run into the fray. I saw Alex again, still standing, face-to-face with Tank, their noses nearly touching. Coach Clark stepped between them and shoved them apart, shouting too.

Alex turned his back on the whole thing and stomped toward the locker room. Tank shouted something after him, restrained by a hand on his barrel chest by Coach Clark. Another boy threw a cup full of Gatorade at Alex's back, hitting him with a splash of orange-colored liquid.

Alex didn't even stop walking.

A bunch of kids laughed, Coach Clark uselessly barking for order.

How fast he had fallen, I thought. Not that long ago he'd been carried on their shoulders.

I WAS SURPRISED TO see Alex walk into art class after gym. His hair was still wet from the shower, dark curls dampening his collar. He seemed calm. But word of the altercation with Tank had preceded him, and the other students stepped out of his way more quickly than was necessary. He didn't say anything, just walked to his desk and dropped his backpack on the floor and pulled out his drawer to get his self-portrait out.

I had no idea why, but I felt like I should say something to him. Do something. It made no sense. For all I knew, he *was* the one who had killed Jade. I shivered for a minute as I imagined those big hands of his holding a knife. Just twenty minutes ago, he'd looked like he could take Tank's face off with them. Of course, I'd felt that way about Tank myself a time or two.

I gathered my pencils and took them to the sharpener, not looking at anyone as I walked across the classroom. I stuck the first pencil in and listened to the industrial whir of the sharpener. Alex was hard at work on his portrait, ignoring the whispers. A girl who normally worked at the table right next to him and had been trying to catch his eye picked up her things and took them to another desk, half the room away, like she thought he was going to bite her. I could tell he noticed when she moved. His eyes flicked up to the now-empty desk and then did a quick circuit of the room, landing briefly on mine and then, more determinedly, back on his art. I was the master of the quick glance. I knew it when I saw it.

I pulled out the pencil, which I had sharpened down to half its original size. Useless. I stuck in the next one and watched it this time, pulling it out before it, too, disappeared. I worked quickly through the rest and gathered them up in my right hand.

My stomach gurgled, a lingering reminder of my earlier upset. If this kept up, I was going to waste away to nothing. The shapeless yellow dress I was wearing already hung from me, too large and too square for my angular frame. I walked back towards my desk, my left hand rubbing my stomach, trying to get it to settle. Maybe Mrs. Rogers would give me permission to get some peanut butter crackers from the vending machine in the teachers' lounge.

I wasn't paying enough attention to where I was going, and I walked into the corner of Shelley's desk, my hip bumping it and sloshing her painting water. A few drops splashed onto the desk, missing the elaborate and gaudy collage she was working on entirely, but she sneered at me anyway.

"Watch where you're going, you freak," she said, pulling her picture farther away from me.

"Sorry," I said, even though I really hadn't done anything wrong. It was easier than arguing. I stepped back, my hand still cradling my stomach as it knotted in pain again. I could really use a Sprite.

"What, are you pregnant or something?"

"Something only, only something, something is nothing to me," I said, my shock at the question not enough to stop the inevitable nonsense. How could she even ask that? I'd never even kissed a boy. But my nonanswer only served to ratchet up the look of distaste on Shelley's face.

"Totally preggers," chimed in a girl behind me: Lucy, the last person I'd have thought would say something in this class, since she deigned to sit near me sometimes. "I saw her throw up in gym today."

Shelley leaned toward me, her eyes narrowed. She looked me up and down as I tried to think of something, anything, to defend myself. "Who'd sleep with *that?*" she finally said and then laughed, a few other girls joining in.

"Someone," I whispered, prepared enough this time, at least, to not speak loudly. But it only served to make my answer all the more plaintive and pitiful. A dull flush spread across my face. I forced my hand away from my stomach, even though it roiled even more under their scrutiny. I burned to say something back and spill her dirty secrets. How she had lost her virginity at thirteen to a high school boy. That her current boyfriend had slept with two other girls. That scare she'd had sophomore year when a condom had broken and she'd cried every day in the girls' bathroom until her period.

But I said nothing. Anything I said would only lead to questions, more questions, and nothing good ever came of that. And who would believe me anyway?

"Leave her alone." I felt a warm hand on my shoulder, moving me to the side. Alex stepped in front of me, solid as a wall.

"Oh, I see," said Shelley with a smirk. "And here's the answer to the big question. *You* must be the dad. Congrats, Alex!" The other girls laughed with her, a crueler edge to it. She leaned to the right past Alex so she could look me right in the eye. "Better be careful. Don't want to wind up like his last date."

I couldn't see his face, standing behind him, but I saw his fist clench. Without thinking, I grabbed his hand and pulled him away.

"Don't," I said. I kept pulling until we were through the door and out in the hall. Mrs. Rogers didn't bother stopping us. I dropped his hand as the door shut behind us, blocking their laughter. He looked at me a long moment, his dark eyes hard. Did he expect me to say thank you?

"You shouldn't let them talk to you that way," he said.

"*You* shouldn't, either," I said, perhaps more sharply than I needed to. What was I supposed to do anyway? Threaten them? But I knew not to ask. Questions inevitably led to more questions, never answers.

Alex looked me up and down like he was measuring me. "*I* can take care of myself," he said.

I swallowed.

He opened his mouth as if to say something more, then turned, his footsteps echoing in the empty hallway.

TRICK QUESTION

No one was home when I got back after school, and I let myself relax in some music and the chance to collect my thoughts. I had hung out in the girls' bathroom until after school ended, going back into the art room to grab my backpack only once I was sure everyone had gone. Alex's things had been spread out on the desk, untouched. I had hung around for a few minutes, unsure what I should do. In the end, I simply put his art supplies back in his drawer and left his backpack sitting on top of the desk.

He had made a lot of progress on his self-portrait, more than I had made on mine. The strong, bold shape of a phoenix was taking shape, practically leaping off of the canvas. At least I hadn't dissuaded him from using that symbolic bird to represent himself.

This day had been too crazy. This *week* had been too crazy. I'd had more real conversations, if you could call them that, with people at school than I'd had since I had started prophesying. A boy had stood up for me, though I still wasn't sure why. Another boy had sat with me at lunch. On purpose. Delilah and I had even shared some moments.

It gave me hope.

When this curse was finally gone, maybe life could actually get back to something approaching normal. Gran had lost the ability at seventeen, but my birthday had come and gone in January. "*Anytime now*," Granddad kept telling me. Any time now I could have a life again. Of course, I knew I shouldn't read too much into it. Both boys had been on the wrong side of public opinion for perhaps the first time in their lives, especially in Will's case. And Delilah was lost without Jade.

I found Gran's sewing kit and took my dress off. I wanted to fix it before they got home so Gran wouldn't feel she had to buy me a new one. Not that the dress was anything special. The faded floral fabric was thin in more than one place, and the stitching was already uneven. But it was the principle of it. The best way to repair it would be to add a thick ribbon or sash around the waist to cover up all the bad spots. I found an old dress in the scrap bin to act as a donor. I carefully removed the brightly colored lilac sash. It didn't really match the washed out tones of the dress, but it would have to do. I wasn't exactly high style anyway.

My wardrobe was yet another thing that set me apart from the other girls at school. I didn't like shopping—it was too public—and Gran's taste ran from the 1940s to the early 60s. And after I'd been dumped here, I'd outgrown all my old clothes, like I had outgrown my old life.

I no longer owned a pair of jeans. Actually, the only pants I owned were a pair of very retro capris that Gran insisted on calling "pedal pushers." That, combined with my reputation for spouting random nonsense, had helped keep the boys far away, which was generally okay with me . . . and with Granddad. The way I figured it, I would go shopping when I was rid of my curse, if we could afford it. A brand-new start all the way around. Something to look forward to. Something to hope for.

Sitting next to Will today had been the closest I had probably ever been to a boy who wasn't sticking an elbow in my back. Thinking about it brought back the heat of his shoulder, and I blushed yet again.

I shook my head and managed to poke myself with a needle for my trouble. That felt right. Thinking about boys only brought pain.

I wondered if I would ever find a love like Gran and Granddad's. They had been married for over fifty years. Would I be marked forever by my curse, even after it was finally gone? Would I be doomed to repeat my mother's mistakes? My parents' marriage had crumbled like a child's sand castle hit by a wave. No relationship could withstand utter truth.

Just ask my mother. "Why is your dad always late on Fridays?" she'd chirped one night not long after the prophesying had begun. I was twelve, just like Gran had been when her "gift" started. Mom wasn't really expecting an answer from me, just puttering around the dining room table making sure things were pretty. She liked things to be just so.

I answered anyway. Up until that day, she hadn't noticed that I had begun answering every question I heard, no matter what it was. In and of itself, this wasn't surprising, though. She'd never paid much attention to me, anyway, so long as I stayed out of her way.

"He's banging Daisy Rodriguez."

I clapped a hand over my mouth, but the words were out. I was a relatively innocent kid, but even I knew what that meant. It wasn't something I would ever have said in front of an adult until my gift had taken choice away from me.

All I remember was a sharp intake of breath from my mother. "What did you say?"

I repeated it. I'd had no choice; she'd asked.

She slapped me once, hard across the face, then bundled me off to my room and slammed the door. I cried until Dad came home. He didn't come to console me or check on me. No, after he came home, there had been a lot of screaming, but none of it directed at me—not that it mattered. I spent the night hiding in my closet, hugging an ancient stuffed teddy bear as each shouted question brought a new answer from my lips. I knew before they did that it was over and that we'd never be a family again, if we ever had been.

That was the first time I truly learned that most answers are better left unsaid.

OH WELL, OH WELL

By the next morning it was official: Jade's death was murder. She had been found at the edge of the woods off of Laurel Creek, leaving a trail of blood behind her. Even after being stabbed three times in the chest and stomach, she had managed to crawl a good distance before she bled to death. The weapon had missed her heart and her lungs, but it hadn't mattered in the end. If you lose enough blood, there's nothing you can do but watch as your life drips away. I knew that Jade had curled herself into a fetal position and stared unbelievingly at the thin but steady stream of blood leaving her body until finally her eyes had gone dim.

I should have stayed home, the way lots of the other students had, even those who weren't close to Jade. They were just taking advantage of the suspension of roll call. But something had made me come, so I stuck it out, not willing to admit defeat. Maybe Alex's advice, I don't know.

My MP3 player made little difference today. Teachers let students talk things out in class, presumably thinking it would help them cope. For once, I was grateful to Mrs. Pratt for her enforced cheerfulness. She handled the situation perfectly, only allowing talk of flour, eggs, and sugar during home economics. That suited Delilah, too. Strangely enough, she'd come to my table again in silence, head down, all the fire gone from her.

We stood side by side, mixing things in bowls, dropping in ingredients, reading the recipe—together, but also apart. I opened my mouth half a dozen times, wanting to say something, but unable to think of what that might be. At the end of the class, we had a perfect batch of peanut butter cookies to show for our time together. Neither one of us took even a single bite. As she was gathering up her things to leave, Delilah finally spoke. "Thanks for not making me talk." I nodded like that had been my intent all along and patted her shoulder when we parted ways.

THE HALLWAYS WEREN'T AS kind to me as home ec, though. The big question of *who* did it was asked many times. I had only one answer: "Water is like life. It arrives madly, then recedes away faster, faster . . . leaving everything silent." It became like a mantra to me. I could hear it in my head even against the pulsating rhythms of The Maine cranked as loud as it would go. And yet that answer had no rhyme or reason to it and an Internet search had turned up nothing. The only thing I could figure was that she had died near the lake, but it certainly wasn't water that had killed her. A blade had done that.

No, a person had. Someone had stood over her with a cold smile, striking first at her stomach and then at her chest. And then they had watched as she had fallen to her knees, begging.

When people asked *why* Jade had been murdered, however, three different answers came.

"Silence never killed anyone," I murmured the first time someone had asked, which wasn't so much an answer as a statement, albeit one that didn't mean anything.

Then:

> "Once begun, can't be undone.
> The itch must be scratched,
> The fire must be fed."

That made even less sense.

And finally: "There are so many little dyings that it doesn't matter which of them is death." I stole away to the computer lab between classes and learned that the last was a quote from a poet, Kenneth Patchen. But figuring that out did nothing to shed any light on the reason someone had killed her.

LUNCH ARRIVED, AND I escaped to my oak tree. I didn't trust myself to eat anything beyond crackers, not with the rest of the afternoon stretching ahead of me and doubtless more questions. The stomach churning was starting to lessen with repetition, but I didn't want to take any chances. I looked more pale than usual. Better to keep clear of everyone and everything. It was blessedly quiet in the courtyard.

I watched as a lone bird made loops around the upper branches, trying to choose a perch. I slowly chewed another cracker. What was I even doing here? I was circling, like that bird. I'd almost made up my mind to leave campus after all when I heard footsteps behind me.

"Hello again, Aria. Were you waiting for me, or do you always sit out here?"

Will sat down in front of me cross-legged, his knees almost but not quite meeting mine. He balanced a lunch tray across his lap.

"Yes, yes," I said, my tongue the traitor. Hopefully he thought I had answered only the last half of his question and not the first, though I knew in my heart it was the answer to both. I blushed, cursing myself inside, and tried to recover. "I like it out here. It's quiet."

"Hmm," he said. "I brought you some crackers, in case you'd run out." He took a handful from his tray and put them on my plate, then picked up his own sandwich to take a bite.

"Thank you," I said, not sure how to respond. No one had given me crackers before. I picked one up and took a bite. It was as dry and tasteless as the ones I'd already eaten.

Now that he was here, I could admit to myself that I had wondered if he would show up again. I watched from behind my hair as he chewed slowly, easily. Surely Jade's death should be affecting him as well? At the very least, you'd think he would be feeling the pressure of public opinion. The tide seemed to be turning more against Alex now, but I'd overheard a few girls wondering how he could be so calm and cool. I did have to agree on that, at least. The Florida heat didn't even seem to make him sweat.

"You know you are what you eat, right?" He had noticed me watching him. I quickly looked down at my plate. "I'm not sure what crackers say about you." He grinned at me, probably expecting a witty response.

Instead he got a stanza of poetry. "It's a very odd thing, as odd as can be, that whatever Miss T eats, turns into Miss T."

Dear God, what was that? My eyes widened in horror at what had come out of my mouth. There was no way to recover from that one. It was cryptic and silly. *Stupid, stupid, stupid.* My face glowed until surely I looked as red as a tomato.

Will looked at me a moment and then burst out laughing. The sound filled the courtyard, sounding alien. The circling bird flew off, startled.

"What was that?" Will asked when he had himself under control again.

At least this time the answer came out directly, even if I did sound like an encyclopedia. "From the poem, *Miss T* by Walter John de la Mare, English poet, died the twenty-second of June, 1956."

He laughed again. "You're not stupid at all, are you?"

"No," I said, and this time I flushed in anger, not embarrassment. I took the plate of crackers off my lap and placed it on the ground. Had he just come out here to make fun of me? I'd thought it might be to get away from the speculation of the other students, but I was all too familiar with being the target. I moved to get up, and he grabbed my wrist to pull me back down, tethering me there.

"I'm sorry," he said, not laughing anymore. "I didn't mean that the way it sounded. It's just, well, there are lots of rumors about you. That you're . . . you know."

"Not all there?" I asked through gritted teeth. I knew people thought that, but it still hurt to have this boy right here in front of me saying it. I wiggled my wrist, but his hold was firm.

"Yeah," he said with a small smile, letting his fingertips drag across my skin as he finally let go. I let my hand drop to my side and shifted from my knees to sit back down.

"Well, you know how rumors are," I said pointedly.

He was silent for a moment. "Yes, I do. But you and I know what value rumors hold, right?"

"The value of a rumor is only held by those who would believe them," I whispered. Who was I to judge? They called me crazy and stupid and bumped me in the hallways, but they didn't think I was possibly a murderer. Someone had scrawled KILLER on Alex's locker this morning. Will's locker had been egged, the yellow yolk dripping down the front. Students were taking sides and picking a team to root against, not for.

"And they're obviously crazy," he continued, picking up his sandwich again. "There's nothing wrong with you."

"Oh, sure," I said bitterly. "I'm perfectly normal."

"Who wants to be normal?"

"Me," I said. There it was. That was one answer that certainly had the ring of truth in it. It was all I had ever wanted since all of this started. I'd had friends and all the trappings of a normal life, even a mother and father. Once lost, could I ever regain them? Would my mother or father be willing to welcome me back once I stopped spouting inconvenient truths? I didn't think so. Some things you can't forget. Too many bridges had been burned. Did I even want to go back to them? They were as good as strangers to me now.

"Well, not me." He leaned back on his hands and studied me. "Normal is for people who don't know any better. Normal is for people who believe rumors. Normal is for idiots."

Blushing was getting to be a habit for me around him. Was I being too sensitive, or had he called me an idiot? Maybe he realized what he'd said because he smiled. "And you are obviously not an idiot. If anything, I'd say you're pretty special."

I laughed at that. *Special.* Yes, that was one word for it.

"Yes," he said, nodding more to himself than to me. "Definitely out of the ordinary. I think I need to get to know you better." He picked up his sandwich again. I was left without words. He wasn't at all like what I had expected, not that I'd had any clear idea. I struggled to come up with something, anything to say.

"I'm sorry about Jade," I said at last, which was probably the last topic I should have brought up.

The slight grin melted away. "I . . . don't really want to talk about it." He took another bite, a faraway look in his eyes. "First loves stay with you forever, don't they?"

"First loves are bittersweet," I said, almost sounding like a normal person but not quite.

He nodded. "We were supposed to meet that night," he muttered, avoiding my eyes. "I keep thinking that if I'd gone, maybe I could have stopped whatever happened. But I'll never know." He sighed and put his sandwich down, eyes lowered to the ground.

It was my turn to reach out. I squeezed his hand. "Don't blame yourself. You couldn't have known something was going to happen."

"I know, but I can't help but wonder who did it and why. Jade wouldn't hurt a fly." He clutched my hand like a drowning man.

"A stranger, I think. There's no way of knowing why." Not unless someone could decipher my proclamations, but I wasn't about to share them with anyone. If the answer was clear, then maybe I could have called in an anonymous tip or something. But how could anyone make out anything from the randomness that came out of me? "It's not your fault. There was nothing you could have done. Just remember that."

"Thank you," he said, bringing his eyes up to mine. "That means a lot to me, especially coming from a friend of Jade's. I really need that right now."

He looked so intense that I blushed again and had to look away. It was ridiculous. At this rate, if he kept talking to me I'd have to start wearing makeup to hide my blushing. I'd never been so transparent before. I was too embarrassed to even correct him about Jade. I hadn't been anyone's friend since this curse started. They had all abandoned me as I spilled their secrets, large and small. By the time my grandparents had taken me in, I had nothing and no one but them.

"Can I ask you something?"

"That's why I'm here," I said. I bit back a bitter laugh. At last, my purpose in life had been revealed. Why was I not surprised?

"I've always wondered. What is it you're always saying under your breath? Are you making fun of people or what? I can appreciate that, given where we live."

"The truth," I said. "There's no fun in it." I dropped his hand and shifted away from him, managing to embed a root or rock into my tailbone at the same time. "Look, I'd really rather not talk about that. Can we talk about something else?" Anything else. Or not talk at all. I didn't want to spoil the moment.

"You can't leave it at that! Now I'm really curious. What do you mean, the truth?"

"I answer questions with the truth," I said. I clapped a hand over my mouth, not that it had ever helped me before.

"You answer questions," he said slowly, like he was chewing that over in his mind. "What questions?"

"All questions. Every question. Any question I hear. Yours, theirs, hers, his . . . never mine," I whispered through my fingers. "Please stop." He was too close. Too near. It didn't matter how quiet I whispered, he could still hear me. I felt his breath on my cheek as he leaned closer, trying to catch every word. My entire body felt cold now, even though a thin trickle of sweat was working its way down my backbone.

"Stop what?" He looked genuinely confused.

"Asking questions." I removed my hand. "I have to go to class," I said.

It was already too late. I had said too much, been too strange. I got up quickly before he could stop me with either his hands or another question. My knee caught my plate as I scrambled to stand up, scattering broken crackers everywhere.

"Wait!" he called after me. "I don't understand! What did I say?"

"I don't understand!" I repeated back, which was true enough. That was what he had said, but it also defined my life. I had so many questions of my own, but they were never answered. Why was I this way? When would it finally end? I didn't know. I pushed through the door and back into the cafeteria, not caring that I was causing a scene. People scattered, for once getting out of my way. I kept going until I got to the parking lot and didn't stop until I got home.

BANG, BANG (MY BABY SHOT ME DOWN)

I sat in my car staring at the relentlessly tacky exterior of the Clamshell Restaurant. Then Granddad knocked on my window, making me jump. I rolled it down.

"Aren't you coming in?" he asked. He wanted to celebrate his track winnings and had insisted I come along. But sitting there looking at the restaurant, I knew I couldn't join him. The last time I'd been here, I wound up telling some poor woman that her husband thought she was a fat cow. The resulting scene hadn't been pretty.

"I can't," I answered. See, even my inner oracle agreed with me.

"Aria," began Gran, "Are you—"

"It's okay," I said. "You guys go without me. I'll come next time, I promise." If next time was after my curse had ended and I could avoid ruining anyone's dinner. "Besides, I'd really like to relax at home. With everything going on at school . . ." I trailed off and did my best to look pitiful. It wasn't hard. The last few days had taken their toll on me.

"Of course," said Granddad, giving Gran a look. "But Aria, you be careful driving home, okay?"

I LEFT AND DROVE aimlessly around Lake Mariah, not yet willing to go home to our empty house, but not daring to stop anywhere there were people. I finally turned in the direction of the lake and parked my car in the gravel lot at Three Oaks. The lake was usually a popular meeting spot, especially for kids my age, but everyone usually stayed near the dock and beach area. It was supposed to close when it got dark, but no one ever paid any attention to the posted signs. The local police had given up long ago and now just drove by once or twice a night to knock on steamed-up car windows if they found any. They didn't have to bother tonight. I only saw one vehicle, a Chevy Suburban, on the far side of the lot, and it looked empty. Jade's murder was likely keeping everyone inside. A few people were off drowning their sorrows at the party I'd heard Tank was having tonight. He was calling it a wake for Jade, but that was only an excuse to get wasted.

If Granddad knew this was where I'd gone, he'd probably be mad. But I needed to get away and the woods were my favorite escape.

I walked down one of the paths that flirted with both the edge of the lake and the forest surrounding it. It was getting dark, but I always kept a flashlight in my car for times like these. Even when everything was quiet, the forest still murmured: little furry things rustling through fallen leaves, the wind in the branches, every now and then a deer leaping away in confusion. All those little noises made me feel less alone, like I was a part of something in some way. Something I couldn't hurt or ruin.

I walked gently, taking care not to disturb anything. When I was younger, I had practiced my "Indian" walk; balancing lightly on the balls of my feet and rolling into a step rather than just setting my feet down. After years spent walking in the woods by myself, I was as close to silent as you could get. Of course, the woods here were different than ones I had grown up in. Very few pine needles, for starters. The feeling was the same, though.

The deeper I went, the darker the woods became. I finally switched on my flashlight when I stepped on a twig, and the sharp snap sent a sleepy bird to chirping. I was almost to my favorite spot on the lake, the place where the trail dipped back to the shore halfway around from the beach area. There was a tree there that had grown crooked. Over the years it had formed itself into a knobby bench where you could sit and watch the lake but be far enough away to keep anonymous if there were any beachgoers. I turned the final corner before my tree. I had my flashlight pointed at the ground so I wouldn't trip over the big cypress root I knew was lying in wait in the middle of the path. It had gotten me more than once.

"Who's there?" a voice called.

I brought my flashlight up to shine on the tree, managing to stub my toe on the root at the same time after all. It was Alex, possibly the last person I had expected to see. The light illuminated him in a hazy glow. He blinked against it. I caught myself against another tree, and I juggled the flashlight in suddenly clumsy hands. If it weren't for my problem, I might not have managed a reply at all. But I said, *"La voce della verità."* Whatever that meant. I cleared my throat and spoke louder. "It's Aria. Just Aria."

"What are you doing here?" he asked. "You're not following me, are you?"

I couldn't tell for sure, but he sounded more bemused than annoyed. "Looking for peace," I responded, relieved the truth didn't sound too stupid. "I don't follow anyone." I got the flashlight under control and righted myself, pointing the light in his direction again. He squinted, not bothering to hold up a hand to block the light from his eyes. I lowered the beam.

It was my turn to ask a question. "What are *you* doing here?"

"Just . . . remembering."

I heard a *clink* as he shifted on the tree and allowed the flashlight beam to drift lower. He was grasping the neck of a nearly empty bottle of vodka. He shifted, trying to hide it behind his back, but almost dropped it instead.

Oh, I thought.

"I'm sorry. I guess I should leave you to it." The beam of light wobbled.

"Whatever," he said, looking away.

I hesitated. He wasn't asking me to stay, but he hadn't told me to go. I took a step closer to him. He shrugged and took a swig from the bottle, swaying slightly. I kept going.

What was I doing? I sat down near his feet, not willing to sit next to him on the tree. It was comfortable for one but far too close for two. I set the flashlight on its base so it was pointing towards the sky, a makeshift searchlight towards the emptiness.

He laughed softly, bitterly. "What, do you think I'm going to bite you?"

"What long teeth you have," I said, grateful for the darkness. I kept saying the strangest things, even by my abnormal standards. If I didn't know better, I'd think my "gift" was out to get me. Maybe it was.

"The better to eat you with," he said and slipped down unsteadily from the tree to sit next to me. "Don't worry, I don't actually bite. And look, now we're on even ground. "

I doubted that would ever be true.

For a few peaceful moments, the only sounds I could hear were the croaks of frogs and the gurgling bellow of a nearby bull alligator. There was no other noise quite like it. I shivered a little despite the warmth of the Florida night and Alex's closeness. Primeval was the only word to describe the sound. Even after all these years of living out here, it made my heart race a little.

"What was it you said when you first got here?" asked Alex. "I didn't quite catch it." His words slurred at the end, turning the last two words into one.

I was hoping he hadn't noticed that. "*La voix de la vérité*," I answered. Wait, *was* that what I'd said before? It didn't sound the same.

"What?"

"*Ağızin gerçeğini konuşuyor.*"

What was with all the languages? The first time had sounded a bit like Spanish, which I'd taken in school, though I was completely awful at it. Maybe it had been Italian? Then French? But I had no idea what this one was.

Alex tried to whistle but gave up to take another quick drink from the bottle instead. "How many languages do you know?"

"One," I said.

He laughed again. At least someone thought I was amusing, even if that someone was obviously drunk out of his mind. "You are one strange girl, Aria."

"Truer words were never spoken," I said. Close up he smelled of alcohol and some kind of musky body spray. Or maybe it was just him.

"But then, I'm strange, too. We're the same, you and me. Just the same."

"Oh?" I said.

I'd heard there were a few different types of drunks. He was obviously the maudlin kind. At least he wasn't angry or violent or amorously inclined. Sad and introspective I could deal with. He held up a single finger on the hand that wasn't clutching the bottle. "No one wants us," he said. He added another finger to the first. "We're both on the outside, looking in."

"You're not," I said, surprised. "Or you weren't anyway." Before Jade.

He grunted or maybe he laughed. It was hard to tell. He simply held up another finger to make three. "We want to get out of this shithole town."

"And go where?" I had nowhere else to go. At least, not

until my curse was gone. Here was bad, but there wasn't anywhere that would be any better, not for me.

He ignored what I'd said and stretched all his fingers out. Five now. He'd skipped four. "And we're both alone," he said.

I shook my head. "I have my grandparents. And you have your dad." I wanted to say that he'd had Jade, too, but that would have been rubbing salt in the wound. Was it really better to have loved and lost than never to have loved at all? *Had* he loved Jade?

"Right," he said. "My dad." His voice was flat and dead. "I suppose I ought to drink to that." He raised the bottle, but I grabbed it before he could get it to his mouth and took it away.

"Have a sip," he said with a crooked smile. "Be my guest."

"No, thanks. I don't think you need any more either."

"Probably not," he slurred. He slumped down against the tree, using it and me to prop himself up. "It's my dear old dad's, you know. Stole it from him."

"Yeah," I said. "I guessed that."

He picked up my flashlight and shone it directly on the bottle. For a second it was like a prism of fireworks going off in my eyes, then the beam wavered off to the side as his hand shook. "Never touched it before. Never had a drop. Can you believe it?"

"I am a believer," I said.

"Tastes like shit. Burns." He dropped the flashlight and leaned forward, groaning.

I poured the rest of the bottle out into the waiting ground like an offering and set it down off to the side. I patted him gingerly on the back. He felt even more solid in person than I had imagined. Not that I had ever imagined touching him, exactly. Never in my wildest dreams, actually, would I have predicted this situation.

"So why are you drinking it?"

He sat up and turned to face me, misjudging the distance so that his face was only inches from mine. "It's all my fault," he said. "Me. My fault." He leaned forward even more until his forehead was touching mine. He brought his hands up to my face, one on either side. His hands were so big they covered the sides of my face.

"What's your fault?"

"Jade," he whispered. One word, sad and lonely, swallowed by another roar from the bull gator.

I jumped, knocking the empty bottle over. It rattled a warning against the roots of the tree.

"You should run away from me, too." He let go and drooped back against the tree, deflated. "Run," he repeated again, softly this time, but that only made it sound more menacing.

My heart was pounding. I wasn't sure if it was his words or his closeness or even the bass call of the alligator still rumbling inside of me. I scrambled to my feet, grabbed the flashlight, and took a few steps and then stopped. How could I leave him like this? How could I not? Had he just admitted to killing Jade? It was impossible to tell. If he really did kill her, there would be nothing to stop him from killing me. Nothing. And no one would mourn, other than Gran and Granddad. No one else would even notice. He was right. I was alone and unwanted.

"Alex," I said, too quietly and then louder, "Alex!" I pointed the flashlight right at this face.

His head lolled around, and he blinked at me, his eyes glassy. Why was I doing this? "Thought you were going to leave me, too," he said, his words even more slurred now.

"Ask me what I should do," I said.

"What should I do?" he asked, sounding forlorn and lost. And very drunk.

"Trust me," I answered. I sighed. I needed to know whether I could trust *him*, not the other way around. "No, Alex, ask *me* what *I* should do."

"What should you do?" he managed to get out before his head dropped back down to his chest.

"Always do what is right," I said. I closed my eyes in frustration for a moment, but it had been a stupid idea anyway. It never worked, like when I'd lost my keys and asked Gran to ask me where they were. It was like my "gift" knew and wanted to mess with me. "Where I left them," though, was slightly more helpful in that situation than what I was getting in the one tonight.

"Okay," I finally said, more to myself than to him. "Let's get you home." I bent down and managed to get one of his arms around my shoulders. He came to his senses enough to help me get him standing. We stumbled down the trail. Maybe I was wrong, but it felt right.

EXTRAORDINARY MACHINE

I dreamt of oak leaves blowing in the wind, making patterns as they drifted in the air. Just as they were about to form a picture, a new gust of wind would blow through and rearrange everything. I woke up feeling unsettled, as if right on the edge of discovering some ancient truth.

It was a reoccurring dream of mine, though it meant nothing to me and had never left me with any earth-shattering revelations. At least it was a peaceful dream. Sometimes my sleep was broken by nightmares of smoke and ashes, and I would awaken with the taste of soot in my mouth. Gran said the dreams would go away, too, someday. She'd had them herself.

I lay in my bed staring at the watermark on the ceiling while I tried to will myself to get up. It reminded me of a serpent snaking its way across my room, watchful and staring. I shifted, and my back ached. Alex had been beyond heavy. It had probably only taken twenty or thirty minutes to get him to my car the night before, but it had felt like hours. I had left his truck at Three Oaks. From his condition when I left him on his porch, I wondered if he would wake up wondering how he even made it home.

"Aria," called Gran. "Up and at 'em! I need you to help me out at the store today."

By "store" she really meant her roadside stand: one of those ubiquitous greying half-building, half-shack stands that dot the roads all over Florida, shilling everything from orange juice to saltwater taffy and discounted Disney tickets. Gran sold fruit from our pitifully few trees, as well as her homemade jams and jellies, and pretty much whatever else she and Granddad could scrounge up. But Lake Mariah wasn't a prime Florida destination, nor was it directly on the road to one. Very few tourists made it through our part of the state.

If she wanted me to help out, that really meant she wanted to keep an eye on me. Luckily, even with the whole Alex situation, I had arrived home before Gran and Granddad's celebratory dinner ended. It was only her normal concerns that drove her. She had no idea what I'd done after leaving the restaurant. With the morning sun streaming in through my old lady lace curtains, the whole thing felt surreal. Had I really helped a drunken murderer get home? Was he really the culprit? Or had I just dreamed the whole thing?

"Okay, Gran," I called, knowing she was waiting, probably standing half in, half out of our front door, letting in the mosquitoes like she always did. "I'll meet you there. Half an hour, I promise."

"Great," she yelled back. "Porter's gone fishing. Says he's going to catch dinner, so maybe you should get something out of the freezer. See you in a few." The screen door wheezed shut as she left.

I allowed myself a smile as I got up. Granddad never caught anything unless I went with him. He had as much luck with the fishes as he usually did with the dogs, though I was usually more help with telling him where to cast his line than telling him what dog to pick. I went to the kitchen and pulled some hamburger out of the freezer so it could thaw.

I made it to Gran's stand in twenty-five minutes with my hair still wet from the shower. It hung heavy down my back, making my dress stick to my skin from my collar to my waist. With the humidity, it would be over an hour before it dried completely. Gran was always telling me I should cut it all off. Long hair didn't make sense in Florida, she said. But I couldn't do it.

I handed Gran the fresh thermos of coffee I'd brought with me, and she grunted her thanks. To me, my long hair made more sense than Gran drinking gallons and gallons of a hot beverage during the heat of the day, but she'd no more give up the caffeine than I would my best feature. It made me think of Alex and my self-portrait and whether or not he would indeed be able to step beyond his father's shadow and rise above it. Definitely not if he turned to the bottle again. But it wasn't my problem to think about.

"Quiet today," said Gran.

It was quiet every day around here, but I nodded and climbed up on a stool next to her.

"About last night," she started but stopped when I held up a hand.

"It's okay," I said. "You don't have to say it."

"All right," she said. "I won't. But you know—"

"I know, Gran," I said. "I know."

We sat in silence for a few minutes. A pickup truck drove by, slowed down almost imperceptibly and then went on without stopping. We did sometimes get a little local traffic for the vegetables and herbs Gran grew in a tidy little plot behind our house, but it was so hot this time of year that there wasn't much to harvest. No reason for anyone to stop other than pity.

"I've been thinking," I said, startling both of us.

"Dangerous," said Gran. She grinned at me, her eyes crinkled at the corners.

"What if I just took my GED? Then I wouldn't have to go back to school." I'd actually been thinking about this since she'd quit homeschooling me after eighth grade. School was nothing but embarrassment and pain. Going out in public was the same. I had to figure out a way to shield myself better.

"Aria, you've made it so far. You can't give up now."

"I know. But—" I couldn't think how to put it into words. How frustrating it was walking the halls every day, my head down, mumbling nonsense. How the only time anyone looked at me it was with disgust or distrust and I wasn't sure which hurt more. Alex's words came back to me again. No one wanted me. Even dead drunk he could see that. Why couldn't Gran? I sighed. "I don't see why I can't just get my GED for now. Then, when

I lose the 'gift' I can start off new, maybe at CFCC or something."

There was no way I could afford a four-year university, but I could probably swing a small community college, especially if I was able to get a job. But there was no way I could get a job until my gift was gone. I was seventeen now, the same age as when she'd lost her gift. Why wasn't mine gone?

"Aria," said Gran. She reached out her hand, knuckles swollen with arthritis, and patted my shoulder. "I know it's hard. I've been there. But you've got to *live* your life. Don't give up on everything. You can't squirrel yourself away. Who cares what people think?"

"Everyone," I said.

She lightly punched my shoulder. "You're a beautiful girl, Aria. A beautiful person. You should be out there, shouting your truths from the mountaintops."

"Gran, this is Florida. There are no mountains." I tried out a small smile so she'd know I was teasing. Next she'd be telling me what a wonderful personality I had.

She laughed. "I'm serious, girl. It's time you showed the world who you are. It's not everyone who has a chance to make a real difference. Grab that bull by the horns."

"And do what? Tell women that their husbands think they're fat?"

"No, of course not. Though that will happen, too. I remember that woman. Maybe she needed to hear that. Maybe that lady has diabetes and needs to watch her diet."

"Maybe she just looks bad in a bathing suit, and now she'll never get in one again."

"Fine," snorted Gran. "Maybe she was destined to drown at the beach, and you changed that. Now she'll live to be a hundred and three, fat and happy, with over twenty great-grandkids."

I giggled. I couldn't help it. Gran let out her hyena cackle along with me. She had the kind of laugh you could hear for miles. It always surprised me. It was such a big, joyful noise coming from such a small person. We leaned into each other on our stools until our laughter had died down to a sputter. Gran wiped her eyes and gave me a quick squeeze before letting me go.

"You'll find your place in life, Aria, don't you worry. I did. Now, no more talk about getting out of school. We'll get you through it."

I nodded, but the good feelings I'd built up during our laughter faded. She'd found Granddad after she'd lost her gift. When she talked about how it had been for her, she never seemed to have any bad stories, just happy ones. Her first prophecy had been about the end of the war back in 1945. She'd been twelve, just like I was when my curse started. But my first prophecy had been about something stupid, not momentous. I couldn't even remember now exactly what it was, though I could remember the feeling of surprise and dread that had filled me when I found that my voice wasn't my own.

"Look alive," said Gran. "We've got a customer." She got up and bustled around rearranging jam jars on a rickety shelf.

I stayed on my stool and watched as a black car slowed down and then actually stopped. It was so clean it practically shone. I wondered who the crazy person with a black car in Florida was. Then the door opened, and Will climbed out. What was he doing here? He couldn't possibly want grapefruit preserves. I sat up straighter on my stool and picked up an old magazine lying on the counter.

"Hey, Aria," he called out as he came towards us in that smooth easy lope that reminded me of a panther.

"Hello, Will." I put the magazine back down and tucked my hair behind my ear. I could feel a blush threatening to break out on my cheeks, just thinking about the last time we had talked. I'd had no choice but to cut and run. He'd come far too close to discovering my secret. Gran might say she wanted me to shout my truths from a mountaintop, but did she really mean it?

"Well, Aria, you should introduce your old grandmother," she said, dropping all pretense of rearranging the shelves.

I stood up and waved vaguely between them. "Gran, this is Will Raffles. He goes to school with me. He was Jade Price's boyfriend."

Why had I added that? Gran shot me a pointed glance as Will stepped forward with his hand out.

"Nice to meet you . . . Gran," he said with a slight smile.

"Oh, sorry!" I said, and the blush bloomed after all. "Ellie Porter." I waved my hand again and then let it drop.

"But you can call me Gran, if you like," she said and met his smile with one of her own. "And I'm sorry about your girlfriend. Terrible thing, just terrible."

"We actually weren't really dating anymore," he said,

glancing at me. "But thank you. It is a terrible thing." He swallowed, his voice hoarse. "That's the only way to put it."

Gran nodded, then dusted her hands off briskly and turned to me like his arrival had interrupted a conversation we weren't having. "So, Aria," she said. "I've got to go run and get that . . . thing. I'll be back in a while. Half an hour at least." She smiled again at Will. "Maybe your friend can keep you company?"

"No problem," he said. "I'm excellent company."

"Wonderful! It's been a real quiet day, but I always hate to leave Aria here by her lonesome, especially with what happened . . . There's been hardly anyone by at all today. Great for talking, though."

Gran was about as transparent as mud. I was surprised she hadn't added a wink for good measure.

"Gran," I said, not even sure what I was going to say. But she just smiled real big at me and practically ran for her car. I shrugged as she drove away, keeping my eyes on her disappearing taillights.

Will was silent for what seemed like a very long time.

"I'm sorry about lunch the other day," I said, deciding to get it over with. Besides, I meant it. I was sorry. Not necessarily for running away, but for the whole situation. I shouldn't pretend to have normal conversations when I can't.

"Don't be." He shifted into my line of sight, not taking his eyes off of mine. "So," he said intently, "let me see if I've got this right . . . whenever someone asks you a question, you have to answer?"

I tried to bite my answer back, with no luck. I almost

didn't recognize my own voice; it came out with such strength.

"I am the voice, I am the truth. Ask me, I will speak." My breath caught in my chest, and I sat down hard on the stool, looking anywhere but at Will.

He grabbed my shoulder to steady me. "And you *have* to answer them, is that right? You have no choice?" His voice was calm but firm.

"The truth compels me. I must answer. What is choice but an illusion?" The words came out with forceful strength, but my tongue felt foreign to me.

"Who—*what*—are you?"

No one had ever asked me *that* before. I raised my eyes to his, not sure at all what I was going to say and half afraid to hear it. "I am Aria. I am Sybil. So my ancestors before me, so my daughters after me. I am the vessel of truth, and the truth flows through me." My body shook, and goosebumps rose on my arms despite the heat of the day.

Will let go of my shoulder and sat down on Gran's stool, his eyes faraway. I didn't know whether to laugh or cry. I felt drained and weak. Insubstantial. What was I? I was a freak. Gran had always told me we came from a long line of seers, but this, this was too much. A Sybil? An actual, honest-to-God, real oracle? I wasn't a person. I was a *thing*. A mouthpiece.

"Well," said Will. I looked at him. He had that slightly twisted smile on his lips. "That was weird. But it wasn't wholly unexpected."

I laughed in spite of myself, but it didn't last long. Maybe this was what hysteria felt like. The shock would be setting in soon. "Sorry you asked?"

"No," he said. "Are you sorry I asked?"

"No," I said, surprised at my answer. "And this is me talking now, too, not . . . *whatever.* I really don't know how I feel about it. You're the only person other than family who knows my secret." I was torn. I was terrified but at the same time, relief washed over me. *Someone* knew, and that someone hadn't run away screaming. Yet. It wasn't a mountain, and I wasn't shouting, but . . .

"I guess I see why you don't really talk to people at school. How does—" He stopped. "Maybe I shouldn't actually *ask* my question." He cocked his head at me, some of his hair flipping into his eyes. "Maybe you could *tell* me how it works."

"Thank you," I said. "It's nice to have a choice and be able to pick my own words." I closed my eyes for a moment to gather my thoughts. I wasn't used to talking about it. Gran wanted me to use my gift, but she didn't want me to actually tell people about it and neither did Granddad. He said people would want to use me. Most people are decent, he'd say, but there are some things human beings can't resist.

Maybe I shouldn't tell Will anything more, but I found myself continuing. "I've been this way since I was twelve. If I hear a question, I have to answer it."

He opened his mouth and snapped it shut again. I nodded, accepting his unasked question and pleased that he'd remembered to not ask it.

"It doesn't matter if someone's asking me directly or not. I have to answer *any* question I hear. You asked why I was always mumbling under my breath. That's why."

"Go on," he said and reached out to hold my hand.

I stared at our fingers as he entwined his with mine. It didn't even feel like it was my hand; it looked so unfamiliar being held in his. "My Gran had it, too. But my mom never did." I looked straight into his eyes. "I hate it. It's a curse. I don't have any control over my answers at all. My *truths*." Some sullenness leaked into my words, and he squeezed my fingers. "And I don't know what any of it means. Sometimes my answers make sense, but a lot of the time it just comes out so much nonsense." He raised his eyebrows at me, another unspoken question. "Okay, not nonsense exactly. It's always the truth, but sometimes the answer comes out kind of like a riddle and you can't figure it out until afterwards."

"Like those Nostradamus prophecies."

"Yeah, kind of like that type of thing." I fell silent, watching his thumb make circles on the back of my hand.

"You're *always* right?" he asked.

"The truth is in me," I said in that deep voice again. I sighed. "Yes, always. If you can puzzle it out. The rhymes are the worst."

"This is pretty amazing, Aria," he said.

He didn't understand. "I wouldn't call it that."

"Why—sorry." He stopped to think. "Can—" He stopped again. "This is hard."

"Tell me about it," I said. Granddad had been struggling with it for years.

"I have so many questions," he said.

"Everyone does. Trust me. I would know." That was my feeble attempt to make a joke. He didn't laugh. I didn't either. "Why do you think I was eating all those crackers this week?"

"Crackers . . ." He raised an eyebrow, avoiding the inflection in his voice by proxy.

"The really hard questions . . . the tough ones . . . I *feel* them. All the stuff about Jade . . ." I trailed off.

He was silent a moment. "I suppose everyone has been asking who did it." He let go of my hand and stood up, turning away from me. This had to be hard for him to think about. Even if they really weren't going together it was obvious he still had feelings for her. He'd said as much. Besides, they'd known each other all their lives.

If it was hard for me to think about, I couldn't imagine what it was like for him. I nodded, even though he wasn't looking at me. "And why and . . . how."

"I need to know what you know, Aria." He turned and looked at me, his eyes unblinking and bright. He stepped closer. I picked up an orange from the counter and stared down at it, picking at the peel and releasing the sharp scent of citrus into the air. How much should I tell him? How much would it hurt him to hear it?

"Aria," he said. "Tell me. *Please.*"

I took a deep breath, filling my lungs with the sweet smell of the orange. "Well, she was stabbed, like they reported. Three times. She . . . crawled for help, but she didn't make it." Obviously. I was terrible at this. "And then she just . . . stopped." A long sliver of orange peel twirled between my fingers, twitching.

He let out a long breath, deep enough to disturb the hair hanging in front of my eyes. I blinked as they brushed against my eyelashes. "There must be more." His voice was shaking.

I didn't want to tell him any more. Not about the blood or the pain or the despair she had felt and especially not the emptiness at the end. "Well, if you wanted an example of how stupid my answers can be, every time someone asked who did it, it was just this weird bit of poetry. Same thing every time." I had no trouble reciting it from memory; I'd whispered it to myself so many times. "Water is like life, it arrives madly, then recedes away faster, faster . . . leaving everything silent."

"Hmmm," he said, taking the orange from my hand and working a segment loose. "Water is like life . . ."

"It's not from anything. I looked it up on the Internet while I was at school. I don't know what it means." I watched as he took a bite of the slice of orange and chewed it slowly.

The entire stand seemed filled with the smell of it now. I knew I would never again be able to eat an orange without thinking of this day, this moment in time.

"Interesting," he finally said. "Your answers really always mean something?"

"I only speak the truth. It is up to the listener to bring meaning." I cleared my throat. He'd forgotten that time, but I could forgive him. It was hard to remember not to ask.

He began pacing back and forth within the small confines of the stand, in between the pickled green tomatoes and the orange marmalade. Dust motes danced in the air, disturbed by his passage. "There are just so many possibilities," he said, hands waving in the air.

A Chevy sped by, kicking up sand and rocks as it vanished

down the road. A missed customer. I didn't let it bother me. I relaxed my shoulders, realizing for the first time that I must look like some kind of troll all hunched over on my stool. "It's really not that simple," I said. I tried to think what this must seem like from his point of view. It would be like finding out magic existed. But from my point of view, I knew the magic didn't bring happiness, only tragedy. The fairy tales were right about that.

"I don't see why not. You know, you could change the world."

He sounded like Gran. I looked away. "I don't want to change the world," I said quietly. "I just want—" I stopped short. I didn't know what I wanted. I really just knew what I didn't want.

Will pulled himself up to sit on the counter next to me. It let out a loud creak, making us both jump. "No offense, Aria . . . but I was wondering . . . I was wondering why you guys . . . do this." Will looked embarrassed for me as he waved a hand around at the shack.

"You mean, why haven't we won the lottery a few times?" So we didn't have to live like poor white trash? I stared out into the sunlight. "Granddad does try, but the answers never work out. I mean, they're always right and every-thing, but nothing you can figure out ahead of time. The last time he asked for the numbers, it was something about how the devil's chance is a pious man's dream." I left out the part about how there had been three sixes in the win-ning numbers that week, so that answer had made at least a little sense later, but definitely not at the time.

"Ah," he said. "But it is possible."

"I suppose," I said. "Gran doesn't like that we even try. She says it's practically an abomination. A crime to use my gift that way. She says it should only be used to help people."

"Well, you're people, too. Even oracles have to live." He managed a sad grin. "You deserve something nice."

"I did help Granddad win a thousand dollars at the dog track this week."

"That's great! You just have to ask the right question or be smart enough to figure out the answer," he said.

"I guess." I wasn't stupid, and neither was Granddad. Some of my answers, in my opinion, really weren't meant to be figured out, like my inner oracle was trying to be unclear on purpose. But Will was new to this. He'd heard some strange answers from me, but nothing as off-the-wall as some of the stuff I'd said over the years. He'd be scratching his head soon, too.

"No worries," he said, and his smile brightened. "We'll figure it out. The two of us."

CANDY CASE

*I feel better than I did yesterday.
I think it's 'cause you came.*
"Candy Case" by Last Summer

Granddad was already at the house when Gran and I got back from the stand. He was busy filleting some perch and whistling a jaunty tune. He'd been lucky today after all. He was on a streak. I snuck past him to move the ground beef from the fridge to the freezer again so he wouldn't notice that our faith had been lacking. I kissed him on the cheek, his stubby whiskers scratchy against my lips.

"Good day today?"

I didn't even mind that he'd forgotten and had asked it as a question. "Surprisingly so," I answered. "Sometimes the truth really does set you free." Granddad didn't bother asking me to explain, being used to my weird utterances.

"Aria had a visitor come by today," said Gran. She paused for impact. "A boy."

"Oh, must have been the boy who stopped by here earlier. I sent him over that way. Big fellow, dark hair."

Dark hair? Couldn't be Will. Alex? Apparently, he

actually remembered last night. I was kind of surprised. But why was he looking for me? I remembered the sudden growl of gravel being kicked up as a truck had sped by the stand while I'd talked with Will. Had that been Alex? I'd left his Chevy at the lake, but maybe he'd picked it up.

"No, different boy," said Gran, lifting an eyebrow at me. "The one I saw was blond. Our Aria is popular today."

"Hmm," said Granddad. "I suppose I ought to make sure my shotgun is clean then." He grinned at me, but I knew he was at least partly serious. He didn't keep a baseball bat in his car because he liked to play ball. He looked frail, but he was wiry and his time in the Army had taught him some dirty moves. Just ask the guy who'd tried to rob him the last time he'd been down in Miami. Granddad had walked away unscathed, but the robber had lost three teeth.

"Well, the one I met seemed very nice," said Gran. "Maybe you should invite him over for dinner sometime." She stopped what she was doing and took my face in her hands, looking deep into my eyes. "Talking to him . . . worked out okay, I'm guessing."

"Yes," I said, not looking away. "More than okay." I didn't tell her he knew my secret, saving that for myself. She said she missed her gift, but I could only imagine that she had forgotten what it was like to actually have it. She'd met Granddad well after she'd lost it. She'd never been forced to tell him something unpleasantly true, only what it was like to live that way. And he'd always believed her, even before he saw it in me.

Gran went back to wandering around the kitchen,

straightening this, moving that. She never knew what to do when Granddad was doing the cooking.

"I went downtown to give you kids a chance to talk," she said. "It was deserted." I snorted, and she amended that. "Even more deserted than normal. The only people I saw walking around were some police, and they didn't look overly happy. Don't think their investigation is getting anywhere."

That brought me down again. Maybe I should have asked Will more about his relationship or lack thereof with Jade. I wasn't used to asking questions myself. I wasn't used to *talking*.

"Yeah, on my way back from fishing I saw some highway patrol out by the road where the first guy was hit. Not sure what they're gonna find out there now, but they had police tape up. Looked like something out of a TV show."

"Maybe I should pull out the old stones and bones and see what I see," said Gran.

I wasn't sure if I wanted her to go to this secret place. I had only seen Gran do "her thing" a few times since I had moved in with them after my parents divorced, and neither one of them wanted me. She said throwing the bones looked flaky as anything, but it worked. At least, she thought it worked for her. She didn't have much respect for palm readers and those who read tarot, with their flashing neon signs and ridiculous turbaned headgear, like the lady up the road. "Anyone can check out a book from the library and learn to do that," she'd said time and again, "and most of it is pure New Age bullshit. It's rare that people have an actual gift like us."

Granddad had admitted to me once that he thought Gran had taken up the stones because she missed her gift. I really didn't get it. When my "gift" was gone, I was never going to look back.

"Gran," I said, "I wanted to ask you something about that." Talking with Will had gotten me thinking, especially about that response I'd given about being descended from a long line of seers. About being a Sybil.

"Ask away," said Gran.

"Not the casting thing, but, well . . . you know, I was wondering about our family history. About the stuff we can do."

Gran dropped the dish towel she'd just picked up and clapped like an overjoyed seal. "I've been waiting years for you to ask me that," she gasped. She sat down next to me and scooted her chair in close. "We're from a long line, you and me, Aria. I bet you're still not quite sure what to make of that."

I shook my head, relieved she didn't phrase it as a question, relieved she still knew better.

"I'll make it as plain as I can," Gran said. "In the beginning, there were ten Sibyls. We are descended from the original Erythraean Sibyl."

"Try saying that three times fast," said Granddad, still preparing the fish like we weren't sitting there talking about people out of mythology being related to us.

"Shush," said Gran, but she gave him a smile. "She predicted the Trojan War. You know, Michelangelo even painted her. Imagine that! Our ancestress is up on the wall in the Sistine Chapel!"

"Whoo!" said Granddad, twirling a gnarled finger in

the air. Gran reached behind her and gave him a whack without even looking. He chuckled and went back to working on the fish.

"Everyone has heard of the oracle at Delphi, but that was just the most famous location where people would go to ask questions. There were lots of others. There were traveling Sibyls, too. They roamed the countryside and helped people."

My heart leapt. "If there were ten originally . . . does that mean that there are more now?" Was I not the only person with my particular problem? Were there more girls out there like me?

"Definitely possible. It's hard to say how many of us are left. We're the last in this line, and sometimes the gift is not passed on."

"Like Mom," I said.

Gran frowned. "It often skips a generation, but the knowledge is passed down all the same."

"But then why—" My voice cracked a little, and I cleared my throat. "Why does she hate me so much? If she knew?" She had to have realized it wasn't my fault. I didn't make Dad cheat. I had just been the one to tell her.

"She never believed, Aria, and she doesn't hate you," said Gran softly. "If anything, she hates herself."

"And your father," added Granddad. He gave a vicious chop with his knife and severed the head of a fish with the blow.

Well, *I* was the one she wouldn't talk to. The daughter she couldn't look in the face. It had been over three years since I had even seen her.

"Don't trouble yourself with your mother," Gran murmured. "You have me. I'll help you, Aria. I promise. I'll share everything I know. We'll do this together."

My eyes moistened, but I smiled. Funny, Will had said the exact same thing. All of a sudden, there were people I could trust. Stranger still, they'd been there all along.

THE ICE IS GETTING THINNER

Gran and Granddad tried to talk me into helping out with the stand again on Sunday, but I refused. I told them I had homework, but mostly I wanted to be alone to think. Plus, Jade's service was later in the afternoon. I wasn't entirely sure whether I wanted to go or not, but I felt like I should.

Once they finally left, I turned on some music to fit my mood. It was a playlist with Death Cab for Cutie and Radiohead with some old school Thelonious Monk. If Granddad had been home, he would have laughed at me and put on "something you could tap your feet to." But I wasn't in the mood for laughter, either with me or *at* me. I picked up *Hamlet* and started reading on to the next act. Tragedy was something I could relate to.

I had just reached the scene where Hamlet learns Ophelia is dead when there was a sharp knock at the door. I jumped and dropped my book. Was it Will? He hadn't said anything about coming over, but I couldn't imagine who else it could be. No one ever came to visit us. I ran to the door and made myself stop before I got there long enough to pat my hair down. I took a deep breath and steadied myself. I was probably being stupid. Watch it be some Jehovah's Witness or something, way off the beaten path.

I looked through the peephole. It was Alex.

He definitely didn't have any religious tracts in hand. He must have run. I hadn't heard his huge old Chevy, and his dark curly hair was damp with sweat. What was he doing here? I hesitated for a moment, but he'd probably heard my book fall to the floor. I couldn't hide now.

He knocked again, louder this time, and I jumped. I opened the door and stood in the doorway. He didn't need to see into our tiny little living room.

"Aria," he said at the same time I said, "Alex."

It was my house, so I cleared my throat and asked the obvious. "Why are you here?"

"Can I come in?" he asked.

"I wouldn't be able to stop you," I said. Crap, there I went again. He frowned. I sounded like such a bitch. "Come on in," I said and opened the screen door, too.

"Are you sure?"

For heaven's sake, would he stop asking questions? "Today I am sure of nothing, tomorrow drifts in mist. Someday soon you will open a door, and I will walk through." I held up my hand before he could respond to that, whatever *that* was. "Just come in," I said. "*Please.*"

He stepped through, close enough to me that I had to step back or risk coming in contact with him. I could smell the sweat on him, and it was more earthy than disgusting, which surprised me. It wasn't a locker room smell. Mostly, he smelled like *guy* to the nth degree.

I let the screen door swing shut but left the front door open. Alex stood in the middle of our tiny living room looking like a giant come to visit. He was just so *solid.* I was used to being the big one in the family. I got my height from my dad's side of the family, and Gran and Granddad both had shrunk over the years.

"You want to sit?" I gestured at our old brown couch, though looking at it, I almost doubted it would hold him.

"I ran," he said. He took out a blue and white patterned handkerchief and wiped at his forehead then stuffed it back into his pocket. It looked just like the old-fashioned ones Granddad always carried. He never went anywhere without one. Maybe it was a guy thing. "I'm a little sweaty."

Like I hadn't noticed. He was like a gladiator or something but more real than Hollywood could ever be. "That's okay. It's old." Not that I'd needed to draw attention to that, but it was what it was.

He sat down, and the couch let out a massive creak but held. I stayed where I was near the door. I hadn't turned the music off, and suddenly the introduction from *Carmina Burana* came bursting out of the speakers. I'd had an opera phase a few years back when I'd first looked up what my name meant. We both jumped, and I ran to turn it down.

"Sorry," I said and shrugged. "Um, nice," he said. "Very, uh, bold." I nodded but didn't say anything. I was pretty sure he hadn't come to chat about my love of music. Friday night seemed like a dream. Having him here in my living room didn't feel real. He finally cleared his throat and got to the point. "I came to apologize."

"That's not necessary."

"No, it is." He looked down at the floor and used the toe of his sneaker to flip the edge of our raggedy throw rug up and down. "I know what drinking can do. I know better. I just . . ."

"It happens," I said. I'd never been drunk, but goodness knows it was a sport with some of the kids at school. I knew more than I wanted to about hangover cures and praying to the porcelain god. Tank was a true disciple, on his knees on a regular basis.

He brought his head up and stared at me, hard. "Not to me," he said.

I didn't have a response to that. Obviously, it *had* happened to him, but I wasn't going to push it. "You didn't have to come all the way out here to tell me that."

"I wanted to say thank you, too," he said, looking back down at his feet. "For getting me home." If he kept worrying our ratty old rug, it was going to fall apart.

"You're welcome," I said.

Silence fell between us. I didn't know what he was thinking about, but I was remembering how it had felt there in the dark with him, in the woods. Would a guilt-ridden murderer come to my house to apologize? It didn't seem possible, unless what had happened with Jade had been an accident.

But you can't accidentally stab someone. Not three times.

I took a few steps toward the door before I even thought about what I was doing. I had to say something. "I guess I should thank you, too," I said. "For . . . for sticking up for me."

He shook his head. "You already thanked me for that. It's no big deal."

Maybe not to him. "And I wanted to say I was sorry, too."

"What—"

"Stop." I cut him off before he finished his question. I didn't want to have to go into a long spiel of what I was sorry for. There were too many things. "I'm sorry for that thing I said about your dad the other day. I didn't mean anything bad by it."

He was quiet for a moment more, a silent and unmovable bulk on our couch. "I hope you're right, actually."

"You do?" There I was, asking more questions.

"Yeah." His eyes were dark and unreadable. "I am not going to be my dad. I'm not. I'm going to get out of here."

"So what were you doing drunk in the woods?" Oh, God, what was I, some kind of inverse oracle today? I couldn't believe I'd asked him that. I remembered how broken his voice had sounded as he'd told me how we were the same. *No one wants us*, he'd said. *We're both on the outside looking in. We want to get out of this shithole town. And we're both alone.* Was I alone now? I had Will. Will knew me. He knew my secret. I had someone.

He flushed a deep red. "That was the first time I've ever done that," he said. "And the last."

"Of course," I said, nodding like some kind of idiotic bobblehead doll. I had to get him out of here before I either asked or answered something else stupid. "Um, anyway, I really need to get ready for Jade's service so . . ." I jerked my head toward the door.

He didn't get up, but at least he stopped messing with the rug. His eyes were still on mine though, dark and intense. "One more thing," he said. "Stay away from Will."

I froze. What the hell was that supposed to mean? And what business was that of his? What did he know? "Alex, I think you should go," I said firmly. "I'm really busy."

"I mean it," he said, standing up. "You should stay away from Will. He's bad news."

"And what, you're good news?" Wasn't he the one who'd told me to run from *him*, Alex, just two days ago?

"No, I'm not." He took a step toward me, and the phone rang.

It was a rare occurrence in our house. I nearly jumped out of my skin. He flinched, too. I scrambled to find the phone buried under a couple of yellowing newspapers by Granddad's favorite chair, glad to have an excuse to end the conversation. "Hello?" I said, watching Alex as he stood there watching me.

"Missed you at your grandparents' stand today," said Will.

"Oh," I said and then I couldn't think of anything else to add. It seemed forever since I'd seen him, even though it was only yesterday. I looked away from Alex, uncomfortable. He was too close, and our phone was one of those old clunkers. Could he hear who was on the other side of the line?

"So," Will said when it became obvious I didn't have

anything more to contribute to the conversation, "would it be all right with you if I came over? Gran said it was okay, and you could use some cheering up anyway. I could drive you to Jade's service later."

"Whether it will be okay or not remains to be seen. The future is not yet clear, but you'll arrive in twenty-two minutes and seven seconds," I said. I smacked myself in the head. *Stupid.* I looked at Alex again and narrowed my eyes at him.

"Will," Alex said, not a question but an accusation. He grimaced, almost as if he were in pain.

I shook my head and pointed at the door. It wasn't any of his business. But he didn't move. Will laughed in my ear, the sound jangly and discordant over the phone. "I see it works over the phone, too. Okay, I'll see you in twenty-two minutes and seven seconds then." He hung up, still chuckling.

Well, at least I knew exactly how much time I had to get Alex out of here and to clean up a little. I hung up the phone. "Alex, really, you need to go."

He watched me for a long moment, his brown eyes inscrutable, and then finally went to the door. "I'm serious," he said. "Stay away from Will or you'll regret it, just like Jade." He opened the door and let it bang shut behind him. I went to the window and watched him run down our drive, his stride long and easy. I hoped he'd be far down the road by the time Will drove over.

HEY SOUL SISTER

I straightened up our small living room and opened the window. It was probably only in my head, but the room smelled like Alex, all sweat and earth and sunshine. I switched the music to something more cheerful, too, leaving it low in case some more opera showed up in the playlist. I didn't have time to change clothes, but there wasn't anything better for me to wear than the pale blue sundress I was in anyway. At least the color suited me. I was in front of the mirror pulling my hair into a loose ponytail when I heard Will's car hit the gravel on our driveway. I opened the door and met him on the porch.

He was wearing a crisp white shirt and black slacks. He looked clean and new, especially out here where everything was old and grey. There was a speck of grit on his shirt, probably kicked up from our drive. I brushed it off before I thought about what I was doing.

"Sorry," I said. "It's really dusty out here. Gets into everything."

"It's fine," he said. "You know, you're always apologizing for something. You don't have anything to be sorry for."

I opened my mouth to say sorry again and stopped. How lame was I? Apologizing for apologizing too much.

"So, can I come in? I promised your grandfather I'd be a perfect gentleman."

"You can," I said in what I was coming to think of as my prophetic voice, a little deeper than my normal tones. It seemed to be more obvious when I wasn't trying to conceal myself. And I didn't have to conceal myself with Will. "But we probably ought to sit out here. We don't have any air-conditioning. Sorry."

I winced as he shook his finger at me. There I went again. It's not like it was my fault we were too poor to have air-conditioning. Well, it kind of was. Gran and Granddad had lost a lot of money when they'd sold their retirement place in Tarpon Springs. The housing market had been terrible, and they'd had to take a huge loss after they'd saved for so long to be able to buy it. It had always been their dream to retire somewhere warm after living in upstate Michigan for so long. Our little shanty house in Lake Mariah had been all they could afford. But that was neither here nor there. I shook my head and vowed to not say I was sorry for anything else again today.

Instead I said, "How about we sit on the swing?"

He had that crooked grin on his face. I wished I knew what it meant. Was he easily amused or always laughing at me? I squeezed past him to step outside, but he took my hand and led me over to our front porch swing instead of letting me lead the way. It was as well weathered and grey as the house and it moaned and creaked something wicked, but it was sturdy. It was one of the things that had appealed to Gran about this house.

We sat down, but he didn't release my hand. I curled my legs under me and smoothed my dress down with my free hand. Will pushed us off, and the swing groaned into motion. I could feel my hand starting to sweat and I wanted to wipe it off, but I didn't want to move it either. I settled for relaxing my fingers as much as possible, my hand lying in his like a limp, dead fish.

I was obviously overthinking this.

"So," I said, looking out over our front yard with its overgrown tufts of grass and patches of sand, "you and Jade really weren't dating anymore?"

I swallowed. Maybe it was none of my business, but he *was* holding my hand. Jade hadn't even been dead for a week. I couldn't really call her my friend, but she definitely hadn't been my enemy either. I really didn't know how all of this worked, but it seemed too soon somehow. On the other hand, maybe that was because of how she had died. Of course, if she hadn't, we wouldn't be sitting here or going to her service later. Or maybe the hand-holding didn't mean anything at all, other than consoling someone who needed it. Maybe I was reading too much into it.

He didn't flinch. "Well, we were going to be graduating soon, going off to college, and all that. We always knew it was just a high school thing. And Jade and I didn't have much in common. I know people thought we did, but we really didn't." I could feel his eyes on me, but I didn't turn my head. I probably shouldn't have brought this up. "She'd been acting kind of weird anyway. I don't know what was going on with her. Probably that guy Alex. You know she'd been seeing him." He paused a moment and gave another push to keep the swing going. "You know, I was thinking about it last night. Maybe you could tell me why. Maybe we could even figure out what happened to her."

"Me? I didn't really . . ." I trailed off, realizing what he meant. "I guess so, if you want to try."

"We don't have to if you don't want to."

"No, it's okay. It seems it's what I'm here for, right?" I laughed, but it fizzled before it really got started. A future as a stand-up comedian was definitely not in the cards for me.

"If you're sure you don't mind."

I shook my head. If he really wanted to, I could try. It's not like he didn't already know I was a freak, like one of those fortune-telling machines. Just stick a question in me instead of a quarter. Really, I wasn't surprised that he'd asked. If anything, I should be amazed that he hadn't asked as soon as he figured out what I could do.

"Go ahead, shoot," I said. "Give it your best shot. But don't get weirded out by anything I say." At least we were sitting, in case things got intense or I fainted.

Please, God, don't let me faint in front of Will.

"Okay," he said. "Let me think a minute for the best question to ask."

I chewed on my lip, still looking out at the yard. Like

Gran said: *Worry about the things you can change and screw the rest.*

"Did something happen recently to make Jade act differently?"

I sat up straighter. My cue. "Yes," I intoned. The prophetic voice was kind of creeping me out. It seemed to be getting stronger and less like my own voice every day. Of course, I'd been having more conversations with people in the last week than I'd had in ages. I'd also been trying to conceal it less.

"Did it have something to do with the guy that died in the hit-and-run?"

I turned to look at him in surprise. I hadn't seen that question coming. "Guilt has everything to do with it," I heard myself reply.

He didn't look at all shocked by the answer. He smiled grimly at me. "I suspected something. She said a few things that were . . . strange." He thought a minute and tried a few pointed questions, but the answers were more riddle than fact. He seemed to be getting frustrated, but so was I. Something was close, so close underneath all my nonsense answers. I could feel it, like it was on the tip of my tongue. I felt heavy, weighed down, almost pinned to the seat.

The swing let out another croaking groan as Will swung it back with more force. We rocked silently for a moment.

"Okay, let's try this a different way. Can you tell me: Was Jade involved in the hit-and-run somehow?"

"Yes," I said. Finally, a simple, clear answer. I could hardly believe it, but there it was. I itched to say something, but what? I felt numb inside, and my mouth was dry.

"She was out with Alex last weekend," Will said quietly, so low that I could barely hear him over the swing. "I told her she should stay away from him." He turned to me. "You should, too."

I shivered and looked away. Had he seen Alex running from my house? Did he know Alex had been here to see me? Did he know what Alex had said?

"I have art class with him," I finally said, watching my skirt flutter as we swung. "But I don't really know him or anything." It wasn't a lie exactly, but I felt guilty all the same. I hoped Will wouldn't ask me anything directly about Alex. I snuck a peek at him. He was staring off into the trees, his eyes unfocused and faraway. "Didn't you . . . I mean, I heard that you went out with Jade last weekend, too." I went back to concentrating on my skirt, barely breathing. The pattern was circle upon circle, connected to each other in an unending chain. I traced a line with my finger, winding up back where I started.

"I need you to trust me," he said, his thumb once again slowly working its way back and forth across my hand. "Jade and I really were through. But we did see each other this past weekend, just as friends—on Friday. The guy was run over on Sunday."

I was sure he must have noticed how hot and sweaty my hand was. I couldn't stop thinking about it. What was I doing?

"Wait," he said. "I know. How about this . . . Aria, did I go out with Jade on Friday?"

"In, not out, Friday last. A comedy that no one enjoyed . . . no laughs, no smiles to be had," I said softly.

"Yes," he said. "Exactly. We watched a movie at my house. It was terrible."

"Okay," I said, nodding. "Friday."

He let my hand go, and I almost breathed a sigh of relief. I wiped it quickly on my skirt, just in case, but he didn't pick it up again. Instead, he cupped my chin in his hand and turned my face to his. "Did I love Jade?"

"No," I whispered. The answer probably should have made me feel better, but instead it made me feel lost and sad.

"Did I ever think there would be a future for me and Jade?"

"Never," I said. I felt even emptier than before. Jade didn't have a future, not now.

"See," he said, and his voice caught. "You said it yourself, and you only speak the truth."

BOYS WITH GIRLFRIENDS

Will waited in the living room as I went into my room and changed into a drab grey dress. Unflattering, as most of my clothes were, but the most appropriate thing I owned for a funeral service.

Even though he obviously couldn't see me from where he was, I felt self-conscious, changing as fast as I could, my back to the closed door. I almost pulled out the small stash of makeup I had hidden in my closet, sent by my stepmother to me when I turned fifteen, but I decided not to. It seemed wrong to try and make myself pretty for such an occasion. I settled for brushing my hair until it lay flat and shone.

"You look nice," said Will as I came out of my room. He was sitting on our couch, flipping through an ancient fishing magazine, looking far more at home than I would have thought possible.

"Thanks," I said awkwardly. I picked up my backpack

and then set it back down. I didn't actually own a purse, but it didn't seem right to take my pack. I fished through it and took out my keys and slipped them into my pocket. I hesitated for a moment and left my MP3 player behind. I couldn't very well attend Jade's service with it.

"I really don't know if I should go," I said.

"Of course you should," said Will. "Everyone's going."

"But I might . . . say something," I said.

He went to me and brushed a strand of my hair from my cheek. "It will be fine," he said, taking my hand and leading me out of my house. "I'll be there. Let's go. You can do it."

He opened the car door for me and gave me a wink as I climbed in. "If it will make you feel better," he added, "we'll sit in the back when we get there."

I nodded as I got in, taking a breath against the heat that had built up in his car. Black was a cruel color in Florida.

It felt strange to be a passenger in Will's car, buckled tight into the unscuffed leather seats, the windows rolled up and air-conditioning gently blowing my hair into angel wings. I usually drove myself places, unless I was going somewhere with my grandparents and Granddad always insisted on driving. I felt like a spectator.

He drove faster than I did, faster than the Colt could go, and we were pulling up at the church before I was ready to face everyone. Small groups of mourners were gathered outside, with a snake line of black-clad students making their way inside the double doors. There were a lot of people there. Everyone, it looked like.

He parked in a corner of the parking lot and turned to

look at me. "Do you want to sit here a minute before we go in?"

"It makes no difference to the world, though the eyes upon me will be lessened," I said. I let go of the door handle. "Ignore that. Yes, I'd like to, please."

He turned the car back on, and we sat in silence for a moment, the only sound the air-conditioning. I watched as more people arrived, and the parking lot filled up, glad of the tinting on Will's windows. It was almost time for the service to start when I saw Alex pull in. There were no spaces left, and he turned clumsily onto the grass and hopped out, hurrying across the lawn. He'd cleaned up from his run and wore a suit, though I could tell from where I was that it was a little too small for him and stretched tight across his back. It was probably the same one he'd worn to his brother's funeral.

Will's hand on mine tightened. "He's got some nerve showing up," he said.

"You really think he . . . had something to do with it?" I asked.

"I'm sure of it," he said. "I told the police to take a good, long look at Alex, but I don't think they believed me." He gave a snort of laughter. "Why believe another suspect, I guess. Hopefully they figure it out before it's too late."

Too late? Wasn't it already too late? It was definitely too late for Jade. I shivered, and Will switched off the car.

"Anyway," he said, "are you ready?"

"Not yet," I said. Honest, as always. "But let's go." We couldn't sit in the car all day. I put my hand on the door handle.

"Hold on, I've got it," he said. He got out and went around to open the door for me. "What kind of gentleman do you think I am?"

"The kind that cloaks himself in mystery." My eyes widened at what I'd said, but he just laughed and took my hand to pull me out of the car. The humid air hit me like a wall after being in the air-conditioned car.

"You've got nothing to worry about," he whispered in my ear.

That wasn't true. I had a billion things to worry about. Like getting through the next hour without saying anything else idiotic or insulting someone.

He steered me through the parking lot with his hand in the small of my back, into the First Baptist Church. I had never been inside before. Actually, I hadn't been inside *any* church in longer than I could remember. After a cousin had once asked me about God and caused me to pass out, I was wary of something similar happening in public. Too many big, unanswerable questions in church.

The pews were completely full, a testament to Jade's place in our small community. It was surprisingly quiet considering the number of bodies packed into the space; people were even standing at the edges. An overweight woman in a shapeless hat was playing a piano, and there was the rustle of too-formal clothing and the miserable sound of prolonged weeping, but other than that, it was very still. I was grateful for the lack of questions.

Will led me to one of the last open spots near the door. I had a potted plant on a pedestal on one side and him on the other. I stepped back so that the leafy fern provided some cover for me, but I still felt exposed. It was probably my imagination, but it felt like everyone had stared at us as we walked in. I took a quick look around the room. There was only one person actively looking in our direction: Alex. He was only about twenty feet away, but his eyes were so intently focused on us that I felt like he was right in front of me. I shrank back into the plant, wishing it was larger. Will's hand was warm on my back.

The last bars of "The Wind Beneath My Wings" faded away, and a black-clad preacher stepped forward to the podium.

"We are here today to honor the memory of Jade Price. I had the privilege of knowing Jade ever since her first days in vacation Bible school, and it was a true pleasure to see her smiling face among my congregation every Sunday." He paused to clear his throat and look down. "I must admit that this is one of the most difficult eulogies I have ever had to deliver." He raised his head, and tears were visible, magnified behind his glasses. "Not only have we lost a beloved member of our community and church, but in such a manner as to make even the most devout of us question the meaning behind it."

I shuffled uneasily at the mention of the "q" word. The muted sobbing grew louder. Will spread his hand flat against my back and shifted his weight so that his side pressed against mine. I couldn't help it, I peeked through the foliage to see if Alex or anyone else had noticed, but almost everyone was focused on the preacher. I did find Delilah's eyes on me. She was seated in a pew to the far right and had turned around, for what I didn't know. She gave me a sad, lost smile then bent her attention back to the preacher.

"Whenever we lose someone we love suddenly, especially in such a horrific manner, we are left distraught and angry. Why, we ask. Why did this have to happen?"

I saw Delilah nod.

"Nothing had to happen," I said under my breath, ducking my head behind the plant, glad that I'd had at least a little warning, "it was the will and the way."

Will leaned toward me, like he was trying to hear what I was saying better. "Sorry," I whispered. "I'll try to be quieter."

He turned his head so his lips were just above my ear. "Maybe you were right," he said. "Maybe this wasn't such a good idea. We can leave, if you want."

"I think I'm okay," I said. I hoped that was true.

"We may not know the answer to that question today or ever," the preacher continued. "Some questions have no earthly answers."

I could argue that one.

"When someone is taken from us so young, someone with so much potential and love in their heart, the temptation is to dwell on what could have been, what should have been. We imagine all the experiences we would have wished for Jade, all of the things we hoped for her." The preacher motioned towards the front row, and I saw Jade's mother and father, their faces sallow and drawn in the light of the stained-glass window. "We should strive to remember Jade for what she did accomplish in this life. She was an excellent student, well loved by everyone who knew her. She had a wonderful sense of humor and was a truly charitable individual, selfless to a fault, and always willing to give of herself and her time." He leaned forward, both hands gripping the pulpit. "Jade was loved, and she will be missed, as evidenced by the crowd I see before me today. I urge you to remember the good times and the beauty of Jade's life, even in these dark days of anguish. We should endeavor to rise up and not dwell in the darkness, always looking backwards, seeing only fear and bemoaning our loss. Let us celebrate her life, cut short as it was, and pray for justice as well."

He bowed his head, and everyone joined him. "Our Heavenly Father," he intoned, "you have not made us for darkness and death, but for life with you for ever and ever. Without you we have nothing to hope for, but with you we have nothing to fear. Speak to us your words of eternal life. Lift us from our despair and grief to the light and harmony of your presence and set the glory of your love before us, through Jesus Christ, our Lord. Amen."

I said "Amen" along with everyone else and raised my head.

The preacher motioned for Jade's mother to come forward. She clutched a crumpled tissue in one hand as she made her way to the podium.

"Thank you, everyone, for coming today," she murmured. Her eyes were red-rimmed and fresh tear tracks were visible even from where I stood behind the plant. "I—" she started and stopped. "I appreciate what Reverend Jones has said," she choked out, "but I just want to know: What kind of God allows things like this to happen?"

She broke down, but I barely noticed as an intense heat spread from my stomach all through my body. I opened my mouth, and I could feel my tongue beginning to form words, but I had no idea what I was saying as I collapsed sideways into Will.

ENCE NEVER KILLED ANYONE. ONCE BEGUN,
CAN'T BE UNDONE. THE ITCH MUST BE
SCRATCHED, THE FIRE MUST BE FED. THERE
ARE SO MANY LITTLE DYINGS THAT IT
DOESN'T MATTER WHICH OF THEM IS DEATH.
WATER IS LIKE LIFE. IT ARRIVES, MALES, THEN
RECEDES AWAY FASTER, FASTER, LEAVING
EVERYTHING SILENT. THE VALUE OF A RUMOR
IS ONLY HELD BY THOSE WHO WOULD BE
LIEVE THEM. THE TRUTH COMPELS ME, I MUST
ANSWER. WHAT IS CHOICE BUT AN ILLUSION?
THE TRUTH IS IN ME, I ONLY SPEAK THE
TRUTH. IT IS UP TO THE HEARER TO BRING

ESCAPE MYSELF

SOON, YOU WILL OPEN A DOOR AND I WILL
WALK THROUGH. GUILT HAS EVERYTHING TO
DO WITH IT. NOTHING HAD TO HAPPEN. IT
WAS THE WILL AND THE WAY. THE TRUTH IS
SLIPPERY. PROBLEMS, PROBLEMS, HERE,
THERE, EVERYWHERE. ANSWERS, ANSWERS,
SOON ENOUGH.

The first sensation I had was one of heat bearing down on me. I blinked a few times and finally managed to drag my eyes open. Unbroken grey. Fuzzy. I was in Will's car, reclined back in the passenger's seat, staring up at the roof of the car.

"Quite the drama queen," said Will.

"What?" I tried to sit up and fell back down as a wave of nausea hit me.

"Whoa," he said, putting a hand on my shoulder to hold me down. "I was only kidding. Take it easy."

I took a deep breath and closed my eyes. "How long was I out for? Did anyone see me?"

Will started the car. "Not long. And don't worry about it. We were close to the door. Delilah saw. She made me promise to let her know you were okay. She was pretty much the only one. I got you out of there pretty quick."

"Thanks," I said, keeping my eyes closed. "I'm sorry about that."

"It's okay. Not like you could help it."

I stayed quiet for a few minutes, keeping my eyes closed and feeling the road pass beneath us. It was a much smoother ride than in the Colt, but I could feel it more now that I was on my back with my eyes closed. And my stomach was in revolt.

"Did you—" I cleared my throat. My voice sounded rusty even to my own ears. "Did you catch what my answer was? To Jade's mom's question?"

"Sorry," he said. "I was too busy trying not to drop you. You were kind of mumbling anyway."

"That's okay," I said. "Probably wasn't decipherable anyway."

GRANDDAD POKED HIS HEAD in the front door with his hand over his eyes. "We're comin' in," he called out, "so you better be decent!" I threw one of the lopsided pillows from the couch at him, and he laughed as he threw it back.

"Porter!" said Gran. "There you go again!" She bumped him through the door with her bony hip and carried some bags into the kitchen.

"Will's gone now," I said. "And he was a perfect gentleman, like he told you he would be."

He'd gone beyond the call of duty. After driving me home, he'd sat and talked and stared at me with concerned eyes and only left after I had reassured him about fifty times that I was okay. He'd texted Delilah. (Why did she even care so much if I passed out?) He'd even dug up some crackers for me from the kitchen.

"That's suspicious," said Granddad, sitting down next to me. "Something must be wrong with the boy then." He patted me on the head like he used to do when I was a little girl.

I groaned at the lame joke of a hidden compliment. Granddad knew full well there wouldn't be any boys in my life, not as long as I was cursed with Gran's gift. Will was the first boy I had talked to pretty much ever and definitely the first I had ever had more than one semi-successful conversation with. But I was starting to wonder if the real reason Will kept coming back was because my weirdness intrigued him and not really because of *me*. And after what had happened today, I doubted if he'd want to be seen in public with me again, no matter what he said about it not being a big deal. Like girls fainted on him all the time.

Gran came back in and handed Granddad a glass of juice. She sat down on my other side, and the couch let out a squeak. "Everything good," Gran stated. She looked at me, leaving off the question mark and asking it only with her eyes.

"Yes," I said. "*I'm fine.*" I was a little annoyed that she kept asking. I wasn't about to tell her I fainted in front of half the town. She'd probably tell me I needed to be stronger. "How was your day? Any customers?"

"No," said Granddad. "Slim pickings. The cops came by, and that was our excitement for the day. Ellie did get one of the state troopers to buy a jar of marmalade, though."

"What did they come by for?"

"Just seeing if we'd seen or heard anything, I guess," said Gran. "I offered to do a reading for them, but they didn't take me up on it."

That didn't surprise me. Gran didn't try to hide her belief in prophecy, but people just thought she was a kooky old woman and humored her. I'd bet the trooper had offered to buy the marmalade *after* she'd said she'd do a reading for him. Another sympathy purchase. I sometimes wondered what would happen if people actually took her seriously. Had they ever when she was younger and had the true gift?

"I think they're hoping the girl's death was an accident somehow or a transient or something," said Granddad. "They've never had this kind of crime happen around here before. First that hit-and-run and then that poor girl. They just aren't set up for such things here, beyond setting up a tip line." He jerked his head toward the couch, strewn with newspaper. "Called in for some help from down south. They're no strangers to death down there."

That pricked my conscience. I was positive Jade's death was no accident, though I still didn't see how exactly the two deaths were related. But they obviously were. Or, at least, so my inner oracle said.

"When I was talking with Will, he asked something, and I think I know something about that. About the first guy, I mean. The guy that got run over." Gran and Granddad both looked at me, waiting. I stared down at my lap, uncomfortable. "I'm not sure what to make of it, but I think Jade was involved in the hit-and-run. Her car. It was the one that hit him. I'm sure it had to have been an accident." I couldn't wrap my head around it, honestly. "Maybe when Jade was out on a date with this guy Alex from school . . ." The last part tumbled from my mouth the way my prophecies did, even though it had come from me.

They both started talking at once, and for a few minutes it was pandemonium as they were asking questions and I was trying to answer them. I held up my hands, and they stopped. I took a deep breath. "Thanks," I said.

"Sorry," said Granddad. "I'm always—"

"Forgetting. I know, Granddad, it's okay. Anyway, that's all I know. We were just talking about her a little bit. Will said she'd been acting really strange." I didn't mention that he'd specifically used me to find out why she'd been acting so odd. Thankfully, my grandparents were so preoccupied by the news that they didn't think to ask. And I didn't mention that he blamed Alex for Jade's death. I still wasn't convinced. Even if Alex and Jade were somehow involved in the hit-and-run, that didn't mean it had to be connected to Jade's death, did it? Maybe I was grasping at straws.

"You have to tell the police, Aria," said Gran finally.

It had not occurred to me that she would suggest such a thing. I suppose I should have expected it. She had, after all, offered to do a reading for an officer without blinking an eye.

"Gran, that's all I know. And I don't even know anything, really. Not exactly. Just that she was involved somehow. Her car, I guess, or something. You know how unclear my answers can be. Maybe she just witnessed it, and that's it.

Besides, I'm sure they'll figure it out for themselves." I looked at Granddad. "Didn't you say you saw them investigating the hit-and-run site?" I was babbling. I couldn't help it. "This has nothing to do with me."

He nodded, but it was Gran that took my chin in her hand. "Aria, that man has a family. He may not have been from around here. He may not have been the kind of person that most of the people around here would even care about. But he was a person and his family deserves to know what happened to him. And that boy Alex may have more information." She narrowed her eyes at me. "Who ran that man over?" she said quickly, before I could prepare myself.

"Water is like life," I said, my voice filled with gravel. "It arrives madly, then recedes away faster, faster . . . leaving everything silent."

That same nonsense again. I was sick of it. Though it did show that there was a clear connection between the deaths, for what that was worth.

I swallowed. "Gran," I managed, once I was in control of my own speech again. "I just can't. I can't go to the police with stuff like . . . like *that*." True, Will had learned about my gift, and it hadn't been the disaster that I had always thought telling someone would be. But this was different. I could just imagine the look on the police officer's face as I told him what I knew and how I knew it. Would he offer to buy marmalade from me? Or would he howl with laughter? He would probably think I was making fun. What would I think if I were in his shoes? It's not like I could pretend to be a friend of Jade's just now coming forward with the information. Anyone who knew me at school would punch holes in that story right away.

Or maybe they'd lock me up in a mental institution.

She kept staring at me, her eyes sad, until finally she dropped my chin and nodded. "Think about it, Aria. This is important. Think long and hard. You know what it's like to be on the outside." She got up and went back to the kitchen. Granddad gave me a small smile and a pat on the shoulder and followed her.

Here I was again, alone. I ruffled through the paper and ripped out the tip-line number.

SLEEP WAS OUT OF the question. I turned over and looked at my alarm clock for what must have been the fiftieth time. It was two thirty in the morning. I had been staring at the watermark on my ceiling, watching it staring back down at me, enigmatic snake eyes. There were no answers there. The only answers I had were inside me, and they weren't helping now. They never had.

I blew out a breath and got up, putting on a thread-bare bathrobe I'd inherited from Granddad. Years ago it had been flannel. Now it was a blue-and-grey plaid whisper of itself. I took the screen out of my window and quietly climbed through so the creak of the front door wouldn't give me away. Neither Gran nor Granddad had particularly good hearing anymore. I could hear them both snoring, but I wasn't going to chance it. I didn't feel like making a speech.

I walked over to my car and got in and sat for a few minutes, still not sure what I wanted to do. My car was so ancient that it had a real clock as opposed to a digital one. I could hear it ticking. After a full five minutes had passed with the insistent *tick, tick, tick* echoing in my ears, I stuck the key in the ignition and turned. The Colt sputtered to life, and I rumbled down the drive, an anxious glance back at the house in my rearview mirror. No lights came on.

Gran was right. I didn't even remember what the guy's name was who had been run over. I would be willing to bet that no one at school did either. No one, certainly, had asked. But somewhere out there was a family missing him. His wife, who had found him, for one. *Gabriella.* That was it. Gabriella and Armando Huerta. I remembered now. She deserved to know. And hadn't Gran said they had three kids? They were just as important as Jade was, and no one was giving them a thought.

If I was honest with myself, I hadn't really, either.

And Will was right, too. The police needed to take a long, hard look at Alex. It wasn't just the hit-and-run guy that needed justice. Jade did, too. The image of Jade's mother at the funeral service had been haunting me, too.

I had the tip-line number in my pocket.

I drove to a gas station on the outskirts of town. It was the only place in town with a payphone. For all I knew, it was the only pay phone still left in the county. Everyone had cell phones now, even the kids in elementary school. Everyone but us. We had our landline, but I didn't want to make this call from a phone attached to our name.

I found a few quarters in my glove box and dialed the number I'd ripped out of the newspaper that Granddad had left on the couch. It rang a few times, and then I got a recording telling me I had reached the tip line for the police. Maybe the cops were all asleep, like normal people. I gripped the slightly oily handset gingerly as I waited for it to get to the beep.

"Hello," I whispered, even though no one was around to hear me. "this is regarding the hit-and-run of Armando Huerta, that guy that, um, died. You should look at Jade Price's car or talk to Alex Walker."

I didn't know what else to say. I hung up the phone and went home, finally able to sleep.

TERRIBLE THOUGHT

I leaned my head against my locker and closed my eyes, exhaustion weighing me down. At least the questions had quieted down after the weekend. People were already starting to move on to other things. Maybe the funeral service had provided closure for everyone. If someone like Jade dying barely sent out a lasting ripple, I could only imagine what kind of impact my passing would have.

I felt a hand on my shoulder and jumped, hitting my head on the side of my locker. Backing up, a hand to my ear, I turned to find Will looking sheepishly at me.

"Sorry about that," he said. "I thought I'd surprise you."

"You did." I rubbed my ear but managed a smile. "I didn't expect to see you until lunch." I bit my lip. I probably shouldn't have admitted that I hoped to see him then, much less *expected* him.

A couple of freshmen girls brushed by us. "Do you really think Casey likes me?" one asked the other.

I wasn't prepared. "He just wants to bone you," I said, far too loudly for comfort. I quickly turned back to my locker, but the girls stopped short. They had heard me. It wasn't my problem her friend was crass, but it was my fault for letting my guard down. Will had distracted me. My MP3 player was useless in my hand, the earphones dangling down.

"*Excuse me?* Did you say something to me?"

I felt a sharp poke in the middle of my back. Even the freshmen had no problem taking me down. "No excuses," I said. "Yes, I did." I didn't turn around, glad she hadn't asked me what I had said and that I hadn't volunteered it. Once was enough for answers like that.

"You *bitch*." She grabbed my arm and spun me around. My MP3 player fell to the floor, and her friend stomped her foot down right on top of it without a second thought. I heard the snap of the case. *Crap.*

Will smoothly stepped in between us. "Girls," he said. "Are you talking about Casey Aronsen?"

I froze. This was *Will Raffles*. Talking to *them*. I heard one of the girls take a deep breath. Either they didn't care about the rumors that had been going around since Jade's death or their hormones had gotten the best of them. I don't think they had noticed him standing there next to me. After all, why would he be standing near the school freak? I doubted if they even heard me whisper my affirmative into my locker. She had indeed been talking about Casey Aronsen, one of the boys I had seen ganging up on Alex the other day during gym.

"Yeah," said the one who had asked about Casey's affections.

The girls' eyes were on Will, of course. I was forgotten.

"He *was* talking about a certain brown-haired girl the other day." I could hear the easy charm in Will's voice. He draped his arms around their shoulders, a girl on each side, and led them away from me. They were spellbound. "I wonder if he was talking about *you.*"

Both girls giggled as he steered them through the hall. The crowd parted as if by magic.

I picked up my shattered MP3 player. It was definitely a lost cause, but I pushed a button anyway, just to see. Not a sound. Not even a click. I stuck it in my book bag, wondering how I was going to get through the rest of the day.

I did know what it was like to be on the outside, didn't I? Anger flashed through me. Well, what if I finally wanted in? I shut my locker, its small metal clang tinny and empty in the deserted hall.

I CARRIED MY PLATE of salad past the tables full of talking, laughing kids and out into the Florida heat. I almost expected the lettuce to shrivel immediately. I felt a little scorched, myself. I sat down on the far side of the tree and picked at my salad. After fifteen minutes, I was done, and Will had not shown. Maybe he wasn't going to. Why had I expected him? Why would he want to spend his time cleaning up after my messes?

I dropped a wilted bit of leftover lettuce on top of a trail of ants circling a dead beetle. A small green shroud for the tiny corpse. I leaned forward, my elbows on my knees, to watch as the ants swarmed up and over it, little black lines crisscrossing the green.

"That's a little disturbing," said Will.

I sat up quickly, embarrassed, but he was smiling at me like we were sharing a secret.

"I didn't think you were coming," I blurted out. Why couldn't I control my tongue around him? Here I was saying stupid things, and he hadn't even asked me a question.

He tossed something small at me, and I sat back to let it fall into my lap. "Don't be silly," he said. "I just ran home to get this for you. Happy Monday."

It was an iPod, fancy white earphones still attached. "I can't take this."

"Sure you can. It's my old one. It's been sitting on my desk gathering dust. I even loaded some songs on it for you. That's what took me so long. I only live a couple of blocks away."

No one had ever given me anything before, other than family. It was too expensive, even if it was his old one. I held it out to him. "No, really, I can't take it. This is too much."

He sat down in front of me and pressed my hand back down into my lap. "Aria, this isn't really a gift. It's a . . . well, let's just call it a necessity."

"What are you talking about?"

"You know," he said, his eyes searching mine. "Like what happened to your MP3 player this morning. Now I understand why you have it. It's to keep incidents like that to a minimum. So you don't accidentally insult one of the idiots we're surrounded with." He patted my hand. "Sorry, that was harsh. But Jesus, those freshmen girls . . .

I pawned that one off on Casey as soon as I could. She deserves him. He's an asshole."

"But—"

"No arguing," he said, leaning back and shaking a finger at me. "Just take it. You need it. Someone else might figure out what you can do. I'm not taking no for an answer. We have to protect you somehow."

I knew what he meant. But this really was too big a gift. "Gran's told me I can learn to control it. Maybe," I said.

"That would be great. Like training or something?"

"Knowledge is power," I said. "Um, I don't know exactly, but she says it's possible."

He nodded. "That's cool. But, in the meantime, take the iPod."

Never look a gift horse in the mouth. That's what Gran often said. But she also liked to repeat Polonius's advice about not being a borrower or a lender. *Hamlet* was one of the few literary things she had ever read. She usually stuck to the *Farmer's Almanac*. I was torn. The thought of being able to plug in again was very tempting. I'd narrowly missed saying something damning where Tank could have heard me an hour before. Walking through the hallways without my earphones in made me feel exposed and vulnerable. I didn't want to have to start hiding in the bathrooms again.

"Aria," said Will, "this is where you say thank you. And take it."

"Thank you," I said. "I owe you. I promise I'll pay you back." I had no idea how, but I would find a way somehow.

"We'll think of something." He grinned at me, a lazy

grin that started slow and finished big. My face burned. He couldn't possibly mean what it felt like he meant.

"You know, I can take care of myself, too," I said. "I've been doing it for years." I felt like I needed to defend myself, even if I hadn't this morning.

He laughed. "I don't doubt it, but I'm here now."

Before I could even think of anything to say to that, he took the iPod back and gave me a crash course in how it worked. He was disbelieving when I explained I didn't have a computer but promised to bring me an adapter so I could charge it without one. Something else I would owe him for.

Thank goodness I had a backup of all my music, though I was anxious to see what Will had copied for me. Mr. Krakowski let me use the computer lab to access iTunes, so long as I came in either between classes or after school and didn't bother him. Maybe I had time to go to the lab after lunch, if I hurried. I really did owe Will, big-time. I stared down at the iPod in my hand. Maybe I shouldn't take it. But how could I not?

"I guess I've rendered you speechless," Will said.

"I called the police last night," I blurted out.

I'd been meaning to tell him since this morning. His grin disappeared. Maybe I should have led up to it. I was terrible at making polite conversation.

"Why?"

"It was the right thing to do." My heart slowed just slightly, and I let out a deep breath. I felt a little better that apparently my inner oracle felt the same way as I did. "You know, about Jade and Alex and the . . . the hit-and-run guy.

I had to tell them. His family deserves to know." I sounded like a poor imitation of Gran. "I'm sorry."

"Stop saying that." He stared down at the iPod, clutched in my hand. "Of course you're right. I'm sure they'll want to talk to Alex again now. You did exactly the right thing."

I sagged back against the tree. I hadn't told Gran and Granddad what I'd done in the middle of the night. I wasn't sure why. I had the feeling Gran would think I was a coward for doing it anonymously.

I was a coward.

My eyes found the stream of ants again. They had managed to dislodge the lettuce, exposing the beetle. I turned away, unable to stomach more death. "I did it anonymously. I used the tip line." Why did I feel such a need to confess? Wasn't it enough that I had to lay bare my soul every time someone asked me a question? Here I was, volunteering.

"The important thing was that you did it." He put a finger under my chin and raised my head. "I knew you had it in you."

I smiled at him. It wavered, but it held. He smiled back. Maybe confession was good for the soul. I felt lighter than I had in ages.

SHE'S MY WINONA

Someone grabbed my arm before I could walk into art class. Not Tank or one of his friends, up to their old tricks, but Delilah. Her grip was gentle, and she let go when I turned around. I stepped to the side of the door so I wouldn't be in anyone's way and took out my earphones.

"Are you doing okay?" she asked.

"I am well enough," I said, my oracular voice strangely formal. I'd seen her in home ec, but we'd had a video today and there'd been no chance to talk. I had noticed her glancing my way, though.

"I saw you faint at Jade's funeral," she said.

"I know. Will told me. He said he'd tell you I was okay." I paused. I could only hope that Alex hadn't seen, too. He'd surely have something to say about me being carried out of the church by the boy he'd warned me to stay away from. But Will would have mentioned that to me, Alex's watching. "I'm okay, really," I added in the silence.

"Too much heat and not enough food or something, I guess."

"I just wanted to make sure," she said. She still didn't look like herself. Her hair was pulled back in a simple ponytail. Without her makeup, she seemed both younger and more world-weary. Lost.

"Thanks," I said. I didn't know what else to say.

"I guess . . . I guess I'll see you later." She left before I could say anything else.

I stayed by the door for a moment, not really wanting to go in. Art had always been my relatively safe class. I didn't like this new situation. Shelley hadn't said anything else to me on Friday either in home ec or art, after the scene in class on Thursday, but that was probably because Mrs. Rogers had actually been lecturing us on technique for once instead of letting us "explore" what we wanted. Alex had avoided me in that class as well, and I hadn't seen him since spotting him at Jade's funeral service.

Today I wanted to avoid him, but at the same time I kind of wanted to warn him. Should I? If the police actually paid any attention to the message I'd left, they were going to want to talk to Alex. I imagine they probably already had before, since he was dating Jade. But this was something more. Will seemed to think it gave Alex motive to have killed Jade. Like maybe he was driving or something and she was going to tell and he needed to shut her up.

I had trouble picturing it. I couldn't imagine anyone I knew doing something so terrible, so cold-blooded. Even though I knew secrets about nearly everyone in school, none of them seemed like the kind of person who would actually kill someone. Draw a fake mustache on you with a Sharpie when you were sleeping, yeah. Stomp on your MP3 player? Sure. But murder?

Then I remembered the look in Alex's eyes while he was standing in my living room, warning me to stay away from Will. How he'd looked facing down Tank. The way he'd told me to run away in the woods, the sounds of bellowing bull gators behind him.

Maybe he'd been driven to drink that night by guilt.

Granddad had a tendency toward that himself. Absolution in a bottle, he called it, but Gran didn't let him get away with it much. Alex didn't have anyone looking over his shoulder. The family tragedy hadn't straightened out his father; it had made him worse. The last time I had seen Frank Walker, he'd been so drunk he couldn't walk down Main Street in a straight line at noon.

It didn't matter. I had to face Alex if he was there, but not without my music. I put my earphones back in and pushed through the classroom door, walking straight towards my desk in the back, not looking at anyone.

Mrs. Rogers wasn't there, which should have set off warning bells in my head after last week. I had almost made it halfway to my desk when Shelley slid her book bag right in front of me. Clutching Will's iPod to my chest, I fell onto my side, hitting my shoulder on a desk on the way down. I wound up blinking at the ceiling with Fall Out Boy still playing in my ears. Someone had managed to splash red paint up there at some point. I'd never noticed it before. It looked like a bloodstain looming over me.

A part of me wanted to just lie there on the cold

linoleum floor, even though I could hear Shelley's high-pitched laughter over the song's refrain, *Oh Oh Oh Oh Whoa Oh Oh Oh,* but I rolled over and clambered up to my knees anyway. The sane part of me insisted I had to get up and keep going. I couldn't stay on the floor forever, being laughed at. I rolled my shoulder back, testing it. It hurt like a son of a bitch. I'd probably be purple by dinnertime.

A rough hand grabbed my elbow and helped me up, nearly making me drop the iPod after all.

Alex. A very pissed off Alex.

Of course. He didn't have the gentle touch that Delilah had. The iPod eased into Snow Patrol's "Chasing Cars," and I could hear everyone clearly over the soothing sound of it. Some more Fall Out Boy would probably have been better. Noisier.

"What the hell is your problem?" he barked at Shelley.

My inner oracle didn't care that the question wasn't directed at me. "The truth is slippery." But it didn't matter. Everyone ignored me anyway. I pulled my arm, but Alex didn't let go, his fingertips biting into my skin.

"Fuck off," said Shelley. "You and her both. You're both freaks. Everyone knows you killed Jade. Your preggie girlfriend here probably helped."

"Shelley," said another girl, looking alarmed, "calm down."

Everyone was staring at Alex. His face was blank, like a mask. No one was laughing now. I pulled at my arm again, but he still wasn't letting go. I didn't want to be here in the middle of this. I had to get out.

"Why?" she taunted. "He's not denying it. Look at him. He looks guilty to me."

"You'll regret that," I said in answer to her question, softly this time.

Alex heard me. He took his steely gaze off of Shelley just long enough to glance down at me. Hopefully no one else had noticed what I said.

"I don't owe *you* any explanations," he growled back at Shelley. He took a step towards her, dragging me along. I almost tripped over her backpack again.

"What's going on in here?" Everyone in the class turned to the door. Mrs. Rogers was standing there, her features twisted in disgust or alarm. I wasn't sure which.

No one said a word, except me, since I couldn't help it. "Trouble," I answered quietly.

A girl towards the front let out a nervous giggle but cut it off short when Mrs. Rogers waved at someone in the hall. A uniformed policeman stepped into the room. Trouble indeed.

"Is there a problem here?" the cop asked. He was short and stocky, not very old, maybe in his late twenties, and solidly built. He shoved past Mrs. Rogers and stepped purposefully toward Alex and me. Everyone but Shelley seemed to melt away into the edges of the room. She stood up instead, tossing back her dark hair.

"Problems, problems," I sing-songed under my breath. "Here, there, everywhere. Answers, answers, soon enough." Only Alex heard me. He finally let go of my arm, and I stumbled back, catching myself on a desk again. I massaged my elbow. It hurt almost as much as my shoulder.

"No problem at all, officer," Shelley said sweetly. "Aria here just tripped, and we were helping her up. She's a little clumsy, if you know what I mean." I was surprised she didn't bat her eyelashes.

I didn't say anything to confirm or deny. The police officer was still walking toward us. "Alex Walker?" he asked, one hand over his holster.

"Yes," Alex and I both said at the same time. The cop stopped, confused. Alex gently pushed me back with one hand. The same girl who had giggled a moment ago let out another snort now.

"I am Alex Walker," he said.

"I was waiting to meet you after class," the cop said, "but looks like we might as well get on with it now." He looked back and forth from me to Shelley. She smiled, all holier than thou. I didn't say anything. The cop looked back at Alex. "We have some more questions for you. I'd like you to come down to the station with me."

"I've already told you everything," said Alex. He didn't move. His back was ramrod straight.

"Some new information has come up. Look, I'd rather not do this here, and I doubt if you do either. So why don't you come with me?"

"Go, don't go," I whispered. "This doesn't matter in the long run."

Alex turned to me, his eyes crinkled at the corners. Confused. I shrugged, barely, my shoulder screaming, and looked down at the floor. I held my breath. *Please let him never figure out it had been me that had provided the new information to the police. Please.*

JAR OF HEARTS

After Alex left with the cop, I told Mrs. Rogers I needed to go see the school nurse because of my shoulder. And my elbow. She didn't argue. I think she wanted me out of the room. No one would look at me, except for Shelley, with her insinuating smirk.

I didn't bother going to the nurse, though. I left campus and drove aimlessly around in circles around town until school was over. It was a waste of gas that I couldn't really afford, but I didn't know what else to do. I couldn't stay there, and I couldn't go home. Being alone was the only way to keep clear of questions.

I dropped the iPod down into the depths of my backpack before I went inside, unwilling to explain away such an expensive gift to Gran. And somehow I didn't think she'd appreciate it the way I did. She'd never understood why I brought my MP3 player to school every day.

"Be brave," she was always telling me. "Don't hide!"

Like that was possible. She had either forgotten what school was like, or once upon a time it had actually been a kinder and gentler place, like something out of a fairy tale. Of course, her school had been about a tenth the size of mine. It was easier to hide from a few than from many.

"You got a phone call already, Aria," said Granddad to me as I came in the door, a smile on his face, his tone light. "Guess that Will boy isn't so strange after all, if he couldn't even wait half an hour after school to call you." He had his shotgun across his lap, cleaning it with great show, though I wasn't the one I imagined he intended the display for. "So I got this out, just in case."

"You old coot," said Gran from the kitchen. "Don't pay him any mind, Aria. I'll make sure he puts it away before Will comes over again." She stuck her head in the door. "He is going to come again, I'm assuming. Porter wrote his number down for you. It's on the fridge."

"Thanks, Gran," I said, pointedly ignoring Granddad. I put my things away in my bedroom and then went into the kitchen to grab the slip of paper Granddad had written Will's number on. He'd doodled a shaky heart in the corner. I couldn't help but smile, just for a second. He might actually be happier about a boy calling on me than I was. I went in the living room and picked up the phone. Granddad had set the shotgun against the wall, the display over for now. But I knew he'd find a way to have it out if he was home the next time Will came to visit, no matter what Gran might say. That was the kind of thing he loved to do. Gran always said that if there were a chain to pull, Granddad would pull it.

He grinned at me.

"Just being polite," I said. That wasn't entirely true. I wished I had a cell phone for the first time in my life. I'd never really needed one before. I considered my options, and finally took the phone into my bedroom, the cord stretching down the hall far enough that I made it through my bedroom door. Maybe I could talk them into at least buying a cordless phone with some of the money I'd helped win. After all, I didn't usually ask for much. And it wasn't like I'd ever had a boy call me before. Clearly.

I closed my door and sat down, my back against it. It was as far away as I could get, tethered as I was to the phone. I dialed the number, committing it to memory.

"Hello," answered Will.

"It's Aria," I said. "Granddad said you called?"

"Hey! Heard it was quite a scene in art class today. Someone said the cops dragged Alex out of there."

"They didn't drag him," I said. "He left with them. One of them. I mean, there was only one cop. Not like a brigade or anything." My hand clenched the curly plastic cord, straightening out a few loops.

He laughed. "I thought that was too good to be true. Anyway, I wanted to tell you that the police towed away Jade's car earlier. So they obviously believed you."

"Oh." I don't know why my mind always seemed to go into full panic mode whenever I talked to Will. Even when I wasn't answering questions I still babbled like an idiot.

"I hope you're liking the playlist," he said.

The abrupt change of subject startled me, and I let the

cord go. It sprang back into shape. "Yes, very much. Thank you again."

"I put a few special songs on there for you. Let me know what you think."

I didn't need a prophecy to tell me I was going to fall asleep that night listening to the music, trying to decipher the meaning behind every song I heard and wondering which one was one of the special songs. I was pretty sure it wasn't the one from Fall Out Boy.

There was a knock on the door, and Granddad's muffled voice came through. "Aria, you've got a visitor," he said gruffly. "Another boy."

My heart froze. Alex? Why? Would the police have told him a girl tipped them off? They couldn't know it was me. I'd been so careful. Would they have told him?

"Will, I have to go," I stammered. "There's—I just have to go. Talk to you tomorrow?"

"Okay," he said. "I'll see you at lunch, if not before."

I hung up the phone and opened the door. I knew it was him, but still my breath caught, seeing Alex again, sitting on our couch, making it look impossibly small. Granddad was back in his chair, cleaning his shotgun. I should have known. Alex was studiously not looking at him.

"Alex," I said, ever the queen of the obvious.

"I need to talk to you," he said, standing up. "Outside?"

"On the outside, always looking in," I responded. I looked helplessly at Granddad. He and Alex both just stared back at me, Alex's face growing darker. He probably thought I was making fun on what he'd said the other night.

Gran came to the kitchen door. "You go on outside and talk, Aria. It'll be fine."

I brushed past Alex, and he followed me out onto the porch.

He didn't say a word, just stayed right on my heels. I almost walked right on off into the woods before I thought better of it. In the woods was where Jade had been murdered. I stopped at the edge, where the scrub pines began taking over and the sandy ground was carpeted with scratchy dead pine needles.

"What is it with you?" he asked softly behind me.

"I am what I am," I said, which, considering everything, wasn't as strange an answer as it could have been. "And you are what you are."

I felt him step even closer to me. He whispered, even quieter now. "You're not really pregnant, are you?"

I swirled around, my face immediately flaming red. He was too close, but I didn't back down, not this time. "No!" Even my inner oracle was emphatic. "How can you even ask me that?"

He didn't answer my question or even flinch. He just changed the subject. "I saw you at Jade's service with Will. And at lunch today, too."

"So?" My cheeks were still burning. Pregnant? How dare he?

"I told you to stay away from him," he said.

I clenched my hand into a fist to stop it from shaking and hid it in the folds of my skirt. "I don't see how it's any of your business who I talk to." I walked a few steps away and then paced back. "And I really don't know why you're here. Look, thanks for standing up for me in art class again and everything, but it isn't necessary."

He reached out and touched my hurt shoulder. I cringed. "Yeah," he said. "I can see that. I saw how hard you hit that desk. You ought to get this checked out."

Like we had money for doctor visits. It wasn't broken. I'd be fine in a few days. I pulled away from him and took a few steps backward to put more distance between us. "Why do you care?"

He was silent for a moment, standing there with his hands at his sides. "I don't know," he said. "I'm sorry."

That made two of us. "I think you should go," I said.

He didn't move his feet, but he leaned toward me. "The police think I had something to do with Jade's death," he said finally. "They said we ran over that guy with her car. That I was with her when she did it. Or maybe they think I ran him over, I don't know."

I didn't know if I should try to act surprised. I held my tongue instead and settled for not moving at all. Caught in the proverbial headlights.

"They think I killed her, but they have no proof." He paused, and I wasn't sure if he was even talking to me anymore. "Why would they even think I would want to kill her?"

"Will," I said and bit my tongue. It was obvious to me now. He had been envious of Will and Jade's history together. Who knows what it had to do with the hit-and-run. Maybe nothing at all. It was all about jealousy. I took another step away.

He seemed to expand in size, drawing his shoulders up, his fists clenched. "What did—"

"Aria!" called Granddad from the porch. "Dinner! It's time for your friend to leave!"

I'd never been so glad that Gran and Granddad liked to eat senior-citizen early. I couldn't answer a question half-asked, though even that small bit buzzed around my head for a minute. I walked around Alex, giving him a wide berth. "I have to go," I said firmly.

I got only a half-growl in reply, but he stomped off to his car. I turned to watch him leave from the safety of the front porch.

"You think I had something to do with it, too, don't you?" he called out to me. He didn't wait for an answer, but my heart sank a little more as I whispered, "Yes," to the silent trees.

HARDER TO BREATHE

I knew as soon as I stepped out of my car when I got to school that news of Jade's role in the hit-and-run and Alex's detainment by the police had spread far and wide. The speed of sound is nothing to the speed of gossip in a small town. Students were clustered in groups, and the air practically thrummed with new questions and accusations. I put my new headphones on and turned up the music as high as I could stand it before I left the parking lot. It had to be one of Will's songs, since I didn't recognize it.

I had my head down checking out the band's name and almost ran into the back of some girl. A noisy crowd was gathering around the front walk, staring at something going on under the overhang. A few boys were standing on the railing and holding on to the edge of the roof to keep them steady while they watched. I went around to sneak a peek at the edge of the crowd, insinuating myself in between the edge of the building and a couple of sophomore boys who were shouting.

Alex and Will stood facing each other, their backpacks discarded at their feet. Will's back was to me, but I could see Alex's face clearly even as the sophomores were jostling for position beside me. His eyebrows were drawn down, his eyes hard and flat. He looked ready to do battle, his fists up and his feet dancing lightly on the ground. Will had his hands up, palms out. He looked small compared to Alex, even though he was nearly as tall.

"Stop it!" I shouted, but there was so much noise I was sure neither one of them heard me. Where were the teachers? I yanked my headphones out and tried to shove past the boys but merely got scraped against the brick wall for my trouble.

"You're making a big mistake," Will was saying. "Just back off, man. I'm sure the police are on their way already. You don't want to get yourself in any more trouble than you're already in, do you?" He sounded calm, lightly bouncing on the balls of his feet, as if poised to dodge out of the way if Alex actually did attack.

"Trouble is welcome to knock today," I said. "It's too late for anything but." No one paid any attention, of course.

"Shut up!" shouted Alex. "You're the one who started this!" He moved forward and took a quick jab. Will ducked, Alex's fist only catching a bit of his hair. Alex struck again immediately, and this time his fist connected solidly with Will's face, just missing his left eye. It was probably my imagination, but I swear I heard the dull smack of flesh even over the noise of the crowd.

Will stumbled back and tripped over his book bag, going down over the top of it. Alex fell on top of him, both fists flying, his face contorted beyond recognition, word-less guttural sounds coming out of his mouth. The crowd was screaming with him, a wave of sound that surrounded me. There were no questions being shouted, just cheers and jeers, but I still felt like I couldn't breathe. Will had his arms up, protecting his head. He wasn't even trying to fight back, though I don't know if it would have done him any good if he had tried. Alex looked unstoppable, as if in a trance.

One of the sophomore boys leaped into the air, his fist pumping. I couldn't tell if he was rooting for Alex, sympathizing with Will, or just intoxicated by the vio-lence. What was the matter with kids at this school? He fell against me as he came down, grinding my wounded shoulder into the brick wall. I gasped and closed my eyes against the pain and the noise. I struggled to worm my way out of the throng, my arm scraping against the wall, leaving some skin behind.

I finally made it out and stumbled a few steps away, then leaned against the wall to catch my breath. The steel door burst open next to me, and I barely caught it before it slammed into me. Principal James, a security guard, and a couple of teachers ran forward and began pulling people out of the way as they worked their way in to the fight.

I put my headphones back in with shaking fingers and slipped into the building. The refrain *harder and harder to breathe* echoed in my head.

I KEPT MY HEAD down all morning, plugged in, ignoring the teachers, and they obliged by ignoring me back. First period was a lost cause anyway. Everyone was consumed by the fight, boys reenacting it and girls discussing it to death. Mr. German didn't even notice me in the back corner. "We're here to talk fistulas instead of fists," he shouted at one point. I almost felt sorry for him.

By my second-period English class, the word was out that Alex had been suspended for three weeks. The police had been called, and it was up to Will's family to decide whether or not they wanted to press charges. There was no real word on Will's condition. From the little I overheard, either he was in the emergency room with multiple broken bones or he was perfectly fine and laughing it off. I knew the only who could tell me the truth was Will himself.

I kept the cords on my earbuds hidden in the strands of my hair and kept the music going until I got to home ec. Mrs. Pratt was eagle-eyed but still firmly living in oblivion. Nothing fazed her.

"Music off, Aria, please!" she said brightly as I came into the room. "Participation counts!"

I complied, hoping she'd get caught in a sugar high later so I could put them back in. I pushed past Delilah, who had once again drawn a crowd—not that I was surprised. I knew she'd be first on the receiving end of accusations about Jade's possible involvement with the hit-and-run. I tried to ignore a pang of guilt, but it was impossible. Delilah was livid.

"There's no way! It's absolutely ridiculous!" she

shouted. Her eyes were dry, and her face was flushed. I had to hand it to her: she, for one, had not yet forgotten or given up.

"So I guess you think the police are making it up," said Shelley smugly. "*I* heard they found part of his scalp on the underside of her bumper, and there was still hair attached!" She looked entirely too happy to be relating such gruesome news. Perhaps she watched a lot of crime dramas on TV, but I didn't. My stomach turned at the image she gave me.

"I don't care," said Delilah. "She didn't do it. Maybe Alex planted evidence or something. *I don't know.* I just know Jade couldn't have been involved! She would have told me!"

I kept my mouth shut. I knew for a fact that Jade had been there. It made sense actually, the more I thought about it. Why couldn't Delilah see that? It explained that whole scene in the bathroom with Jade crying her eyes out. She wasn't the type of person to witness something so horrific without being touched by it. And that was the key: anyone could witness something horrible without participating or even interfering. The fight this morning was proof enough of that.

"Girls, girls," said Mrs. Pratt, "let's move on. Time for a new topic! Today we're going to be learning about how to properly set a table!" She held up a fistful of silverware. "Grab a basket of supplies!"

Shelley couldn't resist one more dig. "You could always ask Alex's new girl toy over there. Maybe she knows." She grinned between Delilah and me, vicious as a feral wolf.

"We're going to start with the plate!" said Mrs. Pratt brightly.

I flushed and pretended to ignore Shelley, though I was sure anyone could tell how much I was starting to hate that girl. Was it possible to train yourself not to go red in the face? I grabbed a basket and walked to my normal table, keeping my back to the rest of the room. Maybe I should start wearing makeup after all.

I took out the pieces one by one, concentrating on the task and drawing it out to waste time. Plate, knife, fork, napkin, another fork, spoon, glass.

"Aria," said Delilah. She was standing behind me, but I didn't turn around.

"Delilah," I said.

She was quiet for a minute. Then she walked around the table to stand opposite me. "I need to ask you something. Do you remember last week in the bathroom?"

"I remember," I said. It was the last time I saw Jade. How could I forget? I stopped shuffling the silverware around.

Delilah picked up the glass, turning it around and around in her hands. "Jade was really upset that day."

"Yeah," I said.

"She never did tell me what was bothering her before she . . . you know." She set the glass down and looked me directly in the eye. "But you seemed to . . . to know something."

"I didn't," I said quickly. "I don't."

"I mean, looking back . . ." She glanced around the room, presumably to see if Shelley was paying any attention, but she had moved on to torturing some other girl.

She leaned toward me and whispered. "Looking back . . . maybe what they're saying about the hit-and-run is true." She cringed, like she couldn't believe she'd said it out loud.

I wasn't sure what to say. So I nodded and said nothing. That wasn't enough for Delilah. "Do *you* think it's true?"

"Yes," I said. Yet another confirmation.

She slumped down, elbows on the table, hands on her head, her hair sticking out between her fingers. A single tear built in the corner of her right eye and trembled there.

I took a quick glance around the room. No one was paying any attention to us, not even Mrs. Pratt, who was dealing with a silverware catastrophe.

"It's not your fault," I said, reaching my hand out but stopping short of touching her.

She didn't seem to hear me. "If I'd just made her tell me, maybe none of this would have happened. Maybe she'd be here, and he'd be in jail. I mean, why did she have to die? Why?"

"To shut her up," I spit out, feeling sick. A fork fell from my fingers and clattered against the table.

That got her attention. She lifted her head to look at me, the tear finally falling. She opened her mouth to say something, maybe to ask something else, but I held up my hand.

"Delilah," I said, my voice shaky, "can you keep a secret?"

SECRET

I wasn't sure if Delilah actually believed me, even after she asked me a few questions and got my typical random responses back. She took it better than I'd thought she would, actually. She didn't question my sanity outright or anything like that. She just looked confused, which turned quickly to anger at Alex. I told her how I'd been the one to call the police.

I knew I shouldn't have told her, but I felt lighter the rest of the day. I didn't even let Will's absence at lunch bother me. I planned to go see him after school to see how he was doing, like any friend would.

And Delilah had left home ec saying she would call or talk to me later. Heaven help me, I was looking forward to it. Gran and Granddad wouldn't know what to think. I was actually developing a social life again. My last girlfriend had abandoned me in the seventh grade. Jen Ashley had stuck by me through that first summer after I turned twelve but had given up once school started, and the true weight of my gift had come to bear. I had never really told her why I had suddenly started spouting nonsense. I wasn't really sure myself, until I went to live with Gran. My mother never talked about the gift, and after the truth about Dad came out, she spoke with me as little as humanly possible.

Maybe the teachers felt everyone deserved a break today, because Mrs. Rogers didn't say a word about my earphones in art class even though she disapproved. And if Shelley had any pointed comments to share, I was oblivious to them. I didn't go near her desk the entire time or even look up from my work. My self-portrait was starting to take shape, emerging out of the murk. Alex was conspicuously absent. I avoided looking at his desk.

I kept my headphones on all the way out to my car, The Pierces oddball tune putting a spring to my step. I had to admit it: in spite of all the terrible things swirling around me, I felt good. I wished it hadn't taken a tragedy to change my life, but my world was no longer just a sea of Shelleys. I had friends for the first time since I'd developed this curse. Maybe, dare I even think it, something more than a friend.

I had just turned that thought over in my mind when I saw Will leaning against my car, parked in its customary spot at the far end of the lot. I broke into a short run before I collected myself and slowed to a fast walk. He was watching me as I approached. He seemed to be smiling, but I honestly couldn't tell. The left side of his face was multicolored and swollen. All you could see of one eye was a tiny slit, surrounded by the deepest purple. Strangely enough, the right side of his face was as perfect as normal, making the contrast all the more startling.

I slowed down as I reached the Colt. "How are you?" I asked. "Are you okay? What are you doing here?"

"You're the one full of questions today," he said. He held out his hand to me. I glanced over my shoulder and took it. I had taken my time at my locker after class, and the parking lot was already half empty. No one was near us. Would it matter if there were people around? I had nothing to hide.

I stopped myself before I apologized. "Well," I said, "shouldn't you be at home in bed? Your eye . . ." I trailed off. He surely knew better than I did how he felt. But he looked like hell.

He pulled me closer, and I took another step toward him. "It looks worse than it is," he said. "And I've got more important things to do than lounge around in bed."

"Oh?" Was that a compliment?

"Yeah," he said, suddenly serious, the half-grin dropping. He took my other hand so that he held them both in his. "After what happened this morning, I've been thinking. If I had been able to talk Jade into dropping Alex, maybe none of this would have happened. I never realized what a violent streak he has." He turned his face to the right, and I nodded. Close up he looked even worse. If I hadn't seen the fight with my own eyes, I wouldn't have believed Alex had it in him. "I need to ask you something." He pulled me even closer and bent his head to look me in the eye. "Who's going to be killed next?"

The question hit me hard, and I gasped for air. "Shelley," I said. "A new blade, a hunting knife, new prey, falling the same way." My knees gave out, and Will gathered me to his chest, tucking my head under his chin. I took a deep breath, taking in the clean, soapy smell of him. It spread through me, giving me strength.

"Shelley," he said thoughtfully. "That wasn't who I expected."

I stayed where I was and spoke into his chest, my words absorbed into the soft cotton of his T-shirt. "It makes sense," I said. "She's been terrorizing Alex and me in art class."

"Both of you?" he said, tilting my chin up.

"One who delights in the torture of others often has much to hide, and the easiest to attack are those that don't fight back." There I went, sounding like Confucius, but it was true enough. Shelley had more secrets than most. "She's always been mean to me," I continued, "but lately she's been really . . ."

"A bitch," he finished.

It hit me then what we were talking about so casually. "Do you really think Alex is going to murder Shelley?"

"You said it yourself," he said. "Shelley's next, and it makes perfect sense, if what you're saying is true." His eyes searched mine. "What do you think?" he asked deliberately.

"As I say it, so it is," I said, my voice dull, the words like lead in my throat. I was surprised at how numb I felt. Only moments ago I'd been on the verge of something approaching happiness.

Will took my shoulders in his hands and pulled me upright. "You get home," he said. "Take care of yourself. Can you drive after that?"

"Yes. What are you going to do?"

"The same thing," he said. "Don't worry about it. He'd be stupid to try something tonight, after getting in that fight with me this morning. We'll figure out something tomorrow. Mom already said I could stay home tomorrow and take it easy." He pointed to his eye.

"Okay," I said. I didn't have any better ideas. Maybe it was time to confide in Gran.

I PUSHED THE COLT and made it home in record time, though I really only shaved off five minutes.

Gran was home alone, baking a key lime pie. The sour tang of lime juice hung in the kitchen, mixed with the smell of the sweetened condensed milk.

"Gran," I said, "I need to talk to you."

"Go ahead," she said. "I'm not like you young folks. I can do more than one thing at a time."

Now that I was here, I wasn't sure what to say. Maybe it was best to get right to the point. "I think there's going to be another murder," I said.

Gran stopped her stirring. Her wrinkled lips pressed into a flat line, her worried eyes on mine.

"Alex is going to kill Shelley. She's a girl at school." I left out the bitch part. What difference did it make? No matter how rude or crude you were, you didn't deserve to die.

Gran carefully set her spoon down on a paper towel. "You're positive this girl Shelley is going to be murdered?"

"Murder most foul, as in the best it is. But this most foul, strange and unnatural." I recognized that from *Hamlet*. I wanted to whack myself in the head. Now wasn't the time for Shakespeare. I sat down at the table, suddenly out of breath. All of these questions revolving around death were getting to me.

"Alex is that other boy that came here to our house?"

"Dark of hair, dark of eye, long of limb," I said and added a "yes" in case that wasn't clear enough.

"You look a bit pale," she said and brushed her hands on her apron.

"It's hard," I said. "All these questions about death." I rubbed my forehead. I was a little clammy, even with the omnipresent heat.

"Aria," said Gran suddenly, "are *you* in danger?"

"My future is unclear, but danger is certain," I said. The same stabbing pain that had hit me when talking about Jade settled in, and I doubled over. "Gran," I gasped, "no more questions right now, please! I can't take it."

"What's going on?" asked Granddad, coming into the kitchen.

I groaned. "Death is coming," I said, my voice stronger than I felt and unnaturally deep. I lowered my forehead to the table and concentrated on breathing.

Gran rubbed my back. "Shhhh," she murmured. "Just breathe, Aria, just breathe. I know what you're feeling right now. Just breathe."

Did she? Did she remember how awful it felt? She only ever talked about how she missed it, that uplifting feeling she would get when she prophesized, that feeling of rightness. I never felt that way. Had she ever been doubled over with pain with the cold fingers of death spreading through her body?

"Ellie, please tell me what the hell is going on," Granddad stated, knowing better than to use the interrogative for once. I heard the scrape of a chair as he sat down at the table.

"Aria is in some kind of danger," said Gran.

"Why?" he blurted, unable to help himself. "Oh, Jesus, sorry, Aria."

His apology wasn't enough to stop my answer. "My gift, my heritage, my meaning . . . my salvation and my damnation." I squeezed my eyes shut, tears leaking from the corners.

Gran's hand stopped moving on my back. "I think it's time," she said. "We need to look at the history. Maybe something in there can help us. Help you, Aria."

I lifted my head from the table as she bustled out of the room. The pain slowly began to subside. Granddad reached for me and brushed the hair out of my face. "I'm sorry, sweetheart," he murmured.

Moments later, Gran came back carrying a huge old book. She set it in the middle of the kitchen table, and I swear a cloud of dust came off of it as she did. Granddad sneezed.

It was bound in some ancient-looking dark brown leather with embossed symbols on the spine. Some I recognized, like a crescent moon; others were completely alien, all surrounded by a motif of vines and oak leaves. Metal clasps held the whole thing together, and they were needed; the whole thing was at least ten inches thick.

Something was written on the front, but in an alphabet I didn't know. Greek maybe?

"What is that?" I asked.

"This is everything," she said. "Our entire lineage, from the first Sybil down to you. This book has been passed down for generations. Someday it will be yours." She pressed something on the side, and the book fell open with an audible creak of old leather, roughly in the middle. "I've tried to show it to you before but . . ."

"I'm in here?" I gingerly touched the top page, almost expecting it to crumble. The paper was thick and rough with a creamy yellow color. It looked like something out of a museum.

"Of course. We're all in here." Gran turned to the very first page of the book. She had to hold it open with one hand as it threatened to flip back to where it had fallen open originally. "This is the original Erythraean Sibyl I mentioned to you before."

She tapped her finger on a hand-drawn sketch of a woman in an ancient robe. She looked wise but also rather stern and imposing. Her hair was long like mine, but bound up in complicated plaits.

"How do you think this will help me?" I asked Gran. I didn't see how learning our history would be of much help right now.

"It has everything," said Gran. "First questions, last questions, dealing with persecution, advice, ways to focus your talent . . . I'll be honest, Aria. It may not help, but it's somewhere to start. You know that saying: if you don't know your history, you are doomed to repeat it."

I don't think this was what whoever said that first had in mind. On the other hand, at least it was something. I couldn't handle any more questions, right now, anyway. But Gran knew that. And she knew me. Maybe I *could* find some answers a different way.

Shelley. It was time to pay her a visit.

My whole body had felt itchy since the fight, like my skin was too tight for my body. I wanted to punch someone, feel my fist sink deep into flesh, stopping only at the bone and maybe not even there. To be honest, I'd been feeling like this since I'd killed Jade. It had been such an adrenaline rush. Way better than the so-called runner's high or any sports metaphor I could think of. Better than when I'd run the guy over.

Alive, that's the only way I can think to really describe it. I'd finally felt alive. And I wanted that feeling again. Bad.

This morning had made it worse. I ached all over, inside and out. It was probably stupid to go for Shelley on the same day as the fight, but I couldn't wait anymore. On the plus side, the police wouldn't expect it. Though, seriously, after having talked with them a few times now . . . they weren't going to figure it out. I'd been careful setting up my alibi, even more so than last time. I'd set it all up. It was amazing what you could do with a little technological know-how. Right about the time I was going to meet Shelley under the bleachers, my computer would be sending out a couple of emails and I'd be leaving a voice mail on that one cop's work voice mail . . . the one taking a vacation day for his anniversary. There was no way he'd be at his desk. Thank you, Officer Pete, for sharing that tidbit where I could hear you. It always pays to pay attention.

I put my shiny new knife and a pair of gloves in my backpack and climbed out my window. Shelley was a perfect choice. I'd never liked her, and she'd been making Aria's life hell lately. She was a waste of space, even if she did have a ready mouth.

A vile mouth, too. I'd never cared what she had to say in public about me. Trashing other people was her hobby, probably to make up for her own crap life. But she'd always been available for a little slap and tickle when I wanted it. It had been beyond easy to get her to agree to meet me for a little rendezvous in her favorite spot. It had always killed her that I was going out with Jade.

Funny how things work out.

I WILL KEEP THE BAD THINGS FROM YOU

I took the book back to my room and cocooned myself into my bed. I still felt wrong, like I couldn't quite connect with the world, my feet floating above it. I opened it at the beginning and flipped quickly through the pages on the first Sibyl in our line. She, at least, had been celebrated. There was no way I was ever going to end up on the Sistine Chapel. It was a different world now.

A good portion of the book was taken up with a family tree of sorts, branches stretching out in every direction. Some ended quickly, others went on for years and years. One twig had been cut down at age fifteen because of a prophecy that displeased a king. *Buried alive,* someone had written. I wondered if the poor girl had known what was going to happen to her, but with the way prophecies worked, there was a good chance she had gone into it blind.

Some had kept detailed records of every prophecy they gave—or at least the important ones. Most included their first and last predictions. I was relieved to discover that I wasn't the only one who spouted nonsense. Lots of prophecies appeared to be gibberish at first, only to be deciphered later (usually when it was too late). I tore through several entries. There were anagrams, phrases uttered in reverse, prophecies written on oak leaves, even substitute languages. I admired the one who wrote out her prophecies on the leaves. She left them outside the entrance of her cave. If the wind scattered them, she would not help reassemble them. They were just gone, lost forever . . .

I paused. My mother's name was in the book with the simple notation "passed over." Had she ever even seen this book? If she had, had she been sad or relieved?

The one that really caught my attention, though, was a girl named Serin. Her name had been written in ink so dusky that it looked like dried blood. There were few details about her. She had died at thirteen because, it read, she had denied her gift. She had refused it. They called her "*Ağız Konuşmuyor.*" The Mouth That Would Not Speak. How had she done it? How many refused answers had it taken for the "gift" to claim her?

Granddad came in carrying a tray with toast and water. "How are you?" he asked, probably on purpose this time. He set the tray down on the end of my bed.

"Weak as water," I replied. He held out a slice of toast to me. I shook my head. I couldn't eat, not yet.

He put it back on the plate. "Well, nibble on something when you can. You're like a ghost these days, Aria, and I don't like it."

Me either. "I think I need to warn Shelley," I told him.

"You're not going anywhere," he said. "No way, no how."

I nodded. Driving was probably out of the question anyway, with the way I felt. But I had to warn her. She was in danger. Maybe not tonight, but something inside me said it couldn't wait. What if Alex did do something rash? He wasn't known for patience. "Can you bring me the phone and the phone book, Granddad?"

He nodded but pointed to the glass of water and didn't leave until I'd taken a big sip. Then he brought in the phone and helped me to it. I slid my back down the wall by my door. He made sure I wasn't going to fall over and then left the room. I almost wished that he'd stayed. I had no idea what I was going to say. But it wasn't like he could call her. Shelley had never met him. The only thing stranger than getting a phone call from Aria Morse would be getting one from her grandfather.

I found Shelley's home number in the phone book and dialed it. It rang three times before someone picked up.

"Hello," said a female voice, at once throaty and hollow.

"Is Shelley there?"

Her mom, or at least I assumed it was her mother, didn't bother covering up the mouthpiece as she yelled, "Shelley! Phone for you! Don't stay on long. I'm expecting a call on the home phone!"

"Who is it?" I heard Shelley yell back.

"The bearer of bad news," I whispered, but I needn't have bothered as her mother wasn't listening to me.

"Some girl," she shouted. "Just pick up the damn phone!"

I heard a click as Shelley picked up. "Who is this?"

Apparently she didn't get many calls on her landline. I couldn't say I was surprised.

"Aria," I said, glad of the simple answer.

"What the hell do you want?"

"Peace and safety," I said. She snorted. "Wait, Shelley," I pressed on, "just let me talk a minute. I've got to tell you something important." I rushed through it before she could ask me anything and derail the conversation. "I'm calling to warn you. You're in danger. Great danger. I think Alex is going to go after you. I think—"

"Oh yeah, Alex is going to come after me," she interrupted. She laughed. It sounded like a bark. "I don't know what game you're trying to play, but I've already got plans tonight and they don't involve this stupid shit. You got issues with your little boy toy, you handle them on your own time. I'm not your relationship coach."

"Wait," I said. "I'm serious! You're in danger! He's going to try and kill you!"

"You really are a freak, you know that?"

She hung up, missing my affirmative answer.

"ARIA," SAID GRANDDAD WHEN I made my appearance at the breakfast table the next morning, "Stay home today. You're looking pretty pale still."

I didn't say anything, just sat down at the table.

"Yes, Aria," said Gran. "Until we know what's going on, maybe you should stay home."

That brought my head up. "*You* think I should stay home?"

"Yes." Gran sat down across from me. "We don't know

what we're up against. But we do know that you're in danger. Bad things are coming. That much is very clear."

I held up my hand. "Bad things are my life," I countered. "I'm going to school. Maybe if I talk to Shelley in person she'll believe me. I've got to try." I grabbed a piece of plain toast to appease my stomach and my grandparents and turned to go.

Granddad followed me out of the house. "Aria, I know you're upset but—"

"Please." I spun around. "Granddad, all I figured out last night is that this stupid *curse* has ruined my life. Or might even be the death of me unless I can figure out what's going on. And did you know that almost every single one of us lost their gift before my age?" The starting ages had varied, seemingly tied to puberty, but the ending age mostly hovered around fifteen or sixteen. "What if it doesn't go away, Granddad? What am I supposed to do with my life?"

He rubbed a hand across his white stubbled cheek, the rough rasp a counterweight to his sigh. He hadn't shaved for two days. The stubble made him look older and tired. "Your Gran was seventeen when she lost it, same as you are now . . ." His voice seemed to run out of steam. "I'm sorry," he said. "I know I can't understand what you're going through. It hasn't been easy for you. But you know your Gran would take your burden from you if she could and bear it for you."

I tried not to laugh. "She wouldn't want my burden," I said. "You know what *her* last question was? Something about lunch." I turned to go.

"Aria," he said again. "Hold on just a minute. I have something for you."

I stopped, even though I really wanted to get away. Granddad held out his old bone-handled army knife to me. "I know you can't take it into school with you or anything, but I'd feel better if you at least had something in your car. We need to get you a cell phone, too. Time to move into this century, I suppose."

"I—" I wasn't sure what to say. He meant well. I took the knife and dropped it in my car. "Thanks, Granddad. I'll see you later."

I turned around and got in my car. Granddad took a few steps away so I could back up. My window was still down from the day before, and I gave him a small wave as I drove away. It wasn't his fault. He'd married into the weirdness. Me, I'd been born into it. I didn't have a choice, exactly, but no matter what, I wouldn't kill something. There are lines you shouldn't cross. Lines I would not cross.

I drove listening to a song by The Damnwells. It was another of Will's picks. I wished someone could keep the bad things away. That's all there seemed to be anymore.

I kept my headphones on all the way through biology class. Mr. German had a cold or the flu or something and kept his head down on his desk through our entire lab. We were supposed to be cutting up earthworms, but I couldn't bring myself to do it, not today. I kept transferring the slimy thing from one dish to another and moving things around my lab table to look busy. I snuck it back into the wriggling mass of worms left in the bin at the end of class while Mr. German was blowing his nose. Someone might pick that same worm out in the next class, but at least its end wouldn't be by my hand.

I kept practicing what I'd say to Shelley when I got to home ec with her. I had to make her understand. Maybe face-to-face she wouldn't be able to dismiss me. And maybe martians would land and take us all away. Maybe Delilah could back me up? Two against one were better odds when it came to Shelley.

I was passing by the main entrance on my way to English when I heard the unmistakable *wheee-yoooo* of police sirens. I stopped and looked through the thin rectangular glass window in the door. Three, no, four, police cars with lights blazing pulled into the parking lot. A few other kids stopped behind me to look through the window as well. Most of the police officers got out of their cars and rushed toward the football field. Then an ambulance came screaming into the parking lot. More sirens. They blended strangely with the ethereal Florence + the Machine song playing in my ears.

"What happened?" someone shouted right behind me. Asking the universe, apparently, but lucky them, here I was to answer.

"Coach Townsend found Shelley under the bleachers," I answered.

"How do you know?" asked the same person, quieter this time, but still trying to compete with the sirens, so I heard her. I turned. A freshman girl I didn't really know, not like I really knew anyone around here.

"I don't," I said, pushing my way through the crowd, my drab floral dress swishing as I fast-walked away. I had a sinking feeling I knew what the next questions would be and where they would lead. I clung to a childish hope that Shelley was merely out there for some weird prank, but I knew that wasn't it. They wouldn't have called the police and an ambulance if that were the case, not even if she were out there dancing naked.

I'd almost made it to my next class for lack of a better idea when an announcement came over the speaker system.

"All students, please report to the gym immediately." It was Principal James, his voice sad and resigned. "This is not a drill. Go directly to the gym for an emergency assembly. Teachers, follow all emergency procedures."

I stopped in place, letting the other students flow around me. I flicked the volume up as high as it would go. I didn't want to go in there. I knew what he was going to say. Shelley was dead. And it was all my fault. I should have gone to the police, should have driven to her house, something, *anything* instead of flipping through an ancient book full of dust and memories. While I'd been reading, Shelley had already been on the way to her doom. How had Alex gotten to her? Who was going to be next? Would it be me? He'd seemed so angry the last time we'd talked. Of course his anger hadn't been directed at me. It hadn't been directed at Shelley, either.

Oh God, no. It was going to be Will. I just knew it. Alex had already tried to beat him to a pulp once. Next time it would be a knife instead of his fists. He could be there right now. Neither of them was here at school, where all the police were. Will was home recuperating, and Alex was suspended. Will had no idea what danger he was in.

Before I could think about it, I was off and running.

ADDICTED TO LOVE

The sole bit of luck on my side: Will's house was only minutes from the school. I pulled into his driveway and scrambled out of my car. My heart was beating fast, way too fast. Was I too late again? I ran up the cobblestone walk and banged on the door, then noticed the doorbell and rang it instead. I was about to ring again when I heard footsteps. Please let it be him.

Will opened the door, his hair messy like he'd just gotten out of bed. I let out a shuddering breath and grabbed him in a hug before I thought about what I was doing.

"Aria," he said, his voice hoarse and groggy. "What are you doing here?

"I had to see you, to make sure you were okay, my fear overcomes me today," I said into his chest. I didn't even care what a loon I sounded like. He wrapped his arms around me, and I felt safe for a moment. His heart thumped solidly in my ear, a slow, calm drumbeat. I took another deep breath and pulled back to look up at him. "Shelley's dead," I said. "The police are at the school now."

His bruised face twisted. For a second, I wondered if he might start crying. He shook his head and drew in a shaky breath. Then he pulled me inside and shut the door.

"I shouldn't have waited," I said. "I should have done something yesterday, said something to the police, or done *something*."

"You couldn't have known." He sounded wide-awake now, leading me by the hand into their living room. It was a far cry from my own, tastefully and expensively decorated with oil paintings on the walls and fresh flower arrangements on nearly every table. Even with everything going on I felt a pang of shame that he'd been inside my house. He sat down on a solid red couch, packed with plump, floral-patterned pillows, and pulled me down to sit next to him.

My Salvation Army-issue dress was floral too, faded and pale next to the vibrant colors in the room. I took my hand from his and put them both in my lap, spreading my hands flat, covering my thighs. It made no difference. What did it matter what I looked like anyway? I shook my head. This wasn't what I was here for.

"He'll come for you next," I said, clenching my hands. "I'm sure of it." I turned to face him. I had to make him understand.

He raised his eyebrows and then winced in pain. His eye looked a little better, but it was still swollen and dark purple, tinged with an unhealthy-looking green.

"We have to do something," I said.

"You can't go directly to the police," he said. "Surely you're not thinking of doing that. They'd eat you alive."

I shook my head. "I don't know anymore," I said. "They'd probably think I was crazy, but if they did believe me, maybe it would stop Alex." I searched his eyes. "You're in danger, Will. I would never forgive myself if something happened to you when I could have done something." I'd definitely had no love for Shelley, but I knew her death would haunt me forever. Even she deserved better. I shut my eyes and took another deep breath, trying not to let it shake as I let it go. "I have to do something."

He was silent for a minute. "The problem with the police is that they wouldn't stop questioning you. They'd want to know how you know so much. I bet they'd even hold you until they could clear your name. And if they couldn't for some reason . . . There's no telling what they'd put you through. I can't let you do that, not for me. Not for anyone."

"But—"

"No arguing," he said, touching a finger to my lips. "I know what we can do. Just let me get dressed and we'll go."

"Dressed?" I said stupidly, blushing as I finally noticed he was still in his pajamas and his rumpled bedhead hair really was from him being fresh from bed. His pajama bottoms were a blue paisley silk, though he wore only a plain white undershirt on top. I wondered if I should avert my eyes, but it wasn't as if he were naked. I flushed a deeper shade of red at the thought and found a magazine on the table to concentrate on. *Field & Stream.* His dad must be a hunter. Most dads around here were. It looked out of place surrounded by the very female touch everywhere else in the room.

He stood up, apparently not having noticed my sudden discomfort. "Yes, we'll go to where Jade was killed and see if we can use your gift to find a clue that the police might have missed. After all, they'll all be over at the school today. The crime scene in the woods will be empty. Safe. If we find something, we'll leave them an anonymous tip or something, like you did before."

I didn't know what to say, so I nodded. The thought of going to where Jade had died made my stomach sink, but it was something. He patted me on the shoulder and left to go change. I sat in the silence of the room, surrounded by the cheery floral patterns, staring down at the muted flowers covering my own dress. They would never be a match.

WE LEFT MY CAR and took his instead. I didn't argue. I couldn't picture him sitting in the Colt anyway. Besides, the day had ripened into a blinding heat, and it wasn't even noon yet. Air-conditioning would be preferable. It was even warmer than normal, but you could see the threat of rain in the darkening sky.

There was no breeze either. Everything lay still and heavy in the heat, eerily like the calm before a hurricane. I'd been through enough of those to know how that felt, though I hadn't heard that one was expected anytime soon. During the season, it sometimes seemed like one was headed towards Florida every other week. We weren't that close to the coast, but it didn't really matter. Nowhere was safe, really, from the storms.

Will drove out of town and headed straight for the Laurel Creek preserve. He'd changed into a pair of jeans and a dark grey T-shirt. He'd run a wet comb through his hair, too, and it was back to its normal perfection. From the passenger's side I couldn't see the bruised side of his face at all. At this angle, it was as if the fight had never happened.

"Do you know where to go?" I asked.

"I think so," he said. He turned on his stereo, and I recognized the song from The Damnwells that I'd heard just that morning. It seemed forever ago. I closed my eyes and listened to the words as we drove deeper and deeper into the woods.

Four songs and three different dirt roads later, Will pulled off the side of the road and parked.

"This is it?" I asked. The trees were thick and close together here, but most of them were fairly young, and almost all were pine trees and scrub palms. That meant there'd probably been a fire here some years ago. It took a devastating fire to take out the oak trees and release the seeds from the pinecones. Probably before my time, given the age of the trees, but this spot had seen its share of tragedies. Unless, I supposed, you were one of the new young trees given a chance at life.

He nodded towards a swatch of yellow plastic almost hidden in the brush. "See, there's some police tape left over there." He opened his door and got out, coming around to meet me on the other side. He waved off to the left of the road, even deeper into the trees. "I think that's where they found her, and I imagine past that is where she, um, crawled from." He bowed his head, and we held a moment of silence together, broken only by the cooing of a dove.

When he lifted his head, I climbed out and then nearly tripped over a rotted out stump. He reached out a hand to steady me and then took my hand. "Be careful," he said. "It's dangerous out here."

I let out a nervous laugh. The sky had continued to darken, and with the added cover of the trees, it felt like dusk out here. The air was like soup. It was going to be a heck of a storm. "Are you sure we should be out here right now?" I asked. "Looks like it'll come down cats and dogs."

He glanced up at the sky. "Better now than later. The rain could wash away some evidence. And we know the police are preoccupied with Shelley right now." He set off into the trees and abruptly stopped, turning to me. "Um, I have no idea where I'm going," he said. "I should have asked . . . Aria, which way should we go to get to where Jade was murdered?"

"East, then north," I said, my voice deepening as I spoke. "You will know it when you come to it. Death was there."

He squeezed my hands and set off in what was presumably the right direction. I wasn't sure which way was actually east. I loved to walk in the woods, but I relied mostly on my inner compass, not on which actual direction was which.

He guided me between the trees, making sure to point out roots and thorny bushes along the way so I wouldn't get caught. It wasn't necessary, but it was kind of nice all the same. I'd never walked in the woods with anyone other than Granddad and I was a better woodsman than he was. I let myself be pulled along.

He stopped after a while and peered into the gloom. A few fat drops of rain fell between the tightly packed branches above us. "Which way?" he murmured.

"Twenty paces ahead, past the oldest oak." That rang a bell with me, with what I'd said before about where Jade was located. He led me on and soon we did come to a massive and gnarled trunk scarred by flames. Whatever fire had come through years before, this tree had survived it. Now it was alone and surrounded by upstart pines.

"We're here," he said. "This must be it."

I nodded. Now what? The storm hadn't really started yet, but more drops were falling. A big one fell directly on my head with a wet plop.

"Well," Will said, looking at the sky, "I guess let's be direct. It doesn't look like we have much time. Is there anything of Alex's here?"

I let myself go as loose as I could. This was no time to hold back. "Something borrowed, something blue." I blew out my breath, frustrated. That made no sense. Wasn't it some sort of hokum people said at weddings?

Will sighed along with me.

"Sorry," I said. "I was afraid this would happen."

He dropped my hand and turned slowly around. "Okay, how about this . . . which direction should I go to find whatever the blue thing of Alex's is?"

"Left, three steps," I said. I breathed a sigh of relief. Maybe this had a shot of working.

Will walked left a few steps forward and stopped by a fallen tree. "Which way now?"

"Down," I said.

He raised his eyebrows at me, and I shrugged. Then he dug into his pockets and carefully removed a pair of household gloves out of his pocket, like the kind Gran cleaned with. He was so prepared. I never would have thought to do that, but it was smart. If Alex had left something, we didn't want to contaminate the evidence. And as he pulled them on, I realized with a flutter that Will had probably done it for me. He wanted to keep me away from the police and didn't want to risk anything that could tie me to this place.

As he got down on his hands and knees and dug a bit into the decaying leaves and pine needles, a dank rotting stench rose into the air. "Ah," he said after a minute. He stopped digging.

I came closer and bent down next to him. Some cloth was caught under the dead tree. Blue and white. I recognized the pattern immediately. I had seen Alex wipe the sweat from his face with the twin of this handkerchief, the day he'd run to our house. Will stared at it a moment and then covered it back up, leaving a small corner of it sticking out.

"What are you doing?"

"The police should find it themselves," he said. "Otherwise, they might think someone planted it." He avoided my eyes. Once again, he was trying to protect me. "We just need to figure out a way to get them to look here again once they're done with Shelley." He stood up and brushed off his hands. "You did it, Aria. Once they find this, it will tie him to Jade's murder."

I wanted his eyes to catch mine, to smile, but it felt like

a hollow victory, considering that it was too late for Shelley
to benefit from the find.

"It's weird that he would have left this," I said, almost to
myself. "It's almost asking to get caught."

"Maybe it's like on those TV shows. Maybe he wants to
be found. Maybe it's got blood on it, and he didn't have
time to get rid of it or something. Maybe he's planning on
coming back for it. But I'll bet he probably doesn't even
know it's missing. I mean, imagine what was going through
his mind at the time . . ." He didn't finish.

"I guess so," I said. Alex didn't seem that stupid to
me. Of course, Alex had never seemed like a murderer
to me before either.

The rain began to fall harder and harder, breaking
through the canopy of trees, drenching us. Lightning
flashed in the sky, and thunder rumbled seconds later, so
close I could feel it in my chest, knocking around in my rib
cage like another heart. Will grabbed my hand and pulled
me underneath the lone oak tree, up against the thick slabs
of greyish-brown bark. The branches were so thick that
only a scattering of drops made their way down to us.

"Aren't we supposed to avoid tall trees in a storm?"

"We're probably supposed to avoid crime scenes, too,"
he said.

My world was reduced to the rough bark of the tree
behind my shoulders and the warmth of Will in front of
me. He was so close I could feel the rise and fall of his
chest.

"I think I'm already soaked," I whispered, suddenly
very conscious of how my thin dress clung to me and how

my hair was plastered to my head. As if he could hear my thoughts, he took his hands and brushed the wet hair away from my forehead. He tucked it behind my ears on either side.

"Just a little," he said. His voice had gone a little raspy.

I blinked in the rain—at his eyes, then away from his eyes.

He shifted back and took my hands, lacing his fingers with mine and then pulled our entwined hands together into the small of my back. The bark scratched my wrist a little, but it was the last thing on my mind. Nothing was on my mind, nothing but how this felt, to be this close to him. I shivered.

"Are you cold?" he asked.

"I'm not cold," I whispered back.

He bent his head towards me, so close I couldn't really see his eyes anymore. "I've been meaning to ask you," he said, drawing each word out. "Do you want me to kiss you?"

"Kisses sweeter than wine," I whispered. Was that from a song? He wasn't fighting fair, two questions in a row. I hadn't really answered, but now my heart was rattling. What meaning would he draw from that?

"Is that a yes or a no?" he asked, whispering so close to my skin I felt each word as it came out, a tiny puff of air caressing my cheek. Somewhere we'd taken a turn into uncharted territory.

"I don't know," I said and for once, the answer was mine on every level. The thought of him kissing me terrified me. The thought of him *not* kissing me terrified me.

"No more questions," he said.

He leaned into me, and at the last second, I turned my head. His lips caught the corner of mine, hovering there until I gave up.

I'd never kissed a boy before. Never thought about how it would feel, hot and wet and hungry, like liquid and fire at the same time. He drew me closer to him, my arms trapped in his, his hands squeezing mine. And then his lips moved on, tracing a damp burning line from my mouth up to my temple. I didn't know when, but I'd closed my eyes and he paused there, placing butterfly kisses on my eyelids.

A bright flash in that perfect darkness, and he stepped away.

"Maybe we should make a run for the car," he said, his voice a husky rumble. If he weren't so near, I wouldn't have heard him at all. "Before it gets worse." As if to agree, the thunder boomed around us. The lightening strike had been close.

I didn't want to go, didn't think I could walk at all. My whole body felt like rainwater, like I was melting. If he let me go, there might not be anything left. I would dissolve into the storm. But I managed to nod. It only made sense. It wasn't safe to stay here. I'd lived in Florida long enough to know that, and this was, by far, the least safe I had ever felt out in the wild. I was lost.

He let go of my hands and stepped away. I thought that was it and then abruptly he was back, his mouth on mine, harder this time. His hands were tangled in my hair, his body pressing me into the tree. I grabbed onto his shirt, not sure whether I wanted to push him away or pull him even closer. Not sure I had a choice.

Then he was gone for real, running through the trees toward the car. Cut loose and unmoored, I stumbled forward a step. The rain had turned vicious, and without him to shield me, the drops stung. I gasped for air, a fish out of water while surrounded by it, and then ran after him to the car.

AWAKE MY SOUL

Will was deathly quiet on the way out of Laurel Creek, his brow furrowed in concentration as he tried to keep the car on the road in the driving rain.

I didn't trust myself to say anything that wasn't stupid. I shivered silently in the air-conditioning, goosebumps all over me. It had taken me five minutes of sitting and breathing to slow my heartbeat, and I was pretty sure it wasn't from the mad dash to the car. My lips still tingled.

He seemed to relax a little as we emerged onto paved roads again. The rain continued to beat an insistent staccato pattern on the roof, turning the car into the inside of a drum. I rolled my shoulder back a little. I winced at the pain, even though this morning seemed impossibly far away now, a past I hardly remembered living through. Being pinned against the tree hadn't helped, but it wasn't Will's fault. He didn't even know I'd hurt it.

He cleared his throat. "Do you mind if I take a little detour on the way back?"

"No," I said. I had nowhere else I needed to be. Nowhere else I wanted to be.

He didn't say anything else, just turned the stereo up. Did he regret kissing me? Had things gotten weird between us now? I wasn't sure what I was supposed to do. I'd never been here before.

Though I had been on the road we were headed onto. "Where are we going?" I asked, afraid I knew the answer.

"I want to do a drive-by of Alex's house and see if the police have picked him up already or not after . . . after Shelley."

"Do you think that's a good idea?"

"Probably not." He turned, a sad smile on his face. Then he slowed as he really took a good look at me, his eyes sweeping me from head to toe. "You look . . . cold." He turned the air-conditioning off.

I crossed my arms over my chest. Maybe that wasn't what he'd meant, but I blushed anyway.

"Just a little," I said. "You know, you don't have to drive all the way out to Alex's house. You could just ask."

"Oh," he said, giving a little laugh. "Didn't even think of that." Lightning cracked again, and he was quiet for a moment as we both waited for the thunder to follow. "Okay, Aria, have the police arrested Alex?"

"No," I said. Short and to the point. Direct but not useful.

Will pulled off to the side of the road. "Maybe they haven't questioned him yet. Have they?"

"Yes," I said, "So many questions, so many answers."

"Did they believe his alibi?"

"Two for, two against, the jury is out, but the verdict is in." I groaned. "I'm sorry, this isn't helping." I wished I hadn't offered now.

He managed another smile and shook his head. "No, it's okay. It's not your fault." He drummed on the steering wheel in tune with the rain. "You know what? We just need to get them to go dig up Alex's rag."

"How do we do that?"

"We have to be careful," he said, his voice faraway.

I wondered if he was thinking of Jade. And I had to admit: I didn't like that I was wondering that.

"I suppose I could leave a message from the pay phone again . . . telling them something like I told Delilah before, that I overheard Alex talking to himself or something." It sounded lame, but it had worked before, more or less.

His eyes brightened. "Perfect." He started up the car again, and we screeched back into the road with a sudden lurch. He drove fast, faster than I would have liked with the way the rain was still pouring down in solid sheets. I held onto the door handle with one hand the whole way.

"Are you sure we need to call *now*?" I gasped. Maybe we could wait until it wasn't pouring rain?

He stared at me, his brow furrowed. "Aria, the police need to get on top of this as soon as possible, don't you think?"

"They need all the help they can get," I said. Ugh.

He was right to ask. Even if he still had feelings for Jade, that wasn't just understandable, it was *human*. Besides, I needed closure, too. The questions would never end so long as Alex was free. Of course it was more important to get the information to them. It's not like I wasn't already wet anyway. I was being a baby.

Luckily I still had the slip of torn newspaper with the number. I read it over a few times to fix it in my head, grabbed some coins, and got out of the car. The rain had gotten so much worse. I was drenched through to the skin in seconds, my dress clinging to my body and twisting around my legs.

I dialed, wondering if the phone would even work in the rain or if they'd be able to hear me over the dull roar of it. As the line connected, I had a brief worry that an actual person would answer, but after a few rings it went to the automated message. I rushed through "Alex Walker" and "blue-and-white bandanna," hoping it didn't sound too incoherent and secretly wishing that maybe they wouldn't even be able to recognize my voice as the one who had called before. Then I hung up and dashed back in Will's car, dripping all over his seat.

"You did the right thing," he said somberly. He drove off as I was putting my seatbelt on. I was ridiculously wet. I wiped my hand over my face trying to get some of the water off. "I hope so," I said.

"We'd better get you warm and dry," he added. "I can lend you some clothes if you want. You know, before you get your car back."

FEELIN' LOVE

I hoped his mom wouldn't come home soon. I'd only seen her once or twice, but based on her décor, I didn't think she'd appreciate my beat-up Colt in her driveway, not to mention my dripping all over their hardwood floors. We entered in through the laundry room, and he handed me a towel from a stack on top of the dryer, then took one for himself. He was still damp, too, though nothing compared to the sopping wet state I was in. The towel worked okay for my hair and arms, but patting at my dress did almost nothing. It was plastered to me. I felt exposed.

I took one more swipe at my face and then pulled the towel down to see Will staring at me intently.

"I don't think that's going to do it," he said. He reached out and plucked at the sleeve of my dress where it clung to my arm. "We should stick your clothes in the dryer. Why don't you take them off?"

"Do I dare disturb the universe?" I responded, my inner

oracle seemingly as dismayed by the idea as I was, though it *would* have to manifest as a bit of poetry. At least I knew what it was from: *The Love Song of J. Alfred Prufrock*, Alex's favorite poem. "What about your parents?"

He sighed. "Dad's never home if he can help it, and Mom's in Fort Lauderdale for some art and antiques show or something. She left last night."

"Even after you got hurt?" I couldn't see Gran or Granddad leaving me home alone if I'd been beaten up and had a black eye the size of Miami.

He shrugged the question off. "I'm fine. Besides, she never misses it. She goes every year and buys a bunch of crap and fills up the house with it. As far as I can tell, that's what she thinks her job is." He grinned at me, but it was a bitter grin. "Go ahead and take your clothes off, and I'll go find something for you to wear."

He left, and I set the towel down on the washing machine and looked down at my dress. He was right. I couldn't walk around like this. I sighed and reached behind my back to unzip it, but it wouldn't budge. The cloth was too wet. I tugged at it, which only made my shoulder hurt.

"Having trouble?" Will was back already, some clothes in his hand.

He'd changed out of his own wet clothes and into a dry pair of shorts but had neglected to put on a new shirt. His chest was tan and mostly smooth, muscular without being too muscular and entirely too naked. I tried not to look at it, with little success.

I tugged at the zipper again and blew out my breath. "It's stuck." Why couldn't Gran buy me normal clothes? If

I were wearing a T-shirt and jeans, this wouldn't be happening.

"Let me," he said. "I'm good with zippers."

He probably hadn't intended it, but that made me blush for the millionth time. At least I had a reason to turn my back. A few short, sharp tugs and the zipper finally began to move, stuttering down for the longest unzipping of my life. When he hit the end I made to move forward and grab the clothes he'd brought, but he peeled back my dress from my shoulder and I stopped.

"Aria," he said in a tone I didn't recognize. "Your shoulder . . . what happened?"

"Shelley tripped me, trippingly so, I fell, oh, I fell, oh woe." I twisted around a little and then stopped short as he used both his hands to pull my dress the rest of the way down over my shoulders. It fell to my waist with a big squelch, held up only by my hips, admittedly not much up to the job. I froze there with my back to him. My bra was some cheap white polyester thing. It was soaking wet and, at this point, practically see-through. I crossed my arms over my chest.

"This looks terrible," he said. He traced a spiral with his fingertips over my shoulder blade and down the back of my arm.

I shivered but willed myself to stand still. "She tripped me in art class, and I fell into a desk," I said, swallowing, feeling like I had to explain, like I had to fill the air with words. "It's not that bad, really. Not any worse than your eye. I mean, it hurts, but . . ." I trailed off. Should I make a grab for the clothes or the towel? Or would that make me look like an idiot? I felt naked. I was as good as naked, nearly.

Will drew my hair to one side. Did he know what he was doing to me? Did he have any idea at all? I concentrated on keeping my breathing normal, the smell of the lavender fabric softener filling my nose.

His fingertips danced over my elbow. "These bruises here don't look like they're from a fall." He tugged gently, and I gave up my left arm, letting him pull it away from the shelter of my body, leaving my right arm a solitary and ineffectual barrier across my breasts. "What about these?"

"Alex's fingerprints," I said, startling myself.

I hadn't realized I'd bruised when he'd grabbed me. Will's grip increased for a moment, then he let go of my arm completely. For some reason that made me feel even more naked. "Alex helped me up after Shelley tripped me, but he was pretty pissed. At Shelley, I mean. That was right before the cop took him out of art class. I don't think he meant to hurt me." I wasn't sure why I was defending Alex at all. I chanced a peek over my shoulder at Will.

He was staring at my elbow, a strange look on his face.

My arm was just hanging by my side now. Should I cover myself again? Go for the towel? The clothes?

Whatever it was, the look passed to be replaced with a dark and determined glint in his eye.

"No one else will ever do that to you again," he said, leaning forward to kiss me softly in the middle of my shoulder, so gently I almost didn't feel it. His lips were warm as he drew them slowly across my neck and stopped behind my ear, his breath tickling me. "I promise," he said.

He kissed my neck. He was still talking in between kisses, but it was hard to concentrate on the actual words. I had lost track of his hands and became very suddenly aware of them as he moved into me, his bare chest so warm against my back and his fingertips drawing a web across my stomach from my belly button out.

"Aria," he breathed into a spot just above my ear, my name like a three-syllable symphony played for me alone.

"Yes?" I whispered back.

"Do you love me?"

My hands flew up to my lips, but the words came anyway: "Too much."

An ache opened up deep inside me. It had been building the entire time, and now it lay there, in my center, laid bare before him. I turned to face him. "Will, that wasn't fair." I hated how my voice quivered.

"I know," he said gently. He lowered his eyes. Then he took my face in his hands, tilting it up to meet his. Where the kiss in the woods had been almost too intense, this one started slow and soft. My arms were caught between us, and I flattened my hands against his bare chest. Maybe the thought had been to push him away after his small deception, but the ache inside me was filling me up. I lost track of time, of myself. It could have been midnight. It could have been next week. I was lost in a place that had come down to his warm breath mingled with mine, his skin against my skin. My whole body was a live wire, humming with electricity.

"Aria," he said again, and I almost braced myself for a question, but what did I have left to hide from him now?

I dropped my forehead onto his chest and took a deep breath, trying to calm myself. It didn't help. So close to him, it was like breathing him in. He smelled like rain and heat. He ran his hands down my back, stopping at my waist. My hips had betrayed me at some point, and my dress had fallen the rest of the way to the floor. It was tangled around my ankles, a heavy weight against my feet.

"We'd better stop," he said. Finally I could hear some hint in his husky voice that I wasn't the only one set adrift. "Unless—" he splayed his fingers so they oh-so-barely went underneath the elastic waistband of my underwear "—you want me to keep going."

I drew in a shivering breath and pulled back. If we went any further, I didn't know where I'd wind up. This morning, I'd never even *kissed* a boy. I didn't say anything, but he seemed to understand. He kissed the top of my head and left the room without another word.

FALL FOR YOU

I tore off the dripping remnants of my clothes and put everything in the dryer, throwing in one of Mrs. Raffles's lavender scented dryer sheets. When they were dry I'd be able to take the smell of the afternoon with me.

Will had left me one of his white T-shirts and a pair of red drawstring shorts, like the kind boys wear to play basketball. I put everything on, wishing I had a mirror to see how ridiculous I looked. I had drawn the string as tight as I could, and the shorts were bunched up in the middle. It felt really bizarre to be wearing them without underwear, but I had no choice. The T-shirt was an undershirt, kind of like Granddad always wore. It was comfortably worn, and I had the feeling it was as good as see-through. Did it matter at this point? I pulled my hair into a twisty knot and went to find Will.

He was in the kitchen making sandwiches. He smiled at me as I came in, composed and calm now. "Hope you like grilled cheese," he said. "It's the only thing I really know how to make. I'm an expert."

"Love them," I said. Who doesn't love grilled cheese? I sat at the kitchen table on a padded bench. The whole set was white and distressed—that shabby chic style where you make things look old and worn on purpose—whereas my kitchen just looked shabby. I tried not to think of my kitchen. I tried to be here, now, away from Gran and Granddad.

I watched Will as he cooked, humming some song I didn't recognize. He paused long enough to pour me a glass of water and give me a look that clearly took in my bra-less state. I pretended not to notice, but I crossed my legs thinking that maybe I should have kept my soaking wet underwear on anyway instead of sticking them in the dryer, too.

He flipped the sandwiches over and got out some earthenware plates and cloth napkins. I hid a smile. Much as I tried to banish Gran and Granddad from my thoughts, we looked the picture of domesticity, other than my underwear-less state. Like we were playing house. I let myself dream for a minute. The two of us together in some better place, another kitchen, another state, far away from here. Me, not hiding and not lost, but found. Will Raffles and me, fifty years from now.

"Here you go," he said, putting the plate down in front of me. He straddled the bench next to me and pulled me closer to him so I was settled between his legs. He kissed my cheek and then picked up his sandwich to take a bite.

I picked up my sandwich, too, but what I really wanted

to do was take another taste of him. Wanting him was like a hunger. I cleared my throat and took a bite, trying to chew slowly. Will put his left hand on my back, making slow, lazy circles. I swallowed, sure he could hear me chewing. I put my sandwich down. I had to kiss him again. He was killing me. If he'd just sat on the other side of the table, I could have made it, but I was dying. Maybe I shouldn't have stopped him in the laundry room.

"You should eat," he said. "Aria . . . you're not anorexic, are you?"

"No," I said and then repeated it again for myself. "I am *not* anorexic. Why would you even ask that?" I picked my sandwich up again and took another bite, the moment gone.

"Don't be mad," he said. "I just . . . You're really thin. Not that thin is bad or anything. But it's important to take care of yourself. You matter. You matter to me."

"I—" I didn't know what to say. My eyes prickled, and I blinked. No one other than my grandparents had cared about me enough to notice anything about me in a long, long time.

He went on eating like nothing special had happened. Maybe it wasn't a big deal for him, but it was for me. I took a few deep breaths and chewed the bite in my mouth, trying to slow my heartbeat with the routine of it. Chew, chew, chew, swallow.

"I, um, have lost some weight since . . . since Jade died." Chew, chew, chew, swallow. "I told you, didn't I, how the big questions affect me? There've been a lot of big questions."

"Oh, right. All the crackers at school." He kissed my temple. "Is there anything you can do to help with that? I mean, with your whole situation?"

"Yes," I answered simply. That brought me back to myself. "Gran did say there were things I could do to control it more. She showed me this book that's been in our family for a long time. A really long time. It's about our . . . condition." I refused to call it a gift out loud. "I started reading it last night. She thinks it'll help."

"Right," he said, nodding. "I can't wait to hear what's in it." He grinned wolfishly at me.

I rolled my eyes, undone again by that grin. I didn't trust myself to speak. He finished a bite and pulled me even closer to him, the hair on his legs tickling my knees. I could feel him down the length of me. Heat like I'd never been warm before.

Chew, chew, swallow.

"I'D BETTER GO," I said after I changed back into my clothes, still warm from the dryer. "If I don't go now, my grandparents will worry."

It was still raining, but softer now, a gentle rain. Determined but gentle.

He finished wiping his hands on a towel and came over to me. "Okay," he said. "I've got some things I need to do anyway. I'll keep an eye on the news, see if anything new gets released."

Oh, yes. Shelley. Alex. Jade. I seriously needed to get my head back on straight. Three people lay dead in the morgue, including a girl I should have been able to save, and all I could think about was Will. I needed to go home, see if there was anything in the book, and talk to Gran. Maybe she had some advice. I was turning into one of *those* girls, something I had never imagined doing.

"Of course," I said. "Um . . ." It seemed silly to just say goodbye after the time we had spent together. What was I supposed to do? What did normal people do?

"One more before you go," he said and took me in his arms. I didn't hesitate this time, just melted right in and opened my mouth to his. He tasted of grilled cheese, but then, I probably did too. His hands settled on my hips, pulling me close.

He let go too soon or maybe just in time. Probably both. I stepped back, my hand touching my lips without me even thinking about it. "Well," I said. "Right. I'm going now then."

He smiled one of those slow smiles at me and watched as I walked away. I felt his eyes on me all the way to my car.

I WAS HALFWAY HOME before it hit me: *Please don't let Gran or Granddad ask me anything about my day.* I couldn't imagine any answer I could give that wouldn't get me into about a billion degrees of hot water. This was a problem I'd definitely never had before.

They were usually pretty good about not asking me questions, but Granddad was always slipping up. Usually the small things like "What?" or "Why?" or "How was your day?" which were exactly the types of questions I didn't need. What I needed was to get my hands on Gran's book and see if there was any actual concrete information in it about how to control my "gift." It was about normal back-from-school time, a little before 4 P.M., so at least they wouldn't suspect anything. I parked and was running to the door with my backpack over my head to try and keep the rain off when Gran came flying onto the porch.

"Aria, where have you been?" She paid no mind to the rain and grabbed me in a bear hug on the first step.

"With Will," I muttered into her shoulder, never more grateful that my inner oracle had kept it brief. "We're getting soaked. Let's go inside."

So much for my plan. This was bad. I wasn't sure why she was so freaked out, but maybe if I kept talking she wouldn't think to ask any more questions.

The rain had let up a bit from earlier, but even that small run had drenched me again, though not through to the underwear like before. I blushed at the memory and busied myself with shaking the water off my backpack out the front door onto the porch.

"What's wrong?" I asked. "Why are you—?"

Gran didn't let me finish. "Aria, they closed the school today. Another girl was murdered, right there on the football field. The one you mentioned. Porter's out driving around looking for you. We were worried sick when you didn't come home."

"Oh," I said. That explained her freaking out. I should have thought of that, of course.

She was working up a good head of steam now.

"I don't know what you were thinking. What were—"

"Gran!" I interrupted her before she could ask

something I really didn't want to answer. Anything that mentioned me mostly naked with Will was not going to help matters. "Gran, I'm *fine*. I'm sorry, but I didn't know. I would have called if I'd had a cell phone. Nothing happened. I'm perfectly okay. Just calm down."

Gran drew herself up to her full height and brought the finger of doom to point at me, shaking. "Don't you tell me to calm down! We thought you might be dead!"

"Well, I'm not. Everything's fine." I turned to go to my room. Maybe some distance would help, not that there was a lot of it to be had in our house.

"Everything is *not* fine, Aria." She grabbed my arm and stopped me. "The police were here looking for you."

I stopped. The police? That wasn't good. That wasn't good at all. What if they recognized my voice from the messages I'd left? I knew I shouldn't have taken Will's advice. But I also knew he'd been right to want to tell the police in the first place.

"They want to ask you some questions," she continued. "I had to tell them I didn't know where you were. You neglected to mention to me that apparently you and this Shelley girl got in a fight the other day."

Who told them I'd been in a fight with Shelley?

"We didn't get in a fight," I said. "Shelley is . . . was just one of the many people at school who makes my life hell on a daily basis. *Made*, I mean . . . Because she's . . . I— damn it." I didn't normally swear in front of Gran, and I half expected her to stop me right there. I yanked down the collar of my dress and turned my back to her so she could see the bruise. If it had been bad enough to freak out Will, surely it would make Gran understand. "See this? I don't fight. I just get knocked down."

"Aria—"

"No, Gran, I just . . . I just don't want to talk about this right now, okay? I'm going to my room." I turned away and then stopped, my back to her. "I'm sorry about Granddad," I added and walked on.

Gran called after me, "A girl called for you, too. Said she was a friend of yours. Delilah. I left her number on your dresser. School's closed again tomorrow, and the police want you to stop by first thing." I waved a hand over my head to show I'd heard her but kept walking. The phone was still sitting near my bedroom door, and I pulled it inside my room with me and shut myself away from Gran.

ALL THE SAME TO ME

First, I went to the mirror on my closet door and took down the dresses hanging in front of it. Since I didn't use makeup and usually kept my hair hanging loose, I didn't often use it. Before Will, I really hadn't had any reason to. I hated myself a little for thinking that, but it was true. It had been a rare week where I'd looked in the mirror more than once. No one cared what I looked like except Gran and Granddad. And as far as they were concerned I was beautiful no matter what the truth was.

I swallowed, trying to remember that as I stepped close to the mirror. Gran and Granddad were better parents than most kids had around here—like Will for starters. Gran was pissed. She had a right to be. I didn't even want to think about Granddad's rage. But they'd get over it.

I stared at myself, trying to see if I looked different. I *felt* different. I touched my lips. Were they redder than normal? Plumper? Rosy with remembrance? Probably not.

It was likely my imagination. Then I took my damp-again dress off and turned my back to the mirror so I could try and get a good look at my shoulder. It was mostly purple. I looked like someone had beaten the hell out of me. I matched Will's eye. We were a pair.

I twisted my arm around so I could look at my elbow. There were five smaller, circular, purple-brown bruises where Alex had grabbed me. *When he was defending me.* I shivered and tried not to think about what he must have done to Shelley. Had he used a knife again? Or just beaten her to a bloody pulp?

I closed my eyes and took a few deep breaths. If I had to admit it, the other reason I'd left school this morning was to escape those answers. I was bone weary with all the questions centered on death and dying. I didn't want to know what had happened to Shelley. That would only bring more guilt. If only she had listened to me. If only I had tried harder to get her to listen.

I picked up one of my dresses from the bed and put it on. It was loose-fitting at the best of times, but I'd probably lost at least five pounds in the last week, maybe more. I put on a belt, but that only made me look like a child trying on her mother's clothes, something I had never gotten to do. Will was right. I needed to take care of myself, or my "gift" would be the death of me. I couldn't just keep counting the days to when it disappeared and gave me my life back. If I wanted to be with him out there in the real world, right now, I had to manage it, to control it, as Gran suggested. I couldn't go throwing up every time someone asked a question about the always-depressing world news or whatever local tragedy was going around. The world was full of death and evil. I had to deal with it. Somehow.

Gran's book—*my book*—was the only hope I had. I had to keep trying. There had to be something useful in there. Why else would it have been passed down for so many years? But I wasn't ready to venture out of my room yet. I could hear Gran puttering around in the living room moving things around. She always rearranged things when she was upset.

I sat down next to the phone on the floor and dialed Delilah's number. One ring . . . two rings . . . three . . . I was about to hang up when Delilah answered.

"Hello," she said.

It felt so strange to be calling someone up. I used to talk on the phone for hours with Jen, but that felt like a lifetime ago. Another life entirely. "It's Aria," I said.

"Aria!" I wasn't sure if she sounded surprised or happy or even angry that I'd called. "Have you talked to the police yet?"

"At not to," I said. I swallowed back the oracle gibberish and gripped the phone. "I mean, I called the anonymous tip line earlier, but I haven't actually spoken to them in person. Gran said they want me to come in tomorrow."

"Me, too," said Delilah, lowering her voice to a whisper. "I heard Lucy telling an officer about something that happened between you and Shelley and Alex in art class."

"It wasn't a big deal," I said. "Normal Shelley stuff. You know how she is . . . was."

"She was a bitch." Delilah let out a short, nervous

laugh. "I shouldn't say that. I shouldn't speak about the dead that way."

"Well, she was," I said. I relaxed a little against the door. The conversation was going okay. It wasn't like talking to Will, but it was okay. I was doing it. We almost sounded like any two high school girls talking, except for the topic.

"People are talking about you and Alex," said Delilah.

"We're not friends or anything," I said. "He just stood up for me." I still didn't understand why.

"He's pushy," said Delilah. "You need to watch out. I mean, besides the fact he's probably the killer." She hesitated. I had nothing to offer in the silence. "I was going to ask you something but then remembered I shouldn't," she confessed.

I laughed sadly. She laughed, too.

"Thanks," I murmured.

"I just never understood what Jade saw in him," she went on. "He really just . . . I don't know . . . I guess I felt like he wanted to control her. He hated that she was still seeing Will sometimes. She said he told her to stay away from Will."

That sounded familiar. "He told me that, too," I said.

Delilah drew in a breath and was quiet for just a moment. "People are talking about you and Will, too."

"Oh?" I said. Noncommittal.

"*So.*" I could imagine her leaning into the phone, anticipating juicy gossip. "Now I have to ask. Is there something going on between you two?"

"Something, not nothing, too much, too little," I answered. I wondered if I should tell her what happened today. I had an itch to tell someone, to make it real, but at the same time I wanted to keep it to myself and hold it close. I hadn't had time to really examine it yet, each word, each moment, each touch. I settled for a diplomatic answer of my own. "I'm not really sure what's going on yet. But let me ask you something. Do you think it's too soon? He . . . he told me he and Jade were pretty much broken up."

"Hm," she said, and I held my breath for what would come next. "Well, they *were*, pretty much. It is kind of soon, though."

"Yeah," I agreed, deflated.

"I mean, other people who don't know would probably think it was too soon."

"What do you think?" I asked, suddenly anxious. For the first time I had a source of girlish wisdom other than Gran.

"I think . . . I think you should go for it. If you don't, I might."

I laughed, relieved. A little. Was she joking about the last part? I didn't feel like I knew her well enough yet to know. "Really?" I said and then immediately thought that I shouldn't have asked.

"Of course not!" said Delilah. "I was just kidding." Had I offended her? But she tempered it with another little laugh. It was okay. I let out the breath I was holding.

"I'm sorry. I'm not very good at this," I said and then wished I could take it back. Will was right. I apologized way too much.

"At what?"

"Trust," I said. It was the oracle, but it was me, too. If I'd had control over my own voice, I would have said "*Conversation.*" Or "*Friendship.*" Or maybe even something normal-sounding, like, "*Talking on the phone.*" I'd done it all before, though. Surely I could learn to do it again.

Delilah was quiet for a moment. "It must be really hard for you," she finally said. "I'm sorry, too."

"For what?"

"For anything I said before . . . you know, before I knew."

"It's okay," I said. I could hardly blame her. She hadn't actually been that bad. I'd barely popped up on her radar screen, not like Shelley.

Delilah cleared her throat. "I am a little freaked out about tomorrow. Are you . . . do you think . . . I'm sorry," she said. "I can't think of how to say it without asking it like a question. And I guess that's kind of a pain for you, huh?"

"The pain only comes with the big questions," I said.

"Oops, I guess I did it there, too." She was quiet, and I could hear a clicking like she was tapping her nails or something.

"Go on," I choked out. *Please don't let her give up on me.* I needed this. "It's not a big deal. I know it's hard. My grandparents just kind of say things instead of asking them. That works. And you've already done it. But they forget all the time, too, especially my granddad. So don't apologize." I smiled at the irony of offering someone else the same advice Will had offered me.

"Well . . . um, I want to know if you think that you'll be okay talking to the police." Her voice went down instead of up at the end, doing her best to make it a sentence instead of a question, but I could still feel it. Perhaps a good time to practice controlling my answer. I could feel the pull of the question inside me, but it was slight, a whisper, the flicker of a candle flame. I tried to choose my words myself.

"I think it will be hard," I said, my voice wavering a little. I had an unsettled sensation for a moment like I hadn't really answered the question after all, but it began to dissipate almost immediately. Maybe this could work.

"Yeah," she said, not realizing how big this moment was, that I'd actually given my own answer for once. It had been a small question and only half of one at that, but it was something. I allowed myself another smile even though she couldn't see me. "They'll probably just think you're crazy," she added.

That wiped the smile off of my face.

"Oh, sorry. I didn't mean that the way it sounded," she said. "I meant—"

"I know what you mean." I'd had the same thought myself. And what if they *did* recognize my voice from my messages? Would they discount them? Would they believe that I was telling the truth? After all, I couldn't tell anything, *but* Will's fear of exposing me to the police in person suddenly made more sense than ever. They'd never stop asking questions.

"What are you going to tell them?" I asked.

"I don't know," she said. "I don't really know anything, I mean other than that thing with Jade being so upset and all. Do you think I should I tell them about you?"

She'd forgotten that time, not that I could blame her.

"Should, could, would, it will not matter, it will not happen, it may not happen, it could happen, it could matter, and that's what you should do." I said, my voice going deep. A hollow feeling settled into my bones.

"Um . . ." she said.

"Ignore that," I said. "I have no idea what that meant. I guess you could tell them if you want to. What time are you going in? If you're going before me, maybe it would even help." Maybe if someone normal told them what I could do they'd be more likely to believe me than stick me in an insane asylum. Gran wouldn't like it, but what else could I do? If they talked to me for any length of time, it was going to come out somehow. She had to know that. And it might be better than if they simply thought I was insane.

"I think I'm supposed to be there at ten. Hey, what should I wear? I have no idea what's proper for a visit to the police station—oops!"

"Wear clean underwear," I said. We both laughed. Apparently, Delilah could also bring out the playful side in my inner oracle.

She took a deep breath. "I just want this to be over," she said, and I thought of how inseparable she and Jade had always been. Would we ever be friends like that? Could we be? I swallowed hard, nodding, even though she couldn't see me.

"Will it be it over soon, Aria?"

"It will be over tonight," I answered.

The hollow feeling inside me grew. Would the police arrest Alex tonight? Maybe a policeman was out in the woods right now digging up a dirty blue handkerchief.

Maybe my phone call had done some good. I searched for something more to reassure Delilah when I heard the creak of the front door opening.

"I saw Aria's car outside. She's here?" Granddad barked loudly enough for me to hear.

"Here for now," I whispered.

"I don't understand," Delilah whispered back, not knowing that my inner oracle was responding to someone else.

"Hey, Delilah, I have to go. I'll talk to you later, okay? Sorry." I hung up while she was still saying goodbye. It was time to face the music.

I NEED SOME SLEEP

I barely had time to stand up before Granddad crashed through my bedroom door, dripping water from the umbrella he still held in his hand. "Aria, what—"

"Granddad," I interrupted, "I'm sorry."

I grabbed him in a hug, and he crushed me to him. I had to keep him from asking any revealing questions, though I really *was* sorry. His face was creased with worry as he released me from the hug. He held me by the shoulders at arm's length and looked me in the eye. I kept myself from wincing, barely, as he squeezed my shoulders and then finally let go. Gran stood behind him, watching us both.

"You scared me," he said.

"I didn't mean to."

"I don't know what's going on around here anymore," he said, turning from me to Gran and back again. "This whole place has gone crazy."

"I know," I said.

"I don't like it," said Granddad. "I don't like any of this. I especially don't like the thought of you being questioned by the police tomorrow." He turned back to Gran. "I don't think we should allow it."

"We don't have a choice," said Gran. "I think they suspect Aria might be involved because of that fight she had in class with the murdered girl, Shelley Roman."

"Wait, what?" I asked, panicking. "Why do they think that?"

Gran shook her head. "It doesn't matter. You have to talk to them. If you don't, they're just going to think the worst. I don't like it, but it's time to go public, Aria. It's time, and the sooner the better before anyone else dies."

Alex, I thought bitterly. He'd found a way to shift blame to someone else. Me. Had he come up with the idea in art class as soon as the police had arrived? Or had it come later, when they were questioning him?

"Gran," I said, "I need the book."

She nodded and went to get it while Granddad stood there unhappily, avoiding my eyes.

FOR A LONG TIME, long after dusk settled into night, I sat against my closed door, sunk down to the floor, the book sitting heavy in my lap. I traced the embossing on the front with a finger, following a gold-dusted swirl around and around. *So much for eating,* I finally thought. That was when I reached for the phone. I needed to talk to Will. I dialed his number and waited impatiently while it rang.

"Hello, Aria," he said, his voice warming me. "Miss me already?"

"Yes," I breathed. I didn't even care that he'd asked. I wasn't going to have any secrets from Will. Life was too short for that. "I have to talk to you."

"Is everything okay?"

"Not yet, maybe never, the future is not clear," I said. What was that? No matter. "The police came by my house today while I was with you. They want me to go in tomorrow for questioning. Gran thinks they think I had something to do with Shelley's death because of that thing in art class. You know, where she hurt my shoulder."

"That's not good," he said. "That's not good at all."

"Well, you may be right," I said. *And probably are.* "But Gran thinks maybe it could work out. She thinks it's time I came clean about my gift, anyway. Besides, Delilah is going in for questioning, too, at ten tomorrow, and she's going to tell them about me, too, so maybe they'll believe me and not be completely freaked out when I go in. It could work. Maybe. Then when I talk to them, maybe they'll believe me about Alex. Maybe they can even ask me questions, and I could help them find the truth." That was a lot of maybes.

"Wait. Delilah knows, too?" He didn't sound happy.

"She knows, she knows, she knows too much, she knows too little," I said. I sighed. This conversation would go faster if he didn't ask so many useless questions. "Yes, I told her yesterday. She believed me. Listen, Will. Why don't you ask me more about Alex? It worked today in the woods, you know? I can handle—"

"Aria." He blew out his breath and was quiet for a moment. "Why did you do that? Tell Delilah, I mean. That was stupid."

I blinked, stung. "I wanted a friend," I said. Ah, the truth laid bare.

"You shouldn't have told anyone else," he said softly. I could hardly hear him. "Especially not Delilah. They don't call her the Mouth of the South for nothing. Here's a question: Has she told anyone else yet?"

"No," I said, a mercifully brief answer. Why was he so mad? "It could help, though, don't you think? I can't not go and talk to them, not when they suspect me. And if she tells them before I even get there, maybe they won't freak out so bad."

"I wish you'd told me about the fight in art class," he said, changing the subject abruptly.

"It wasn't a *fight*. Everyone keeps saying that. It was just Shelley being Shelley. She's been saying all kinds of crap about me and Alex since this whole thing started—"

"*What* has she been saying?"

I had no choice now that he'd asked. "That we were friends, that we were lovers, that I carried his baby."

There was dead silence on the other end of the line.

"She was telling people you were pregnant with Alex's baby." At least he hadn't asked it as a question, though the flat statement somehow made it sound even worse.

"Yes," I said, cringing even though he couldn't see me.

"Tell me what you did that would make her think that."

"Nothing!" It hurt that he would say that, especially in that cold, level voice. "I never even kissed a boy until today, and you were there for that." My attempt at humor fell flat. "You know how Shelley is . . . was. She just saw that my stomach was upset and that Alex was standing up for me, and so she came up with the worst possible story to explain it."

"This is bad," he said. "Very bad."

"I don't have a choice," I said. "I can't *not* talk to the police now. They're going to think I had something to do with it unless they finally figure out it was Alex between now and then."

The more I thought about it, the more I thought it could work. Will had believed me. Delilah had believed me. If the police kept an open mind, they might believe me, too.

"Aria—promise me you'll never keep things like this from me again," he said at last.

"I won't," I said. "Of course not." Couldn't he tell I was hiding nothing from him? Nothing at all? "I wasn't *trying* to keep it from you. It just hadn't come up." It wasn't exactly a good conversation starter.

"Okay," he said, and I could almost hear the smile coming back into his voice. "I've got an idea. We'll talk tomorrow first thing. Don't go in to talk to the police until you talk to me."

"Okay," I said. "I'll call you."

I hung up the phone. Maybe I hadn't gotten him to ask me any questions about Alex, but that was a bit of a relief. I needed to save myself for tomorrow, anyway. It would be so nice when all of this was behind us somehow. When we could talk to each other about something other than murder and the police. Someday.

I picked up the book. There was no table of contents. There weren't even page numbers. I flipped it open to a random page, somewhere past the long list of names.

The word *Choices* was inscribed across the top of the page in large, fancy letters.

There was something in another language as well, but I had no idea what it said. Half the page looked Greek or Cyrillic or something unrecognizable with what I presumed was a translation going down the other side in English.

Most of the handwriting was spidery and faded. There was no telling how long ago the page had been written, either the first time or the translation. I traced my finger under the lines as I read them. It was weird to think that someone in my family had written all of this down, so many years ago.

It is tempting to try to find meaning or decipher our prophecies for those who ask, and ask they will, but we must remember that we are simply conduits for answers and not the solution ourselves. Tragedy follows the Sybil who steps outside her duty.

Well. That wasn't helpful. I flipped forward a few more pages.

I called out to Gran and Granddad, who were in the living room watching TV. "Can one of you ask me what page I should look at?"

"What page would be best for Aria to turn to?" asked Gran loudly in response.

"In the beginning, in the middle, the end. What you seek cannot be found where you are looking." I groaned. I should have known better. "Thanks anyway, Gran," I called back.

"What does Aria need?" asked Granddad.

"To leave fear behind and embrace her own strength." Where was a real answer when I needed one? I hated sounding like a stupid fortune cookie. I slammed the book shut and counted to ten with my eyes closed.

Gran tried one more time. "Will anything in the book help Aria?" she asked hopefully.

"Everything. Nothing. Strength, determination, and will come from inside." I shook my head, even though they couldn't see me. "That's enough, thanks. It's not helping. I'll just have to do things the hard way." Like always.

I took a deep breath and flipped open the cover. There had to be something in here. Why else would all my ancestors have bothered to write all this stuff down? Why else did Gran haul it out in the first place? I started reading from the very first page, determine to scour every word.

GRAN BROUGHT MY DINNER to my room on a tray. I kept reading while I ate. I read about the purification steps used by various oracles. I read about the rituals they used to delay supplicants or the people who wanted to ask questions. I read about how water often strengthens the gift, though no one really knew why. I took extra care reading through the notes on how the Sybils dealt with prophesying. But the few who managed to develop any kind of control over their gift had done it in completely different ways. One had found that she could guide her answers by keeping her eyes closed. Another had removed all meat from her diet; another fasted three days before allowing herself to come in contact with questioners. One bathed in rainwater, while another only answered naked. I'm sure she was quite popular with the supplicants.

Just as I'd feared: the book was of no help. There was no rhyme or reason to it. Basically, it was trial and error. I shut the book and rubbed my eyes. My head ached from trying to decipher all the handwriting, a lot of which was faded or too shaky to be legible.

I looked at the clock. It was after ten. Gran and Granddad would either be asleep or on their way to bed. They were both firm believers in that early-to-bed, early-to-rise thing.

I went to the kitchen to get a glass of water. There was only one solution: I was going to have to practice. If I could figure one trick out before I talked to the police tomorrow, things would go at least a little smoother. I didn't want to bother my grandparents, so I'd have to use the TV and hope I could find a program where someone was asking questions. It wasn't ideal, but it would be something.

I gathered up some of the herbs that had been mentioned in the book just in case. Who knew? Maybe the key was something as silly as breathing in the scent of rosemary. (Talking to the police naked wasn't an option, I guessed.) If I could find something that would actually keep me from *having* to answer a question it would be even better. Something not as drastic as dying, like that girl Serin. I was willing to eat or drink or smell just about anything for that.

Once I turned on the TV, I didn't have to wait long. Commercials were full of rhetorical questions. I tried smelling whatever I could think of between each one. The questions were all pretty mundane, though, and not much of a challenge. I found the scent of citrus actually seemed to make me answer more strongly and not in a good way. Maybe I'd been right to swear off Gran's juice.

I was trying out thyme when the news came on.

The sports report, always first in Florida after the weather, did nothing for me—though I did find out who was going to win the World Series, even though it was still months away. I'd have to tell Granddad on the sly, and maybe he could place a bet. At least *he* could be happy.

Then came the local news. "Our top story tonight is the string of murders occurring in and around Lake Mariah. The question topmost on everyone's mind, of course, is why?"

I took a deep cleansing breath, just like a few of my ancestors had recommended, closed my eyes, and tried to relax and let the answer come out slowly. "Some people are only alive in the midst of death." I breathed out.

My stomach felt okay. Maybe the thyme was making a difference. I held it to my nose again and inhaled deeply. Or maybe I just wanted it to, more than I'd wanted almost anything.

The anchor said a few words about Shelley without mentioning her name and the ongoing investigation. They didn't mention Alex, but then, they probably couldn't legally since he was underage. I opened my eyes as they went to an interview with a police officer that must have been taped earlier today. He was standing in front of the school.

"Any ideas on the motivation behind the murders?" asked whoever was holding the microphone.

The policeman rubbed a hand across his face. He looked tired. I missed his answer as my own came: "Need," I said. "Hunger and wanting, getting stronger each day."

My stomach clenched a little that time, like I was infected with the urgency of the killer. Maybe the thyme wasn't doing anything after all. I took a sniff of the rosemary, the astringent smell filling my nose.

"Will the killer strike again?"

I tried to control it, but the words poured out of me like water, burning my throat as they came. "Like a snake in the night, tonight he hunts at the lake with crocodile tears. O, unsuspecting fools, trust not his promises for he intends to steal your life from you."

I slumped forward, the jar of rosemary falling out of my hand as I did, spilling the brittle needles around me.

I AM A GHOST (ARTIFACT)

I came to with the tang of rosemary filling my head. I sat up and shook myself, scattering needles as I did. They were caught in my hair and spread all over the floor. A commercial was playing now, something about chocolate. I glanced at the clock. It was close to eleven now. I turned the TV off, the sudden silence leaving me lonelier than I'd felt in a very long time.

What should I do? Should I call the police? Wake Gran and Granddad? No. I knew what Gran would say. She'd tell me to go to the police and let them take care of it. Granddad would want to stay uninvolved or anonymous somehow. We'd be up half the night arguing about it, and meanwhile someone else would die. Just like Shelley. And worse, I didn't even have a name for this victim. Not yet.

Maybe I should call Delilah's cell. Maybe she could call the police first? Or Will? But I didn't want to upset him. He might even insist on coming over, at which point Granddad might reach for the shotgun again.

I grabbed the phone and dialed Delilah's cell. Hopefully she wasn't asleep already. It rang and rang and then went to voice mail. I tried not to read too much into it. Just because I was up didn't mean she would be. But it was way too late to try her landline. Still, I was anxious enough about not being able to reach Delilah to forget about upsetting Will.

"Aria," he said, picking up on the first ring. He sounded out of breath, like he'd run for the phone. I pictured him in his room, in his pajamas, grabbing the phone before it woke up his parents. "Is something wrong?"

"Not yet," I said. An unhelpful answer but one that made me feel even worse, a feeling of despair settling into my stomach like it was there to stay. "Will, Alex is going after someone again tonight."

"Are you sure?" he asked.

"Only of the water . . . Water is like life."

"The lake," Will said.

It wasn't a question. I wasn't sure what it was. I shook my head, fighting back the oracle. "I don't know, but I have to do something," I gasped. "After what happened with Shelley—"

"Aria," he interrupted me. "Just stop. Would you do something for me?"

"I would do almost anything for you." I let out a little gasp. I couldn't believe I'd said that. No, I *could* believe I'd said it. I just couldn't stand that I'd actually said it *to* him.

"Good," he said. "Stay home. Stay safe. You've told me

everything I need to know. I'll take care of it. I'll talk to you in the morning like we planned." His voice sounded far away, and there was a sudden bang, like he'd slammed a door. I winced. He hung up, leaving me holding the phone to my ear listening to the *beep beep beep* of the disconnected line. I hung up and redialed immediately, but he didn't answer this time.

No. He couldn't do this to me. He was the next most likely target. I would never forgive myself if something happened to him. Never. And now it sounded like he was going to take matters into his own hands. I hesitated for just the briefest of moments. I had to call the police. Didn't I? I dialed the emergency number, my hand shaking.

"Nine-one-one. What is your emergency?"

"Nothing yet, but give it time. The plan is already set in motion." I bit my tongue. "Sorry, I'm sorry," I said quickly before the operator could hang up on me. "You know the murders?" Of course she did. I was being stupid. "The murderer is going to try and kill someone else tonight. At the lake. You have to send someone to the lake. Right now before it's too late."

"Miss, what is your name?"

"Aria Morse."

"Can you spell that?"

"Yes, of course. I mean, yes, it's A-R-I-A. M-O-R-S-E. You guys need to get there right away."

"Let's start over here. Where are you located?"

"The living room." I whacked myself in the forehead. If she'd stop asking questions, this would go a lot faster. "Look, I'm at home."

"You're saying that you're at home. And there's a crime taking place at the lake tonight, correct?"

I took a deep breath, trying to control the words, make them sound reasonable and sane, something she would believe. "I have spoken the truth as it is. But . . . *not yet.*" I wrenched the last two words from my belly, my voice deep and almost guttural. "Please, just listen! I'm trying to tell you that the killer—Alex—the one that's been killing the girls at the high school—he's going to try and kill someone else tonight. Maybe at the lake. Probably at the lake. Maybe Will Raffles, probably Will . . . and it's my fault, I told him it was going to happen, and I think he's going to go out there and try to stop him." I was almost sobbing now and breathless. My throat burned. I wasn't making much sense. The operator probably thought I was crazy.

"Miss, calm down. Can you tell me why—"

"Wait!" I jumped in before she could finish whatever it was she was going to ask. "Look, I know this sounds crazy. That I sound crazy, but I just *know*, okay? You need to get to the lake before someone gets killed."

There was a small pause. "Exactly who is it that's going to be killed, and who is it you say has been killing the girls over at the high school?" Was that a hint of derision in her voice?

I doubled over with a sudden piercing pain in my stomach. "Will—" I managed as all the air in my lungs seemed to disappear as his name crossed my lips. I dropped the phone and it fell, landing on the base and hanging up. *Click.* I couldn't catch my breath. Breathe.

Breathe. I had to hold on. I couldn't afford to pass out. Not now. I slammed my hand down on the floor, just missing the phone. The bottle of thyme went spinning off under the couch, but the pain in my hand gave me something to focus on. I wrapped my arms around my stomach and held on tight. Get it together. Get it together.

Beeeeep, beeeep, beeeeep went the phone. I reached out a hand that refused to be steady and hung it up, then crawled to my knees. I had to get to the lake.

POSSUM KINGDOM

The Colt was halfway down the driveway when I realized I didn't even have shoes on. I'd grabbed my keys and run. No time to go back and get them. I floored it, the unfamiliar feeling of the metal pedal strange beneath my bare foot. I could feel the vibration of the car as it leaped forward, the back tires spinning a little in the sand before taking hold.

The rain had dropped to a miserable drizzle. I scraped off the sand stuck to my feet on the car mat and swore as I stubbed the big toe of my left foot against something hard and cold. I reached down and fumbled around under the seat until I found what it was.

Granddad's knife, the one with the bone handle. I set it in my lap, the weight of it somehow reassuring. I had no plan, no ideas, but at least I had something. I couldn't count on the police coming, not after that call. They probably thought I was insane.

The car skidded a little as it hit the main road, but I didn't slow down. I had no time. Why did we have to live out in the middle of nowhere? I drove. The moon was out, peeking behind a curtain of clouds hung so low they felt like they were hovering just over the road, waiting to swoop down and suffocate the earth.

All I could think about was that it was my fault. Again. I'd set the series of events in motion. If I hadn't called Will, he wouldn't be in danger. He wouldn't be out there right now trying to stop Alex. Why had I called him? Why hadn't I called the police first? Why couldn't I have managed to say something coherent to the police when I did call them?

It didn't matter now. I wasn't going to dwell on it. I held onto something I'd read earlier. One of my ancestors had said the future, no matter how prophesied, is not set in stone. Even the very act of prophecy can change the course.

Not always, but sometimes.

Please let it be so tonight.

I came to the crossroads and hesitated for a second before turning to go directly to the lake. I didn't want to waste precious time checking Will's house first, even though I didn't like that bang I'd overheard. Was Alex trying to break in? Had he already? But then why had the lake popped up as the place to go to, something Will had responded to, something even now I could feel with certainty?

I drove as close as I dared to Three Oaks and parked a little way down an abandoned dirt road that led to nowhere. I took Granddad's knife and my flashlight with me. Then I cut through the trees and across dog trails and came out near the entrance to the parking lot. The gate was open, but I slipped in under the fence away from the solitary streetlight that shone there.

There was a single vehicle parked at the far side of the lot. It was huge. Alex's? Yes, it was his rusted old Chevy Suburban, nearly in the same spot where he'd parked that night I'd found him drunk. He was here already. Oh, God.

But Will's car wasn't.

My heart froze. Maybe Alex had already killed him in his home. Maybe he'd dragged Will's dead body here . . .

Granddad's knife felt solid in my right hand as I crept through the brush along the edge of the lot on the border between the gravel and the trees. When I got closer, I could hear that Alex's Chevy was running. There were no other sounds, just the low rumble of the engine, drowning out the insects and the owls and the breeze. The drizzle had almost stopped. Was that Alex in the driver's seat or just a dark shadow? Nothing moved, and I didn't dare turn on my flashlight yet.

I walked slowly over to Alex's truck, my shoulders hunched. My heart was pounding so loudly in my chest I felt like he must be able to hear me coming. I stayed focused on the windows to see if there was any movement, but I saw only nothing and more nothing. I gripped the handle of Granddad's knife tight to stop the trembling in my fingers. I had to get myself together.

I was nearly there when I tripped over a sharp rock in the dark. I leaned into the side of the Chevy to steady

myself, my hands full with the flashlight and the knife, neither of which I wanted to lose. I was at the passenger's side
door. I righted myself and took a deep breath. Nothing
had stirred inside the vehicle. It was now or never. I flicked
on the flashlight and shone it in, directly on Delilah's slack
face pressed against the window.

"Delilah!" I yelled, not caring if anyone heard or not now.

I dropped the knife and yanked on the handle, but it
was locked. I climbed up on the sideboard and banged
on the window, but she didn't move. I shone the flashlight down her body, trying to see if she had any wounds, if
there was any blood, but there wasn't anything I could see
within the small flickering beam of my flashlight.

Please, please, let her be knocked out and not dead.

I tried the back door behind hers, but it was locked too.
I ran around the back of the Chevy and tripped over something again, this time falling on my knees and dropping the
flashlight. It spun in a circle for a second and then stopped
as it rolled into something. I picked it up and pointed it at
whatever had tripped me. A plastic tube? It was attached to
the exhaust and snaked around to the driver's side. I got
to my feet and followed it around. The tube was duct
taped into one of the windows.

That was why the Chevy was running. Carbon monoxide. Oh, God. I got to my feet and yanked on the door
with the tube. Locked. I went to the driver's door to try it,
and that's when I saw that Alex was in there, too, behind
the wheel.

"Alex!" I screamed, but he didn't move, either. I wanted
to curse him.

That door was locked as well, so I ran back to the tube and pulled as hard as I could but other than a slight ripping sound, it didn't budge. He must have used an entire roll of duct tape. Where had I dropped my knife?

I ran back to Delilah's side, my feet skidding in the gravel. I dropped down on my hands and knees with the flashlight to find Granddad's knife. I was cursing that it had that dull black handle when the beam of the flashlight finally caught a glimmer of the edge of the steel blade. It had fallen behind the tire. I grabbed it. Was I too late? How long had they been in there? How long did it take before the fumes killed you? Why was Delilah there at all? Did Alex know that she was my friend? Was it my fault she was there?

Granddad's knife was solid, heavy. An old Army man's knife. He'd had it since basic training. I remembered the stories he'd told me about it when I was little, the action it had seen. Instead of wasting time running back around the car and trying to hack at the web of duct tape covering the window, I bashed the solid end of the knife into Delilah's window. The glass cracked immediately, but didn't shatter. I hit it again and again until the glass gave way in a glittery diamond shower. I fumbled finding the door lock and finally found it. I flung the door open, stepping back as the shards of glass spilled out around my feet. I dropped the knife into my pocket where it clinked against my car keys. I wasn't going to lose it again.

"Delilah!" I screamed again.

I yanked at her arm, only to be drawn up short as she hit the limit of the seat belt. She was as floppy as a rag doll. I let her go, trying to breathe through my mouth as the sickly sweet smell of the exhaust fumes wafted out of the Chevy and filled my nose. The dome light had come on with the opening of the door. Alex was slumped low over and across the seat. I leaned to the side and took a deep breath, then bent over Delilah, trying to find the seat belt buckle. I pressed the button and muttered a brief prayer of thanks as it came loose. That was a mistake, as the fumes wrapped their cloying fingers around me.

I coughed violently, grabbing Delilah again under the arms and tugging at her.

This time she moved. I hauled her out of the vehicle, ignoring the stabbing pain as a piece of the broken glass embedded itself in my instep and laid her on her back by the edge of the woods a few feet away, propping her head up on a blunt cypress knee.

Was she breathing? I put my head to her chest, but for a moment all I could hear was the roaring in my own ears. I held my breath again, trying to calm down and listen. Was that a faint heartbeat? Or the echo of my own sounding in my ears?

"Delilah, wake up, wake up," I begged.

Her closed lids didn't flutter. I didn't want to shake her. What if I hurt her? What were you supposed to do? I'd gotten her out, but I had to get her to a doctor. I checked her pockets for her cell phone, but they were empty.

I hobbled back to the open door, hoping her cell phone would magically appear where she had been sitting.

Oh, God. *Alex.* He was still in there. For the briefest of seconds I considered slamming the door and leaving him to his fate. He had done this to her. I didn't know why, but he had set this whole thing up. Guilt, who knows? But I wasn't a killer, not like him.

I reached in across the length of the Chevy and shut off the engine, but the inside still reeked of the foul gas. He was too heavy to pull all the way through. I'd have to get him out through the driver's side. I took another deep breath and clambered over him to unlock the door and then ran around the other side to open it. He didn't even grunt when my knee accidentally crushed his hand.

This time I checked for the seat belt first, but he wasn't buckled in. He listed to the side, his forehead pressed against a vent where I'd pushed him to get him out of the way. I grabbed an arm and pulled, but he barely moved an inch. He was over six feet of solid dead weight. The air inside was getting better, but I still had to get him out, somehow. If he was alive at all.

I put my fingertips to his neck, trying to locate a pulse. At first, nothing, but then I found it. Thump, thump, a dull but steady beat. I nearly cried in relief.

"Alex," I screamed in his ear. "Wake up! Wake up!"

I shook him, his head lolling. His upper body collapsed toward me, and I put my hands under his arms, still yelling his name. I locked my arms around his barrel chest and tugged as hard as I could, managing to get his head and shoulders out the door, when gravity started to help me out. I gave one more huge heave, and he slid onto the ground with an unceremonious thud.

I left him there and limped back to check again on Delilah. It might have been my imagination, but it seemed like she was breathing a little easier, but she was still unresponsive. I crouched there for a minute, breathing hard. I needed to find one of their cell phones. I'd gotten Alex out of his truck, but I didn't think I'd be able to get him into mine without gravity to help me out. Of course, I could leave Alex here and take only Delilah, but what if he woke up and escaped? Could I even leave long enough to go get my car?

Now that I had a minute, I limped over to open the back doors of his Chevy and look inside for a backpack or Delilah's purse. I didn't dare look at my feet. I winced with each step. There was a ton of junk in the cavernous back of Alex's Suburban, including a lawn mower, but nothing that would help me get them to the hospital or the police.

Alex would have to help me himself.

I poked him with a bloody toe. He didn't move, but his breathing was steady and loud. I had no choice. I'd have to check his pockets too. If I were lucky there would be a cell phone. If not? I didn't know what I was going to do. I prodded him again. I didn't really like the thought of reaching into his jeans pockets, but I didn't have time to be squeamish. I tried the left pocket first and found only lint. Then I wiggled my fingers into his right pocket and came out with his phone and a sheet of folded paper. I was about to throw it down and use the phone when I glanced at it. *I'M SORRY* was scrawled across the top in large block letters.

I opened it all the way and smoothed it out across his chest. Holding my breath, I read it by the pale light of the flashlight.

I'm sorry. I did it. I killed those girls. I didn't mean to. It was an accident. Jade found out about me and Delilah, and things got out of hand.

I let out a shaky exhale. Snuck a look at Delilah who still lay as if resting peacefully. Sleeping Beauty in the woods. It couldn't be true. Could it? I kept reading.

Shelley confronted me about it, and I had no choice but to shut her up, too. We are sorry for all the pain we've caused and have decided this is the only way we can atone for our sins.

FORGIVE US,
ALEX

"No!" I said, not even realizing I was saying it out loud until my shout echoed back to me from the dark chamber of the Chevy. I beat my fist against Alex's chest, crumpling the paper. He didn't move at first, then he twitched, and I scuttled backward. He coughed a few times and then half-rolled over onto his side, retching into the gravel.

I was numb. I hugged my knees to my chest and watched him be sick. So useless, so useless. Jade and Shelley dead for no good reason, no good reason at all. And Delilah! I'd thought she was my friend, and all this time, she knew. She *knew*. Even when I'd told her my secret, she'd known. She'd played me for a fool. Warning me against Alex! I felt like I should be crying, but I was dry as a desert. A reverse oasis.

The quiet was filled with the sound of Alex heaving one last hacking cough that rocked his entire body. He groaned and tried to push himself up. The letter drifted to the ground as the sour smell of Alex's lost dinner surrounded me.

"I should have left you in there," I said. Until now I really hadn't truly believed he was the one, but there it was in black and white.

He twitched like my words had shot him and swung around until his eyes found me.

"Aria," he said, my name as raspy and rough as sandpaper. "What—?"

"I said I should have left you in there." I straightened my back and lifted my head up. His almost-question swirled inside me and then dissipated. "I can't believe you actually did it. I know I thought you did it before, but I didn't believe it, not really."

"I don't—" Another wracking cough doubled him over. I sat and watched, growing more and more angry. He used his strong arms to pull himself back against the Chevy and slumped against it, holding his head in both hands, the very picture of defeat.

"Where is that bastard?" he choked out. "Where did he go?"

"Near," I answered, even though I didn't want to. "At the gas station." I dragged myself to my feet. "I won't let you hurt him," I said. I darted forward and grabbed the letter for evidence, then kept a wide berth around him. I had his phone, and I knew the woods. He couldn't stop me. "Or anyone else. It's over. I'm going to call the police. It's time for justice." It *was* going to end tonight.

"I don't know what the hell you're talking about," he said, lifting his head from his hands. "But fine, call the police. Maybe they can figure out what's going on. I don't even know what the hell happened. I can barely feel my damn legs." He strained and his right knee barely lifted and then fell again. "And I thought you were dead."

I stopped. "What are you talking about?" I shook my head at myself. Why was I even asking? I couldn't trust anything he said. He was an admitted killer.

He didn't answer me. "I don't know how you're mixed up in all this," he said. "I thought—" He coughed again and leaned over to the side to spit out a mouthful of something foul. He wiped his mouth with the back of his hand and leaned back again, closing his eyes. "He said he was going to hurt you. That's why I came. But it was Delilah lying there, not you . . ."

"*What are you talking about?*" I repeated. For once, would someone answer *my* questions?

He opened his eyes, and that was when he noticed Delilah's prone form a few yards away. She still hadn't moved. "Is she okay? I thought she was you." He tried to get up and failed miserably, instead listing heavily to the side and barely catching himself with an outstretched hand. He lowered himself back down.

"Better now than before, but danger still lurks," I answered. "*Alex.* Tell me what's going on. What are you talking about?" I wanted to kick him. To scream, to shout. I went back and knelt in front of him and took his shoulders in my hands and shook him as hard as I could.

I had his attention now. "I told you," he growled. "*I*

don't know. Will called me and threatened you. He said to meet him here. I got here and found Delilah lying on the ground by Will's car. Then . . . I don't know. It's all fuzzy."

"But—" I started. I looked at the letter still crumpled in my hand. It could be anyone's handwriting. I shook my head. This didn't make sense. Was *this* what Will had meant about taking care of things? But it made no sense. Nothing made sense anymore. Why would Delilah be here? Will had no reason to hurt Delilah but then, neither did Alex. How was I supposed to know what was true, and what wasn't? What good was being the voice of truth when I was surrounded by lies?

"Ask me . . . ask me how you and Delilah got in the truck," I said.

"What are you—"

"Ask me!" I didn't need any unnecessary questions. *"Just ask me."*

He snapped his mouth shut and glared at me. "Fine. How did we get in my truck?"

I took a deep breath and opened up to the answer. "Water is like life. It arrives madly, then recedes away faster, faster . . . leaving everything silent," I said. "Dammit!" I punched the side of the truck. I had hoped to never hear those words again.

He cringed away from me. "What the hell is that supposed to be?"

"An acrostic," I answered. What? "Ask me what an acrostic is!" I grabbed his shoulders again. "Ask me!"

He looked at me blankly, the pupils of his eyes large and dilated. "I don't have to ask you," he said. "You already told *me*, remember? In art class. We had it in English, like, two weeks ago. It's those poems where the first letter of each line spells something. Like that poem by Poe about some woman named Elizabeth."

Two weeks felt like a lifetime ago. Yesterday felt like a lifetime ago. "Will," I said softly. Then I said the phrase, emphasizing the first letter. "Water Is Like Life." I knew the rest by heart, ticking off each letter mentally as I came to it. *Water is like life; it arrives madly, then recedes away faster, faster . . . leaving everything silent.* "William T. Raffles." It had been there all the time, the answer. And Alex had pointed the way. I just hadn't seen it. Couldn't see it. Still couldn't see it. It couldn't be Will. Not my Will.

My mind whirled back to the gibberish I'd first uttered when Granddad had asked about the hit-and-run victim's wife: "*Guts and blood—red is everywhere. Love lost. Anger fills her. Useless . . . except rage takes away . . .*"

Gabriella F. Huerta. How many others were there? How many times had I been too blind to see the answer hidden in the nonsense?

"Are you going to tell me what the hell is going on?" Alex demanded.

"Not yet," I said, despite myself. "Time has flown." I knew, even though he hadn't asked and I hadn't said, that Will must be on his way back. Alex's Chevy had run out of gas and where had I said Will was? The gas station.

THE WAY IT ENDS

Alex stared at me blankly, a study in confusion. I didn't blame him. We had to get out of here and get to the police. Or the hospital. Or both. How to do it? I could probably manage to get Delilah into my car once I went and got it, but what about Alex? Did I even have time to get my car? How close was Will?

"Can you walk at all?" I asked Alex.

"I don't think so," he said. "I don't know what's wrong with me. What did he do to me?"

"He injected you with a horse tranquilizer," I answered. At least the inner oracle had stopped speaking in rhymes. Will's uncle was the town vet, so that made sense in an insane kind of way. Maybe if I got my car and moved it as close as possible to where Alex was he could manage to climb in with my help. Or should I just call the police on his cell phone and hope they got here in time? We were pretty deep in the woods here. The nearest gas station wasn't too close, maybe twenty or thirty minutes round-trip, but I wasn't sure how long Will had been gone. The police would be coming from town if I could get them to believe me and get out here. It would take them at least twenty minutes, maybe more.

My decision was made for me when I saw headlights flickering between the trees that faced the road. I was sure it was Will. Who else would it be this time of night?

"Will's coming," I said to Alex, who couldn't have seen the headlights down where he was, his back to the Chevy. "He's back to finish the job. He was trying to pin the murders on you. Here's 'your' suicide confession." I crumpled the letter into a ball and threw it in his lap. A piece of my heart broke as I said the words, and I shook my head. No time. Never enough time. We had maybe five minutes before Will's car found the turn off and entered the parking lot.

"Look, just stay put. Play dead. Don't move, don't say anything. I'm going to—" I stopped. I had no idea what I was going to do. Alex opened his mouth, but I waved a hand at him to shut up. He was in no condition to help me. It was up to me to save him and Delilah.

I took Alex's phone out of my pocket where it had been clanking against Granddad's knife and my keys. I couldn't overpower Will and neither could Alex, not right now. We needed help. There was only one bar, but I hoped it would be enough. I dialed 9-1-1 for the second time that night.

Someone answered after the first ring. Was it the same woman I'd talked to before? "Nine-one-one. What is—"

"Stop," I said, speaking quickly, my voice low and urgent.

"Just *listen*. We're at the lake, at the Three Oaks parking lot. We need an ambulance and the police. Two people have been drugged and may have carbon monoxide poisoning, too. And Will Raffles is coming to—" I choked a little on the words, "—to kill them." I didn't doubt he was only coming back to finish the job he'd started. "I'm going to try and distract him as long as I can."

"Wh—"

"*Please*. He's here." I took the phone from my ear and hung up. I took a last look at Alex. His eyes were dark and unreadable, but he held out a hand to me. I squeezed it and then handed him the phone. "Stay out of sight, Alex," I whispered. "You can't save me this time."

I quickly slammed the doors of the Chevy. I walked forward, hoping to meet Will as far away from Alex and Delilah as I could. His car turned into the parking lot, the headlights surrounding me in a nimbus of light. I kept walking and waved my arms at him like I was flagging him down.

This was all my fault. Maybe if he believed that they really were dead I could get him away. And then . . . and then I didn't know. But it was a start. One thing at a time.

The headlights bounced toward me, tires crunching gravel. When the black car lurched to a stop and the headlights died, I knew for certain it was Will. Maybe I'd clung to one last desperate remnant of hope. We were a good twenty or thirty feet away from the dark hulk of Alex's Suburban. Was it far enough? In the stillness left behind after the engine had stuttered to a stop, the cicadas had started their ceaseless whine. It sounded like a dirge to me.

"Aria," said Will as he opened his door. "What—"

"Will!" I interrupted, breaking into a run. I couldn't let him ask me anything. "Oh, God, Will, they're dead! Alex and Delilah, they're dead!" My foot screamed in pain with each step but I plowed forward. "I got the doors open, but it was too late. They're gone. I found a note." I crashed into him and buried my face in his shirt. Just hours ago, the smell and feel of him had turned me inside out. It felt like forever ago. Now it made my stomach clench in fear to have him so near.

He wrapped his arms around me. "Aria. Aria, I told you to stay at home." He patted me gently on the back, soft as a whisper.

"We have to get out of here," I said. I pulled back, not daring to look directly at his face. I grabbed his hand and pulled him toward his car. I could barely stand to touch him. All of it had been a lie, every touch, every kiss. How stupid he must have thought me! How had I let myself be taken in like that? I'd told him I loved him! But my inner oracle had known. "Too much," I'd said. Well, there was no love left in me now.

"Let me just see," he insisted, not budging. "I don't want anything that will connect us to here. You should have left them alone."

"No!" I pulled at him again. "Let's just go! The police will never know we were here. I barely even touched them." It was damning to me that his only thought was to conceal evidence and that he showed no surprise at the fact I was telling him they were dead. But of course he knew; he'd put them there. Was he even going to pretend that he hadn't?

He was silent for a moment, rubbing a circle on my hand with his thumb, making my skin crawl. "Wait," he said. "You said you found a note."

In Alex's pocket. Crap. "It was sticking out of Alex's pocket," I babbled. I had no practice lying. "Other than that, I didn't touch them. I mean, other than to check whether they were breathing or not. But they're not. They're dead. Let's get out of here, please, Will, *please.*"

"Where is the note now?" he asked tersely.

"In Alex's hand," I answered. He'd asked too quickly, and I hadn't been prepared. Stupid. I was so stupid. I couldn't let that happen again. Alex must have picked the note up when I'd thrown it at him. I tried to cover over my mistake. "I put it there. After I read it."

He inclined his head and looked in my eyes. "You put it in his hand," he said slowly, softly.

I held his gaze, willing myself to not look away. He had to believe me. I had to make him believe me. "Yes," I said. "Once I read it, I put it where the police would be sure to find it. When they find the bodies. You were right all along, Will. It was Alex and . . . and Delilah." I choked back a sob. I hadn't even realized I was crying.

Will held my eyes for a long beat. Did he trust in my words? Why wouldn't he? I'd only ever told him the truth.

"Are you sure they're—"

"Will, let's go. *Please.*" My voice broke. I didn't need to act my desperation. It was there, all through me. I backed a step away.

"Aria . . . why—"

I opened my mouth to interrupt him again. He quickly

closed the small distance between us and put one hand over my lips, the other on the small of my back, gathering me close to him. My eyes widened as he stared down at me with those stormy grey eyes of his. They had a hard edge in them I'd refused to see before.

"Aria," he repeated slowly and deliberately, "why do you keep interrupting me every time I try to ask you a question?" He loosened the hand over my mouth so he could hear my reply.

I tried to bite my answer back, but it was already coming out. The best I could do was whisper the damning words.

"I don't want you to know that I know what you did."

His hand tightened against my back, pinning me even closer to him. He closed his eyes for a long moment, his long eyelashes visible in the moonlight that had finally broken through the cloud cover. What was he going to do? My heart thudded in my chest. He was too close, too close. I couldn't breathe. At least I hadn't let slip that they were alive. Maybe I could still salvage this. I just had to get him away from them.

Without opening his eyes, he leaned forward and pressed a soft kiss to my forehead. I let out a small gasp. Out of everything, I hadn't expected that.

"Aria, Aria," he whispered against my forehead. "You don't understand. I did this for you." He pulled his head back enough so that he could look into my eyes again.

"What do you mean?" I asked in spite of myself. He sounded so sincere. But he always sounded that way.

"Can't you see—this is the only way. I didn't *want* to kill Delilah, but you had to go and tell her about your gift. I had to think of a way to get rid of her and close the case on the murders, too, once and for all. I killed Alex and Delilah to protect *you.*"

I gaped up at him dumbly. I didn't know what to say, what to think.

"To protect *us,*" he continued, his eyes staring deeply into mine, searching for something. He seemed to find it, because he gave a small nod and kept going. "Once we get past this, everything will be fine. The craziness will blow over and then we'll be free. If we just left without the case being closed, they'd come after us. They'd suspect something. Now we can go anywhere, do anything. With your gift and my . . . talents, no one will be able to stop us. Don't you see that?"

"No, I have been blinded," I whispered. I didn't see, couldn't see what he was telling me. "You killed Jade," I said finally, slowly, each word like a weight on my tongue, "and Shelley. And that man, you ran him over, too, didn't you?"

"Well, yes," he said, the ghost of a smile on his face. "But that doesn't matter now. I've learned from my mistakes. I was . . . sloppy. I didn't think things through. That won't happen again. And now, now I've got you." He kissed my forehead again, gently, his lips lingering too long.

I shivered. I was the one who'd told him that Shelley would be next. It was my words that had killed her. Would she have died if I hadn't said her name? My head swam. Shelley. Alex. Delilah. All my fault.

"With your gift and me asking the right questions, we can do *anything.* We'll be unstoppable." He glowed with a satisfied happiness, the kind that made you think of white picket fences.

I couldn't help it. I had to ask the question. "You want me to help you get away with killing people?"

His grip on me tightened, lost in his plans for the future, our future. My hands were trapped between our bodies. "Sometimes," he said. "But not just that. I've been thinking about it ever since I figured you out . . . we can start small. Work our way up. Win a few Quick Picks, work our way up to a lottery jackpot. Gather information about people." He sounded so casual, like killing someone was on the same level as winning some extra cash, like black-mailing people was an everyday occurrence.

Perhaps he saw the doubt in my eyes. "Aria, don't you remember? I asked. You said you'd do anything for me. *You love me.*"

"I remember," I said. He'd asked that before I knew who he really was. I don't know what my inner oracle would say now, but I knew where my own heart lay, and it wasn't with his. All those lovely little daydreams . . . they were as good as dust. There would be no bright sunny kitchen, there would be no lazy breakfasts, there would be no *us*. And I could see now it had never been an *us*. It had always been *him*.

I fought off the urge to push him away. I cleared my throat, trying to focus on the now. I had to get him away from Alex and Delilah. I couldn't trust that the police were actually coming.

"Why don't we . . . let's go. We should go in case someone comes. We can talk about . . . about your plans."

I tried to smile, but it wouldn't quite stick. He didn't seem to notice. Was he that oblivious to everything but his own desires?

"I knew you'd understand," he said. "I would have told you before, but I wasn't sure you'd get it. Then, this afternoon . . ." He bent down to kiss me. I recoiled.

"Aria," he said, his breath tickling my lips, "what's wrong?"

"Everything," I said before I could stop myself. I tried to recover from it. I wanted to curse my "gift" now more than ever. "We need to get out of here." I pulled away, and he dropped his hands. "Come on, Will, we have to go."

I wondered how much Alex had heard. Would he stay silent? I had to protect him and Delilah. I already had one death on my hands. I couldn't bear to have two more.

"What's the rush?" he said. "The dead can't see."

"The police are coming," I answered. He let me go then, and I stepped back from him. Maybe the truth would work for me for once. "I called them," I said. "I told them I'd found Delilah and Alex, and they had to send an ambulance." I took a deep breath. "I didn't realize it was too late." It had been too late from the start.

I couldn't tell what he was thinking. "Are you lying to me?" he asked, like he couldn't believe it possible. And why would he?

"The voice cannot lie," I said. *Thank God.* They had listened to me. They were coming. I was never wrong. I knew that now. I remembered. The first time we'd talked, Will hadn't asked me if he'd killed Jade. He'd asked me if I *thought* he had and no, I hadn't thought so.

But now I knew beyond a shadow of a doubt. It had

been him all along. It had always been him. And me. It would have stopped with Jade if only I'd been able to keep my cursed truths from him.

Will's face showed the first sign of panic I'd ever seen there. "Okay," he said, "but I have to look first. I was going to do one last check when I came back. I'm not sure I wiped everything down. *Shit.* Did you give them your name when you called?"

"No," I said. Thank goodness I hadn't the second time I called. But I couldn't let him go near them. What if he had his knife on him? He could easily overpower Alex right now, and I didn't trust my strength against his, not even with Granddad's knife. I grabbed his hand. "Just ask me. *Ask me* and we can go." I clenched the hand that wasn't holding his into a fist. I could do this. I would do this. I would be stronger than the voice that lived inside me.

Will stopped. Was it enough? Then, far away we both heard the thin wailing sound of a siren. They were coming. They *were.* Will's eyes grew wide, and this time he was the one pulling me toward his car. "Are they truly dead, and is there anything here that will tie either of us to the scene?" he asked, the words tumbling out of him. He hesitated, waiting for my answer as he pulled the passenger's side door open for me.

I felt the true answer rising in me, but I pushed back. I would not let it come out. No. Not this time. My hand shook in his, but hopefully he would take the struggle as the one that normally came when I was asked of death.

"Yes," I spit out, the word a nail in my stomach, "and no to the last." Perhaps it didn't have that prophetic ring to it, but it was all I could manage. Each word felt like a spike. My knees shook, and I fell into his car. But I had done it. The truth rattled inside my throat, wanting to claw its way out, but I kept my lips pressed tight as I buckled the seat belt. Enough. It would be enough. It had to be. The police were still too far away. Alex and Delilah wouldn't be safe until the police were here.

He slammed the door and ran around to the driver's side and climbed in. "They'll be coming from town," he said, talking more to himself than to me. "I'll head towards Route Sixty and then we can go around the lake and cut through the old Anderson farm."

He sped through the gate and turned left. He didn't even notice when he drove past my car moments later.

A vial of something and a syringe rattled in the cup holder next to me. It must be the horse tranquilizer. Was there still some in the needle?

"*Shit, shit, shit,*" said Will. "This is cutting it way too close." He reached over and squeezed my hand and then went back to the wheel. I let my hand drop down near the cup holder. "We're going to get away though, aren't we?" he asked me.

Another answer clawed at me from the inside, like a beast wanting to burrow its way out. My fingernails dug into the door handle. "Clean away," I said through gritted teeth. I wasn't even sure what the true answer was, though it burned in my throat. My insides felt like they were on fire. That was two now, two lies from the mouth that would only speak the truth. How many questions had it taken Serin before she died? How many truths could I deny?

He was driving fast, faster than anyone should on these back roads, still slick with rain. And I found myself posing questions nobody would ever hear, with answers I'd never understand, even if they somehow came to me. How fast had he been going when he'd run that man over? Why had he even done that? Why any of it?

"What now?" I asked him, my voice shaking with the strain of the truths I held within me.

"I'll get you home," he said. "Wait, how did you get to the lake?"

"A horse brought me," I said and almost laughed. "The Colt. I drove." It felt so good to let the answer come, but the pressure inside me had not let up. The truths I had denied wanted out.

Will glanced at me and then at the rearview mirror. "Crap. Will they find it?"

"No," I said quickly. Maybe they would, maybe they wouldn't. Perhaps the lie wasn't too far from the truth. I did not explode.

"Good," said Will. He let out a laugh then, bright and full of joy and completely out of place in the darkness rushing by us. "You see," he said, pounding the steering wheel. "You see what we can do together!"

All I could think was: *Alex and Delilah are safe.* The sirens behind us had surely found them by now. They would be okay. I shifted in my seat and reached a finger toward the syringe. Will took a corner, and it wobbled around the rim of the cup holder. Close, so close.

"Honestly," said Will, "I have to admit that I'm kind of glad you showed up. I wasn't sure it would work, but something had to be done tonight. I couldn't chance waiting. I couldn't let the police talk to you in the morning. No one else can know what you can do." He grabbed my hand, the one reaching for the syringe, and gave it another squeeze. Not close enough.

Gran had been right. She'd always told me not to tell anyone. To be careful. To know who to trust. I had been so, so wrong.

Will let go of my hand as we came to the turnoff. The syringe wobbled back around as he turned. I grabbed it and held it between the palm of my hand and the side of my leg. Had he seen? No. He was checking the mirror again.

Two demon lies fought inside me now. The truth did indeed hurt when it was denied. I wasn't sure how much longer I could hold it in without breaking.

"You know, Will," I said, "I just realized that there's something I never told you about my . . . my gift."

"Oh?" he said, his eyes still on the mirror looking for flashing red and blue lights that weren't there. Yet.

"Yes," I said. "It goes away. I should be losing mine any day now and then I'll be free." I grasped the syringe in my hand. I was shaking, but I wasn't sure if it was from the pain inside me or the truth that was still fighting to get out.

The car swerved a bit as he turned to me. "What—" he started to say, the shock and horror of a dying dream in his eyes.

"But I'll be free of you *now*," I said and jabbed the needle in his leg, pressing the plunger down. There had been a little left in. Maybe it would be enough.

His question changed. "Why?" he asked. "Why?" And then the car swerved hard to the left and the trees were in front of us, their dark branches seeming to reach out to embrace us as we crashed into them.

There would be no answer to his question.

DON'T ASK ME WHY

I awoke empty. It took me a moment to find my way to where I was. My mouth tasted of ashes and dust. I opened my eyes to a world of white and steel. Where was I?

"Aria. You're awake." Alex's voice rumbled through my body, echoing in the empty space where my heart should have been. I turned my head, and there he was, sitting in a chair next to my bed. The hospital. I was in the hospital. He stood and took my hand. "Everything's okay. You're safe now."

"Delilah?" I asked. My voice didn't sound like my own. It was thin and weak. My throat ached as I swallowed.

"She's okay. She's in a room down the hall. The exhaust and everything hit her harder than me because she's so much smaller, but she's going to be fine. She told me to go get her as soon as you woke up."

I didn't want to know about Will. I wasn't going to ask. But he told me anyway.

"Will broke his leg, but he's fine other than that. He's down the hall, too. They've got a guard on him."

I didn't say anything.

"Delilah and I both told the police what he did to us, but it wasn't even necessary. He told them himself." Alex looked down, shaking his head. "About Jade and Shelley, too. I heard one of the police talking about it. They said he was practically bragging about what he'd done."

I made to sit up and Alex helped me, plumping up the pillows behind me.

"And me?" I asked. I had no casts on, so I must not have broken anything. My head ached, but inside I felt cold and empty. Hollow.

"A concussion, that's it. I could go get your grandparents, if you want. They just stepped out for a minute to talk to the police."

"No," I said. I wasn't ready to talk to Gran or Granddad.

He was silent, waiting.

"I'm sorry," I said finally and rushed through the rest before he could stop me, "for thinking you were the one and for not believing in you." For believing in Will instead.

"I'm sorry, too," he said. "For hurting your arm. I saw the bruises while you were sleeping. And I'm really sorry for making you feel afraid. It makes me sick to think I did that." He took a deep breath. "The truth isn't always easy to see," he added, "even if you know what it is."

"Yeah," I said. I knew that better than anyone.

"Delilah told me what you are. I mean, what you can do."

I didn't say anything. I just waited for it.

"*Is* everything going to be okay?"

The answer flowed through me, from the inside out. "*Yes*," I said, and there was a world in that one simple word. I didn't know how or why, but I felt lighter for it. Everything was going to be okay. The empty space inside me was filling up, maybe with hope. It was going to be okay.

"Okay," he said again. Solid. "Wait. I lied. I've got one more."

I looked at him, really looked at him. He wasn't judging me. Waiting. I nodded, and he nodded back.

"What happens now?" he asked, taking my hand again. His fingers were rough, where Will's had been smooth, but warm, so warm, and the right kind of warm. No one had to ask me. I knew. Alex had never lied to me.

I waited for the answer to come like it always did, but instead there was only me. Just me. "Everything," I said, feeling light as air. "Absolutely anything." And I knew it was the truth. Maybe the truest answer I had ever given.

ACKNOWLEDGMENTS

With much thanks and love to . . .

My husband, who continues to support my writing even when it means scribbling something down at 3 A.M. . . . and my son, Max, the most wonderful distraction ever. And I can't forget C. J. Redwine for helping name Aria . . . not to mention talking me off of writerly ledges, along with MG Buehrlen, Myra McEntire, and Tracey Mathias. Also to Delilah Dawson for letting me borrow her name and my old friend Alex LaFrantz for the same.

And, of course, thanks to my lovely agent, Susanna Einstein, and the equally awesome (but definitely more scruffy) Dan Ehrenhaft, my editor. You guys rock.